Praise for *Lemon City*

A *Black Issues Book Review* #1 Bestseller

"The period details . . . of the 1970s create a vivid backdrop. . . . A pleasant read, light and tangy as lemon meringue pie."
—*Mystery Scene*

"Brown's inspiring, slyly amusing novel marks the debut of a welcome new voice in African-American fiction."
—*Publishers Weekly*

"A warm and witty novel . . . Brown's richly woven characters, with their quirky ways and fierce protectiveness of family traditions, are at once strange and strangely familiar."
—CONNIE BRISCOE, author of *P. G. County*

"A quirky family mystery with loads of tangy charm. A delightful read!"
—VALERIE WILSON WESLEY,
author of *Of Blood and Sorrow*

"A superb debut novel, full of vividly drawn, complex characters. Elaine Brown's writing is gorgeous and beautifully blends romance, black culture, and mystery. This is a treat!"
—YOLANDA JOE, author of *My Fine Lady*

Also by Elaine Meryl Brown

Playing by the Rules

Lemon City

A Novel

Elaine Meryl Brown

ONE WORLD
BALLANTINE BOOKS • NEW YORK

Lemon City is a work of fiction. Names, characters, places, and incidents are the products of the author's imagination or are used fictitiously. Any resemblance to actual events, locales, or persons, living or dead, is entirely coincidental.

2009 One World Books Mass Market Edition

Copyright © 2004 by Elaine Meryl Brown

All rights reserved.

Published in the United States by One World Books, an imprint of The Random House Publishing Group, a division of Random House, Inc., New York.

ONE WORLD is a registered trademark and the One World colophon is a trademark of Random House, Inc.

Originally published in trade paperback in the United States by Strivers Row/One World Books, an imprint of The Random House Publishing Group, a division of Random House, Inc., in 2004.

Cover images: Getty Images/DK Stock (woman), Shutterstock (sky), Getty Images (house)

ISBN 978-0-345-51069-3

Printed in the United States of America

www.oneworldbooks.net

OPM 9 8 7 6 5 4 3 2 1

For my son, David, my parents,
Elmo and Ethele Brown, and the
rest of the Brown family,
who made Thanksgiving
meals memorable.

Acknowledgments

I will forever be thankful to Toni Fay, who led me to Faith Childs, who led me to the wonderful Victoria Sanders, my agent, my dream-maker goddess—thank you for believing in me.

Thank you Sandy Gelles-Cole for the start, and Alice Peck for taking me to the finish.

I'd like to thank my kindred spirits who were with me way back in the beginning, Robin Westen, Charlayne Hunter-Gault, Yanna Kroyt Brandt, Earl Caldwell, and Iris L. Taylor, as well as the inspirational Rosemary Bray, Audrey Edwards, and Susan Taylor of *Essence*.

To my friends Lynette Hoffler, Joyce Coleman-Sampson, Pat Sweeting, Sue Bailey, and Carmen Flowers, thanks for the love and for understanding all the times I needed to say no.

To Bob Gerrard, Gerri Warren-Merrick, Adriane Gaines, Johnnie L. Roberts, Allison J. Davis, Terrie Williams, Lisa E. Davis, and Betti Krukofsky, thanks for all your encouragement and support.

Thanks to Barbara Smith and Dan Gasby for allowing me to make B. Smith's NYC a home away from home. For Joe Rojas, thanks for coming to my technological rescue.

Many thanks to everyone whose best wishes and positive vibes have meant a lot to me during this process. You know who you are.

I'm grateful to Mom and Dad, and my sister, Erica

Oliver, for being my biggest fans. And to my son, David, the first person I shared my story with, thanks for keeping a secret.

Last but not least, thank you to my Random House editor, Melody Guy, for sharing the vision and for being my guiding light. It's been a fun journey and I look forward to walking this road with you again. Peace.

"The history of civilization shows that no people can well rise to a high degree of mental or even moral excellence without wealth. A people uniformly poor and compelled to struggle for barely a physical existence will be dependent and despised by their neighbors and will finally despise themselves."

—*Frederick Douglass, 1873*

One hundred years later:

LEMON CITY CHRONICLE,
*Obituaries, Thanksgiving Day,
November 22, 1973.*

"The passing of Harry Lee Thompson, 1945–1973. Mean as a hound dog. Death due to barking up the wrong tree in the wrong town. Survived by his wife, Faye Dunlap, and various in-laws who wished he'd never crossed the city line, as well as a father who expressed his sincere apologies to anyone his son had offended in life or in death."

The Rules

1. NEVER MARRY AN OUTSIDER. IF YOU DO, THE BOLL WEEVIL WILL BITE YOU BACK.

2. IF YOU CAN'T BE HONEST, YOU MIGHT AS WELL BE DEAD.

3. AIRING YOUR DIRTY LAUNDRY OUT IN THE STREET WILL SMELL UP THE NEIGHBORHOOD.

4. DON'T LET THE MOJO LADY KNOW YOU GOT TROUBLES. IF YOU DO, SHE'LL GIVE YOU MORE.

5. CHEATING MAKES YOU LOWER THAN A DOG SCRATCHING UP A WORM IN THE DIRT.

6. WHAT GOES AROUND WILL ALWAYS COME BACK AROUND AND HIT YOU IN THE HEAD.

7. HELP THOSE IN NEED AND NEVER JUDGE THEM BY THE HOLES IN THEIR SOCKS.

8. DO BUSINESS AT HOME FIRST, THEN WITH OUTSIDERS YOU CAN INVITE INTO YOUR HOME, AS A LAST RESORT.

9. MIND YOUR OWN BUSINESS PERSONALLY AND PROFESSIONALLY.

10. SUPPORT THE COMMUNITY IN EVERY WAY POSSIBLE AND IMAGINABLE.

If you know of anyone who has broken the rules and fallen by the wayside, immediately contact the Ladies of Mt. Zion Baptist Church for reformation instruction, council circle demonstrations, or renewal training.

Prologue

Lemon City was nestled in a valley at the foothills of the Blue Ridge Mountains, sheltered by the range's massive arms, protected from the world. The townspeople claimed direct lineage to Booker T. Washington, not the Booker T. Washington from the history books, but a family whose last name was Washington who had happened to name their firstborn son Booker T. fifty years before the prominent Negro educator had been born. This original Booker T. Washington, delivered into the world in 1806 in Lynchburg, Virginia, was colored, mixed with Powhatan blood. By the time he turned sixteen, he had picked enough tobacco to earn the right to start a family. A mulatto woman with skin the color of fresh buttermilk and hair the texture of sea-island cotton, descended from the union of a house slave and a former president of the United States, caught his attention and became his wife. In 1823, the young Washingtons settled down in Lynchburg and had fifteen children over the span of twenty years. When these children became adults, they married mulattos like themselves, escaped slaves from faraway plantations, and other free Negroes from neighboring towns. By 1865, some of these families emerged as leaders within the new freedmen community: the Washingtons, Dunlaps, Crawfords, Johnsons, and Butlers, family names that would be forever intertwined with the migration, establishment, and history of Lemon City.

At the end of the Civil War, when this new breed of Indian, black, and white people heard that Governor Wiley B. Taylor of Virginia was giving away land as a goodwill gesture to compensate for the ills of slavery, Benjamin T. Washington, Shadrach Mosby Dunlap, Tobias Crawford, Eli Johnson, and Jeremiah Solomon Butler were first in line, followed by many other former slaves eager to get what was owed them. Governor Taylor doled out forty acres of land per person—with a mule thrown in as a bonus—to uphold the Emancipation Proclamation's promise.

The only hitch was that the government land was far removed from Lynchburg, in virgin territory, all the way west toward the Blue Ridge Mountains. But distance didn't discourage them; in fact, many perceived moving away from Lynchburg as a blessing. The "lynch" part in the town's name made the hair stand up on the backs of their necks. Like the prospective miners, who created a rush out West to find gold, these new pioneers made a mad dash to the west of Virginia to claim riches from the land and never turned back.

Having made "reparations" with his generous distribution of land to this former group of slaves, the governor wiped his hands clean. He resumed his charmed antebellum life guilt free, content that justice had prevailed. There would be no Negro retribution for the institution of slavery.

In September 1865, Shadrach Mosby Dunlap, Granddaddy's great-great-grandfather, and Tobias Crawford, Nana's great-great-grandfather, like Moses leading his people to the promised land, led their neighbors from Lynchburg to the wilderness in the valley of the mountains, to the place they would call their new home. Because most of its inhabitants were high-yellow, the first thing they did was to name the town Lemon City, after the color of their skin. The men who would become

known as Lemon City's founding fathers then got to working on putting their home on the map.

Benjamin T. Washington, the eldest grandchild of Booker T., built Mt. Zion Baptist Church, later becoming the church's pastor since he was the only townsman committed to the pulpit and to praying with people full-time.

Making a decision about the town's religious leader was easy compared to making a decision about education: Tobias Crawford had two younger brothers, and both were excellent teachers. Since it was impossible to decide which of the two Crawford boys, Jonas or Ezekial Earl, would run the one-room schoolhouse, the only way to solve the dilemma was to build an annex to the basic structure. At first Tobias thought the older brother, Jonas, should teach the older children and the younger one, Ezekial, should teach the younger children. After giving it more thought, Tobias concluded that solution was too archaic for Lemon City and decided that the girls should have a learning institution all their own. Even though tradition dictated that girls grew up and worked primarily in the home, Tobias saw the value of having a wife who was intelligent, considered to be a partner, an equal. So the Crawford brothers pulled straws from a hat; the older got to teach the boys, and the younger was awarded the girls, which made them both very happy. Tobias made himself principal, overseeing the operations of both schools, and founded the first Committee on Education.

Next, Shadrach Mosby Dunlap was elected mayor, but since the townspeople were always on their best behavior and there wasn't a whole lot of governing to do, he had time to appoint himself part-time sheriff. Since there was also hardly any crime of which to speak, the mayor and the sheriff also had time to read law books, reviews, and write enough made-up briefs to support

make-believe cases around pretend trials, to practice the legal profession and certify himself as a lawyer.

Seeing as how religion, education, government, and the law were taken care of, Eli Johnson made farming his niche. He taught a handful of people how to dig in, get their hands dirty, and plant seeds so they could grow their own food and reap the full benefits of owning land. By teaching them to cultivate the land, enrich the soil, and harvest the vegetables, Eli was determined that the townspeople would provide for themselves.

Solomon Butler had been a slave at the home of a doctor and had paid close attention to enough healing practices and surgical procedures to take over health care. He trained his two sons in medicine, in healing the body, mind, and spirit naturally with plants, herbs, and roots.

Soon after the founding fathers claimed their positions within Lemon City, they established the Town Council and the Division of Commerce. Businesses were born; clothing shops, food and vegetable markets, general stores, and apothecaries flourished and by 1866, Lemon City was booming. The Washingtons, Butlers, Crawfords, Dunlaps, and Johnsons—all founding fathers—continued to inhabit the land, their skin becoming progressively darker over the decades, ranging in shades from eggshell light to ebony black. They prided themselves on becoming self-sufficient into the next century.

Besides it being an all-Negro town, Lemon City was unique for one other thing: its rules. As legend goes, Reverend Benjamin T. Washington, Nana's great-great-grandfather on her mother's side, climbed Mt. Overpeck to find the quiet he needed to hear the whisper of the Lord. When he returned from his weekend retreat, he brought with him a tablet. On it, written in perfect penmanship, were the laws for living, he said, given to him by God. While he denied the appearance of a burning bush, according to what God told him, Washington said

the tablet containing the Ten Rules, the perfect comple-
ment to the Ten Commandments, should be followed as
law. The Rules, everyone would come to believe, were
even more important than family. Families, made of
flesh and blood, might eventually die off, but the com-
munity was the spirit of the town and its values would
live on forever.

None of the parishioners from Mt. Zion Baptist
Church questioned the miracle. They all knew the Rev-
erend's handwriting was worse than chicken scratch,
and the work on the tablet couldn't possibly have been
done by him alone. From that day on, the Lemonites, as
they'd come to call themselves, wholeheartedly em-
braced the Ten Rules, incorporating them into their
daily living. The story of Washington on the Mount was
passed down through the years, and so were The Rules.

Lemon City grew in isolation, prospering under the
Jim Crow laws. Separation made the townspeople de-
pendent on no one but themselves. They had their own
doctors, lawyers, dentists, school teachers, bankers, en-
trepreneurs, policemen, firemen, civic leaders, and
politicians.

The first Lemonites had laid the groundwork for the
future. To build on their existing knowledge, the Town
Council encouraged young people to leave the city to
attend prominent Negro schools. In the mid- to late
1800s, students attended classes in places ranging from
Meharry Medical College, where black doctors, den-
tists, researchers, public health officials and other health
care professionals were born, to the various colored nor-
mal, industrial, agricultural, and mechanical colleges
across the country from as far north as Rhode Island
and as far south as Florida, including Tougaloo College
and Hampton Institute, where the real Booker T. Wash-
ington worked his way through school as a janitor to
earn his degree. Without exception the graduates were

drawn back to Lemon City to share and implement what they had learned and to apprentice others. In doing so, they gave back to the townspeople, adhering to Lemon City's Rule Number Ten: SUPPORT THE COMMUNITY IN EVERY WAY POSSIBLE AND IMAGINABLE.

This cycle continued until the early 1950s, until the end of the Jim Crow era. The Town Council feared the new trend of integration would pull the young people away from the town, causing them to abandon their rich heritage and never to return, and to jeopardize the future of what they had so carefully built. Afraid of losing their young people to the outside world, the Council immediately began discouraging secular education and encouraging home instruction instead. With the assistance of text and reference books, research periodicals and journals, oral teaching methods, and instructional guides and catalogues advertised in the back of academic and scientific research magazines, the young people could master their education inside Lemon City. Now that importing their learning materials had become a priority, the job of Head Librarian would be more critical to the community, and a highly visible role. For the Town Council, it made sense that a descendant of the Crawfords, the town's teaching family, be awarded this newly created and very prestigious position. The Crawfords held this position for the present generation. Louise Dunlap, who also happened to be the great-great-great-great-granddaughter of Tobias Crawford on Nana's father's side of the family, was the town's current Head Librarian for Continuing Education.

Besides their focus on education, a strong sense of patriotism held the town together when it was first settled. To commemorate Lemon City's independence, the founding fathers decided to throw a huge celebration, bigger than any barn dance and jamboree for grownups, and ten times more fun than all the children's

hayrides and three-legged races. What they came up with became the Annual County Fair, which always took place during the first weekend of September, the date the Lemonites first staked claim to Lemon City.

Eli Johnson, the farmer, thought the Fair should be more than just fun and games, selling things, admiring livestock, and displaying musical talent. He added an activity that became one of the Fair's main events: the Tomato Contest. He instituted the title "Tomato Queen for a Day," which would be awarded to any lady of the house who grew the best, biggest, and juiciest tomatoes. To make the contest even more appealing, he recommended the winner wear a red velvet robe with a green leaf collar, topped with the red-and-gold crown that she could keep in her possession for a whole year.

Eli took the contest quite seriously, buying special herbs from Butler's Apothecary and preparing a secret mulch, which he passed along to his oldest daughter, training her in the ways of the land. He taught her how to speak to the plants, encouraging them to grow, how to caress their leaves in such a way that would increase stimulation, and how to find the best time of day to feed and water them, so that she could command them at will.

In the end, all the attention paid off. For the first Annual County Fair, the eldest Miss Johnson unanimously won the Tomato Contest, defeating one of Ezekial Earl Crawford's daughters, who came in a distant second. No one anticipated a sore loser, and everyone was speechless when Miss Crawford threw a fit, lunging for the crown on top of the eldest Miss Johnson's head. A game of tug-of-war ensued, except neither of them was playing. Ezekial Earl grabbed his high-strung daughter by the waist, and Solomon Butler applied a lavender oil–soaked handkerchief underneath her nose, which calmed her down considerably. Eli hadn't imagined how serious this

competition would become, nor did he expect that it would create such an upset between the two families, breeding a fierce rivalry that would continue into the 1970s specifically between his great-great-great-granddaughter by marriage, Lurleen Butler-Johnson—Ole Miss Johnson—and Tobias Crawford's great-great-great-granddaughter Ernestine Crawford-Dunlap—Nana.

In the mid-fifties, *Brown v. the Board of Education* took the town's children away by day, busing them to schools in neighboring towns—"desegregation" is what the newspapers called it. The Lemonites called it a legal form of kidnapping. In the sixties, the United States Census Bureau beamed its radar over the town when the Vietnam War came to a head, taking away their sons—"patriotism" is what the newspapers called it. The Lemonites called it a legal form of kidnapping. As Lemon City was exposed to the social and political changes in the world—the ideas of Martin Luther King Jr. and Malcolm X, and to new publications such as *Ms.* and *Essence*—something was beginning to shift. Toward the end of the decade, Lemon City was divided between two philosophies—"I have a dream" and "By any means necessary"—and aggravated by a few bra-burning and flower-power demonstrations.

By the early seventies, the changes in the world around them would soon climb over the Blue Ridge Mountains, into the valley, finding its way into Lemon City's backyard. Since change was as foreign to Lemon City as a silkworm feasting on a Virginia sun-cured tobacco leaf, the Dunlaps never saw the attack coming until the damage had already been done. Nana and Grand-daddy's youngest grandchild, Faye, became the first family member—since the ban on outside education—to attend college beyond the perimeters of Lemon City. Change picked up speed when she became the first family member to marry and bring home an Outsider. That's

when the real trouble started—that's when change flung itself at Lemon City so hard that it knocked the Annual County Fair right off the calendar. The backlash from the previous decades of turmoil gathered up momentum by 1972, rolling down the Blue Ridge Mountains and landing at Nana and Granddaddy's front door.

CHAPTER ONE

THANKSGIVING DAY, 1973

If Harry were going to die, it was a good thing he picked a holiday. Since the Dunlap family was normally together on Thanksgiving Day, being under house arrest wasn't too much of an inconvenience.

With one eyebrow raised, Louise checked out the activity around the dinner table. She couldn't believe that her family seemed to be more preoccupied with eating food than with facing the possibility of any one of them going to jail. Everyone was carrying on like nobody had died, as if the only dark meat to consider was on the porcelain platter, not lying on a stainless-steel slab in the morgue. If anyone had asked her, that's where she'd say the real turkey lay, frozen on ice, not crispy, oven-baked, and carved on Nana's fine china. She knew they'd have to get their alibis straight. Before they all retired for the evening, she'd have to make sure they'd shared their stories so there'd be no holes when the sheriff came calling in the morning to question them. Even though Louise felt sorry for her sister, Faye, she also felt Faye should never have married her newly deceased husband. But it's hard to advise a baby sister, Louise told herself to prevent from feeling guilty, as she passed the turkey platter to Faye.

Faye jabbed the meat with her fork like she meant to hurt it. After lifting it onto her plate, she used her finger

like a crowbar to remove the chunks of dark meat from the tines, much as she had pried herself away from Harry. Ever since she was a little girl, she'd wanted to have a husband, but she had never once considered that her marriage would end, never mind conclude with her husband on a cold metal slab. Under different circumstances, Harry's death might have been perceived as a tragedy. But toward the end of their relationship, there had been no love lost between them. Because the whole town knew their marriage was falling apart, Faye only hoped the finger-pointing wouldn't be aimed just at her, especially since her family had grown to dislike Harry, much like rust rapidly spreading across a cast-iron pan. She knew the townspeople felt she had picked the wrong husband and believed she had brought this mess upon herself.

Lemon City never took kindly to strangers, but Faye Dunlap was a nonconformist. She had broken the Outsider Rule and now her husband, Harry, was dead—dead as the turkey stuffed with a red apple, lying belly-up on Nana's knotty pine table covered with Lincoln lace. As Faye stared at the turkey, it reminded her of the last time she'd seen Harry, flat on his back on their living room floor with his stomach distended and a tomato lodged in his mouth.

This year, out of respect for the dead, there were no tomatoes tossed into Nana Dunlap's mixed-greens salad. Even though there were bushels of her home-grown tomatoes sitting idle in her backyard, Nana had used freshly picked radishes from her garden to add color to the lettuce and cucumber instead.

Granddaddy Dunlap bowed his head and said the grace. "Dear Lord, thank you for the food on this table this Thanksgiving Day and for bringing this family together—minus one. Amen."

Normally, when death sneaks up without warning

and steals away a family member, the living feel robbed. That wasn't the case with Harry. He was a mean man and had deserved to die, but trouble hadn't died with him, not completely. His demise had raised suspicion about the family, making everyone at the table suspect. Now they were all under house arrest; they had to stay put until tomorrow morning, when the Jefferson County Sheriff came by to start the murder investigation.

If Granddaddy had told his grandchildren once, he had told them a thousand times: never marry an Outsider. It was one of ten sacred rules that had protected Lemon City over the years, insulating the town like plastic wrap from the rest of the world, preserving its sacred customs. He had difficulty with the thinking of today's young people; their whole notion of "self" and "finding one's self" was disturbing to him. As far as he knew, young folks did what they wanted to do and didn't pay attention to the consequences. They totally disregarded the fact that their ancestors had already looked at life for them, so that all they had to do was listen and do what they were told. But no, today's young people acted on their own. And the thing that led them to this independence, the thing they referred to as "discovering their individuality," he didn't think was a benefit to the colored community in general. There wouldn't be a Lemon City if their ancestors hadn't stuck together, keeping the distractions that strangers brought with them at a distance. Being together as one and living life with common goals were the only ways the townspeople could survive. That was the reason The Rules had been invented in the first place.

Granddaddy and Nana were living proof that if you obeyed them, The Rules worked. Their forty years of marriage were the result of being grounded in their roots, being fed the same nutrients from the same soil. On the

other hand, his late grandson-in-law, Harry Lee Thompson, had few roots; the roots Granddaddy had witnessed over the course of a year had grown only for his granddaughter, then withered and died. No, Harry was definitely not the husband he would have chosen for his granddaughter Faye, but she hadn't asked him for his opinion. That's why everyone at the table was in this convoluted mess. He lifted the turkey platter and took a helping of dark meat, and then went back for two slices of white. He then passed the platter to his right, to his grandson, Billy.

Billy felt a sense of relief. The worry lines on his forehead had started to relax and the ache in his trick knee had begun to fade now that his pain-in-the-ass brother-in-law was gone. Harry's sorry ass was out of sight and never coming back. As much as it was his job to uphold the law, Billy knew from experience that there were just some matters that needed to be taken into your own hands. He helped himself to turkey, and then served his wife, Elvira, sitting next to him. Rationing food to Elvira was a habit he had developed at family gatherings over the past few years, as a way of helping her to manage her weight. Even though he loved that she was plump in all the right places, big-boned yet firm like hard rubber, he didn't want her to start jiggling like the jellied cranberry sauce that wobbled on the saucer every time someone bumped against the table.

Moving her eyes back and forth like an eagle trying to get close enough to catch its prey, Elvira watched as Billy calculated exactly how much she should consume at dinner. Knowing he enjoyed a sense of control, she let him go through his ritual thinking he was in charge. She would do whatever made him happy. If she got hungry later, she'd go back for seconds, even thirds, and not pay him any mind even if he cleared his throat or rattled his silverware on the table. There was no mistaking the

meaning behind the way Billy took his time to serve her, the way he picked out each slice of turkey with such care that she understood he catered to her plate purely out of love. She looked across the table at Faye. She felt sorry for her sister-in-law, who hadn't had the chance to experience the kind of love only a good man knows how to give a woman. Now that Harry was out of the way, dead as a slug caught out in the sun after a heavy rain, Faye would find out. Turning her attention back to Billy, she saw he was topping off the turkey with brown gravy, limiting the passage of kidney and gizzard chunks onto her plate with a slotted spoon. He handed the platter to her and she passed it over to Nana.

Sitting opposite Granddaddy at the other end of the table, Nana was happy to have more elbow room, a little more space for resting platters and serving the meal, now that they didn't have to accommodate her granddaughter's recently expired husband, Harry. She didn't miss the tall, lanky, coffee-brown body that reminded her of a stick of beef jerky, squeezing between her granddaughters Faye and Louise at her table. Regardless of the room they'd created for Harry, he never quite seemed to fit in. As she transferred some dark meat onto her plate, Nana noticed the air seemed to be lighter than usual, and the house appeared to be brighter, despite the fact it was an overcast and dreary day outside. Yes, indeed, the darkness had lifted. She was content to have her original family back together again.

Faye daydreamed about her dead husband at the Thanksgiving table, wondering whether or not he would have decided at the last minute to come up North with her, or if he would have chosen to stay in Lemon City. To get her attention, Nana pushed the cornbread stuffing under her nose. Taking the bowl from her grandmother, Faye scooped a tablespoon of the lumpy yellow meal onto her plate and went back to collecting her

thoughts. She couldn't help feeling responsible for Harry's demise, as well as a strong sense of regret. If only she hadn't ignored the Outsider Rule, her situation might be different. How she wished she could start this part of her life over again, pick up from the day she'd met Harry on campus. Instead of stopping to talk to him when he called her, she should have kept right on walking and never looked back. Better yet, she should have had the courage to leave Lemon City on her own to begin with, instead of thinking she needed to be married in order to escape it.

"I still can't believe the Jefferson County Sheriff's Office took me off this case," said Billy.

"Billy, they had to take you off the case because of the conflict of interest," said Louise, not caring that she was talking with her mouth full.

"You can't investigate the death of your own brother-in-law, especially when the Jefferson County Sheriff's Office thinks you may have been involved," Faye added. "But if you're innocent, there's nothing to worry about, right? Who cares about who's doing the investigating?"

Billy's desperation to get involved in the case made Faye wonder if he had something to hide. Maybe she hadn't been the first person to arrive home and find Harry dead on the floor. Her brother's hatred for her husband was no secret.

"*You* got anything to worry about?" Billy shot back at her. "*You're* the one who allegedly found him lying dead on the floor."

"What are you trying to say, that I killed my own husband?"

"You were planning on leaving him, anyway. It would have been easier for you to leave if he were dead. No strings attached that way, now ain't that right?" He winked at his sister and stretched his leg underneath the table to work out the stiffness in his trick knee. When he

snapped the joint back into place, there was a loud pop. Everyone used to wince when Billy released the pressure, as if the pain belonged to them, but now they were accustomed to the interruption and kept on eating as if the firecracker noise was a normal part of the meal and conversation.

"If you ask me, I say he had a heart attack," Granddaddy offered. "The man dropped dead and died. Plain and simple. Don't think that just because you're young that the ole ticker can't stop working." Granddaddy pounded his fist rapidly against his chest and then stopped suddenly when he started to cough. "Then I have this other theory," he added, trying to get back his breath. "Evil just came and got him. Reached its ugly hand up from hell and claimed its own." He lifted his arm above his head, pretending to grab something out of thin air, and dragged it down to the table to illustrate his point.

"Can we stop talking about death and dying?" said Billy's wife, Elvira. "After all, we're at the dinner table, and this is Thanksgiving. Nana, these turnip greens are delicious. Did you cook 'em with pork or with smoked turkey wings?"

"I just don't like anyone messing around in my jurisdiction," said Billy, trying not to make the conversation sound too morbid as a courtesy to his wife. "I know how to do my job and be completely objective. The man was not my blood kin, and on this Thanksgiving Day, that's something to be thankful for." He raised his glass of iced tea in a toast. When he put it back down, he stuffed a piece of turkey into his mouth.

"Well, there's something I'm not thankful for," said Louise.

"What's that?" said Granddaddy.

"I'm not thankful that we had to cancel the Annual County Fair on account of Harry."

"You can say that again," said Nana. "He was bad news in general, but it's a shame he had to get specific and mess up tradition. He always did have a way of spoiling things."

"Ain't that the truth," said Elvira.

"He's still managing to do it, even from the grave," added Louise.

"He's not in the grave yet," said Granddaddy. "He's only in the morgue."

"Can we please stop talking about dead folks while I'm trying to eat?" Elvira's eyes widened. "Y'all hush, now. I'm trying to enjoy my food."

"Yeah, too bad about the Fair," Faye said to Nana, patting her grandmother on the hand. "This was supposed to be your year for Tomato Queen for a Day, winning the grand prize over Ole Miss Johnson, huh?"

"And I woulda done it, too," she said. "This year that crown had my name on it."

Nana took growing tomatoes to new heights, but no matter what she did, she couldn't achieve her dream, to be crowned "Tomato Queen for a Day" by winning the grand tomato prize at the Annual County Fair. There was no limit to what Nana could do with tomatoes. Experimenting with the juicy red fruit had led her to discovering recipes that were a testament to the diversity of her culinary skills. She added tomatoes to potato salad, deviled eggs, omelets, stews, casseroles, breads, and meat sauces. She served them barbecued, baked, broiled, scalloped, stuffed, grilled, canned, dilled, glazed with wine and brown sugar, made them into jams and piccalilli, fried them when they were green and baked green-tomato pie. Here came another year that would leave her without the crown, and she had been so close, which made the cancellation so much worse to bear.

The Annual County Fair was two years away from its centennial; Nana was determined to break Lurleen's

hold as the reigning queen before the fair celebrated its one hundredth year. If she couldn't bring this victory to the Crawford name within a century, it would be time to turn in her garden gloves and tools and teach herself a new hobby. Perhaps she'd have to settle on the knitting she was doing for her unborn great-grandchildren to occupy her spare time.

Saint, who really acted more like a dog than a cat, jumped into Nana's lap, nuzzling against her mistress in a show of compassion and support. Grateful for the display of affection, Nana stroked Saint along her back and scratched the fur between her ears, making the cat purr like an engine. Guiding her gently back down to the floor, Nana fed Saint a piece of white meat from her plate to return the cat's dedication. Because Saint also loved tomatoes, Nana picked a radish out of the salad bowl and held it under her nose to see if she would like this new round red vegetable. Saint took one sniff, turned up her nose, and walked away.

May 9, 1972, the day Faye came home from college, was the day disaster struck. Although Nana wasn't superstitious, first thing in the morning, two things made her think the day wouldn't turn out right. First she awoke with a headache she knew hadn't come from the pink sponge curlers set too tightly on her head. Then, when she went to the kitchen to frost and decorate the three-tiered lemon cake she had made the night before to celebrate Faye's graduation, all that was left were the remains. Nana put both hands to her mouth to hold back a scream so she wouldn't wake up her husband. A mouse had dug a hole straight through the bottom layer of her masterpiece, carving out a tunnel clear through to the other side.

Waking with a headache and finding a varmint had eaten its way through something she had created put her in a foul mood first thing in the morning, and was proof that something bad was gonna happen, especially when it was supposed to be a day of celebration. Although she didn't want to read more into the omen than she should, Nana thought about Faye and prayed that nothing bad had gotten hold of her and eaten a hole through her soul. For added precaution, Nana was extra careful with her comings and goings over the next several hours, just in case the omen was a true one.

Across the street, still in bed in her apartment on the second level of the two-family house, Louise threw off

the covers and peeked out the window. It was too quiet. Ordinarily the wood thrush nested in the old mulberry tree woke her up with its singing. But not today. Not a peep. She wasn't superstitious, but the wood thrush's hiatus on this particular day was odd, and she felt a need to explain the silence. Could it mean that Faye was going to suddenly and without warning leave the nest, too? Or that she wouldn't bother showing up to the family nest at all? Neither answer was good. The lack of birdsong on the morning of her sister's homecoming was a terrible beginning to the day.

Billy and Elvira were in the apartment downstairs making love when they felt the bad luck hit them. While he was on a downstroke, the wedding picture hanging over the bed slid off its hook, hitting Billy on the head. The picture had been secure against the wall for years despite the fact that the headboard always banged whenever they were trying to make a baby. For the picture to come loose today, the same day that Faye was coming home from college, was too much of a coincidence. They both hoped her arrival had nothing to do with being hit with information or anything that could result in physical injury.

Granddaddy didn't have a clue that anything might be wrong, but later that afternoon Nana, Louise, Billy, and Elvira separately began to put two and two together.

What sounded like thunder grew louder and louder the closer it came. Only thing was, the sky wasn't cloudy, there wasn't any sign of rain, and when the noise finally stopped, it came to a halt right outside their front door. When all five Dunlaps rushed to the sunroom window, pulling back the drapes to inspect the unnatural phenomenon, they discovered Faye and a tall man with a big Afro and skin the color of a cardboard box getting out of a 1970, eight-cylinder, two-door white hardtop Pontiac GTO coupe. When Nana opened the door, she

engulfed Faye in a suffocating hug. When Nana released her and Faye finally regained her breath, she made the announcement that nearly knocked her family off their feet.

"This is my husband, Harry Lee Thompson," she said. Nana stepped away, dropping her arms down to her sides as if the shocking news made her limbs turn weak.

"Close your mouths before something ugly flies in," Louise said, trying to lighten the situation with humor. But she was thinking it was already too late; a hornet had just landed in their lives—Faye had brought home an Outsider.

It took a few moments for Nana to collect her composure. She squeezed her eyes shut, clamped her hands together and quickly mumbled, "May the words of my mouth and the meditation of my heart be pleasing in Your sight, O Lord, my Rock and my Redeemer." When she finished her prayer and found her strength, she broke the silence. "Harry, so nice to meet you," she said, faking enthusiasm. She couldn't take her eyes off his lime green double-breasted wide-lapeled suit with matching vest that seemed to compete with the grass outside and the brightness of the day.

Louise sized him up. He was probably Billy's age, in his late twenties. Sweaty from the heat and all dressed in green, the Outsider looked slicker than a wet cucumber. Louise tried to figure out which part of handsome there was about him that her sister could have found appealing, and then he smiled and his whole face seemed to change to halfway decent. The awkward pauses continued, the entire group appearing frozen in time. When no one else made a move forward, Louise took the next step: "Welcome, brother."

After calling him "brother," she cleared her throat. She hoped he hadn't thought she meant it in a nuclear-

family kind of way; she had used the term only in a so-
cial sense. She extended her hand and Harry slapped her
a smooth five. "Tell me your name again." She didn't
like the clamminess of his hand.

"Harry, Harry Lee Thompson. What's happening, sis?
Pleased to meet you."

Granddaddy didn't like Harry eyeballing his grand-
daughter like he was examining a shank of smoked, pic-
nic shoulder ham.

"Willie, what do you say to our new grandson-in-
law?" Nana motioned for Granddaddy to mind his
manners. Granddaddy could sense something slimy
about this guy, and he didn't want to get too close before
further inspection.

"Where's the papers . . . and I don't mean the dern
diploma, either. I mean the doggone marriage license. I
wanna see proof." Granddaddy puffed out his chest as
far as it would go, and stood up as straight as he could
to make himself appear bigger and taller.

Harry scratched his face at the point where his thin
moustache nearly collided with his bushy, triangular
sideburns. When the old man didn't crack a smile, Harry
said, "The document's in the glove compartment."

"Willie . . . that's not what you say." Out of nervous-
ness, Nana smoothed down her dress as if it were wrin-
kled.

"Okay. Then I'll say: How in the hell did you man-
age to marry my granddaughter without my knowing
about it?"

"Granddaddy . . ." Faye had predicted her grandfa-
ther would be angry about her marrying an Outsider,
but she hoped they'd at least get past the door before he
exploded.

"You look too old to be playing 'round in the sand-
box, too dern old to be messin' with college girls."

"I graduated from college with Faye, Mr. Dunlap," Harry said, putting his hands in his pockets.

"That don't make it right," said Granddaddy, waving his hand at Harry like he was fanning away bad breath.

"Now, Willie, invite Harry to sit down in the living room so all of us can hear about how he managed—I mean, hear the story of how the newlyweds met and fell in love. We're all surprised at the news, but we need to go inside and learn more about Harry." Out of anxiety, Nana wrung her hands together and hoped she wouldn't have to beg her husband to calm down and cooperate.

Since his grandfather wasn't doing a good job of pretending to be hospitable, Billy thought he'd give it a shot. "Harry, would you like a beer?"

"Or something cool to drink?" Elvira added, patting the beads of perspiration that had sprouted on her face.

"A cold one sounds real good. Thanks, brother." Harry extended his hand to Billy, who turned abruptly and made his way to the kitchen.

From the way Harry was dressed, color-coordinated right down to his dark green alligator shoes, and based on how he spoke, Billy could tell he had been raised in the North. His sister had not only married an Outsider, but one from unknown parts. Absolutely no one they knew in Lemon City, not even in Jefferson County, would have any information on the intruder.

"I agree with Nana. Let's all go into the living room." Faye grabbed Harry by the arm and led the way.

Granddaddy was devastated. His baby granddaughter had broken the first rule: NEVER MARRY AN OUTSIDER. IF YOU DO, THE BOLL WEEVIL WILL BITE YOU BACK. Trouble had reared its ugly head, materializing from a loud eight-cylinder, two-door white Pontiac GTO—the kind of trouble with tentacles that could sneak up on the whole family and attack. He hadn't had the benefit of a

warning to prepare him for this disappointing home-coming.

Nana had already replaced the mouse-eaten cake and now, thinking quickly, she excused herself while everyone was beginning to chat and warm up to the idea of their newly expanded family. Nana always wanted to know when something was going to happen so she could be prepared, and her family usually respected her preference. What Faye had gone and done without advance notice hurt her to the bone. Nana went into the kitchen to change the letters made of icing on the cake. Fixing the cake would keep her busy and give her time to adjust to the dilemma.

At the moment, the cake read "Congratulations Graduate"; now the words "And New Bride" had to be added. Mixing the appropriate amounts of sugar, corn syrup, and water into a saucepan, she thought about what might have happened to her granddaughter at college that would cause her to commit this act of rebellion. Perhaps Harry had tricked her into marrying him. He looked rather slithery. Surely he had heard all about Lemon City's wealth and its rich folks—must have suspected her granddaughter was from old money, and now he wanted some.

As her heart filled with blame, Nana began to reflect on why she had let Faye out of her sight to begin with. It had started when Faye was still in junior high school. Nana remembered when Faye had been awestruck by all those radical images of the new world that invaded their home on the nightly news on TV. She remembered her granddaughter saying that attending an Outside college could be her way of contributing to something bigger than Lemon City. Then she recalled her granddaughter having the nerve to say she had to "find herself," and Nana looked at her like she was crazy, because she could be "found" standing right there in the kitchen. Day after

day, her granddaughter had bombarded her with the benefits of going away to college. Eventually, and against her better judgment, Nana gave in to the request and sent Faye packing with a brand-new Smith-Corona typewriter just to get some peace. But Faye was thick-headed, always testing the boundaries, crossing the line, and now she was breaking the Outsider Rule, asking for misfortune. Nana was as sure as she was sitting in the vinyl-covered chair in the kitchen with both hands on her hips, getting madder and madder, that mayhem was soon to come.

Faye, seated next to Harry, wished her grandmother would stop puttering in the kitchen and join them. She always felt better when Nana was by her side, especially when Faye was up against her grandfather. No matter what kind of news she hit Granddaddy with, Nana's presence always softened the blow, which was why she had to be with Nana when she broke the second piece of news to Granddaddy. The way he had thrown a fit this afternoon, there was no telling how he'd react to her leaving Lemon City altogether.

She didn't look forward to sharing that information with him any more than she looked forward to sticking hatpins in her eyes. Common sense told her to put off any mention of her travel plans for another day or two. No need to give her grandfather more than he could swallow in one afternoon. Right now he was listening to Harry's version of how they had met. For the moment Granddaddy was sitting quietly, intent on hearing the whole story.

CHAPTER THREE

Booker Trade Community College, located in a small town outside Norfolk, Virginia, way on the other side of the Blue Ridge Mountains and as far east as one could get without falling into the ocean, represented freedom to Faye. Nana and Granddaddy had no idea how confined she felt in Lemon City. She knew they'd never understand why she wanted to free herself from the clutches of her possessive hometown. There was so much going on in the outside world, so many groups, so many movements—Black Power, Black Panthers, civil rights, and the Black Nationalists. Faye couldn't be just a spectator to all the activity going on, the issues being debated—issues that were affecting people of color and elevating their profile and standard of living in the process.

At Booker T. Community, where the focus was teaching the trades, the administration all but guaranteed their students would get jobs in the areas of cosmetology, electrical, mechanical, culinary arts, air-conditioning and refrigeration, plumbing and carpentry, just to name a few. Faye had decided very early on that she had the gift of making people look beautiful, and that would be her path to a better life. Creating hairstyles and products exclusively for black women—not just Lemon City folk—was the way she would contribute to the advancement of her people.

Being involved with the struggle for respect and equality was something she took seriously. It wasn't enough

to sit back and watch all the excitement on TV or read about it in the *Lemon City Chronicle* or quote the rhetoric from contemporary books and literature, like Louise did. Faye had to be *in* it. What she had in mind was not only hands-on styling, but also developing her own line of hair-care products and using the profits to fund organizations that supported black causes—"By any means necessary," as Malcolm X had said.

"By any means necessary" was also how she felt about leaving Lemon City. She couldn't remember how the idea had come to her, but she had always known that she had to run away, not because she didn't love her family, but because leaving was her destiny. That idea stuck and she could never shake it loose.

Learning more about the Black Power movement would be just one part of her education at Booker T. Community. She would also wade through the student population of single out-of-state males, preferably from north of the Mason-Dixon Line. She knew she'd need a ticket to leave Lemon City, and that way of passage would come in the form of a husband. Her grandparents would never approve of her leaving town on her own. In fact, initially, they would not approve of her leaving Lemon City at all—for certain, they'd never agree to her marrying an Outsider.

However, approval or not, Faye was determined to go, and her grandparents would ultimately be more accepting of her move north if she left town to follow a husband rather than a dream. In time, she knew they'd get over her absence. They couldn't hold on to bad feelings any more than they could grab a rosebush with sharp stickers and not let go. Eventually they'd understand and give her their blessing.

Faye felt bad about breaking The Rules and there was no doubt in her mind that she was probably the first person in her family to do so. She didn't like carrying the

burden of that badge of recognition, but there was something inside her that accepted her fate of taking the risk of change. She tossed and turned and suffered through sleepless nights over breaking Nana's and Granddaddy's hearts, but ever since her parents died, The Rules had proven themselves not to be infallible because they couldn't bring her parents back to life. Faye felt The Rules owed her, and she was entitled to break just one.

By the end of September 1970, it looked like college would deliver everything she ever expected. She finally met Black Power in person, the man who would ultimately mark the turning point in her life.

It was Saturday. Fliers were posted everywhere, publicizing the details of the day's rally. Stokely Carmichael, head of the Student Nonviolent Coordinating Committee, was the featured speaker. Music blared, with James Brown singing "Get on the Good Foot," followed by "Say It Loud (I'm Black and I'm Proud)." This brought students out of their beds and set the tone for the event. Throughout the day, committees were busy readying the auditorium, preparing for the cookout, setting up booths to attract new students to SNCC, and decorating the basement at the Carver Hall Student Union building, where everyone would throw down at the afterparty. Faye, who had only seen pictures of Stokely Carmichael in magazines, was looking forward not only to hearing him speak, but also to seeing if he was really that fine in person.

"Philamona Crenshaw, come on. We're gonna be late," she shouted at her roommate, who was sitting under the hooded Sunbeam hair dryer, wire curlers secured with pink pins in rows and positioned strategically on her head. On campus for only a few weeks, Philamona already had a reputation for being slow, and everyone shortened her name to Lamona or Mona

because pronouncing four syllables was just too much trouble. When Faye called her by her full name, that meant her roommate was getting on her nerves.

When Lamona didn't respond, Faye dropped her hand on the dryer hood, and the thud made her roommate jump.

"Go'ne and leave without me." She waved her hand as if shooing a fly from her face. "I'll catch up with you later. I'm not going to see Stokely, as fine as he is, with my hair lookin' raggedy. Plus, I still got to put my face on."

"See ya," Faye said, grabbing her keys and closing the door behind her while shaking her head.

Faye figured she'd catch up with other friends on her way to Carver Hall. Her sandy brown Afro bounced with every step as she walked across campus. The closer she got to the venue, the louder the noise from the gathering students became and the more pumped up with excitement she felt. Midway across the parking lot as she began to pick up her pace, a voice startled her groove and interrupted her beat.

"Hey, my beautiful brown sister. Can you give me a hand?" She turned toward the voice coming from behind the trunk of a 1970 white Pontiac GTO coupe. She backtracked to the car and found the source of the request leaning into the trunk. All she could identify was his bottom half—long legs dressed in bell-bottom jeans that were tight enough to reveal a round, firm behind. She heard him fumbling around in a toolbox. When he found what he was looking for, he backed out of the trunk and casually turned to face her. She liked what the top half looked like as well. He was tall and medium-brown, with skin so smooth it looked like it had been rubbed with cocoa butter since the day he was born. His smile raised his sideburns, lifting the corners of his eyes in a way that made his whole face light up.

"What's happening, lovely lady? My name is Harry—

Harry Lee Thompson." He beamed at her long legs, which were the color of maple syrup. Then, in one swift move, he dropped his Kool cigarette to the ground, crushed it with his sandal, wiped his hands clean on the towel, and then extended a hand to her.

"Hi. I'm Faye . . . Faye Dunlap." She shook his hand, noticing that he looked older than most students on campus and wondering if he were a teacher.

"So dig it, my African queen. Now that we're acquainted, do you know how to drive a stick shift?"

Faye looked at him, raising an eyebrow, not knowing if she should slap him or take his question seriously.

She decided to play it safe. "Personally, I prefer automatics."

"But I'm not taking a survey today, my sister. I need you to help me do something."

"I can't right now. I'm going to the rally."

"Me, too, but just hold up. It'll only take a hot second to give a brother a hand." He closed his trunk. "Besides, isn't that what the rally's all about? Brothers and sisters coming together and helping each other out? Joining in a united front? Working toward a common goal?"

Faye looked at her watch. "This better not take more than five minutes."

He smiled again, showing two rows of perfect teeth. Faye couldn't help but see how handsome he was, not in a college-boy sense but in a grown-man way. He had a lot of confidence as his smile flashed across his face, and she was sure he was the kind of guy who would use it often to get his way. "I hope you don't mind my asking, but are you a teacher here at Booker T.?"

"Heck, no. What made you think that?"

"You don't look like the rest of the guys around here."

"Now what does that mean? That I look old, or do you think I look dumb?"

"You tell me which category fits you." Faye giggled. "My Nana taught me to always be polite."

"I'm old. So mind your Nana, and respect your elders. Not everyone starts college right after high school." Harry unlatched and lifted the hood of his car. "This won't take long at all. Just hop your fine self into the driver's seat—the car's already in neutral and the brake's up." Harry closed the door when Faye settled into the vinyl bucket seat, and then he began his work underneath the hood.

"You know, I've heard brother Stokely speak before."

"You have? Where?" Faye stuck her head out of the open window.

"Even though this is my first year at Booker T., I spent two years at a school not too far from my home, Triborough State, in Harlem. He was there last spring."

"I could tell by your accent that you were from the North." Faye was excited to finally meet a Yankee and the fact that he was from New York City meant that he certainly had the potential to fit into her plans. "What brings you all the way down here to tobacco country?"

As he stood up over the hood and wiped the sweat from his brow, she stared at the tight curls on his chest peeking out over his white T-shirt. Sunlight made the miniature ringlets glisten. He had a nice body. She wondered if he had a kiss to match.

He stepped out from underneath the hood so he could make eye contact with her. "I dropped out at Triborough," he said as he wiped his hands on the towel and then scratched the back of his neck. "I needed a change of pace and different scenery. Besides, this is such a peaceful place to settle down, even raise a family if you find the right mate." Harry winked at Faye, then ducked back underneath the hood.

When he was out of sight, Faye grinned, grabbing the

steering wheel as if she had acquired good fortune and didn't want to let go.

"When we get to know each other a little better, maybe we could plan a trip and go up North together. We could go to rallies, attend demonstrations. You could show me around and introduce me to all your friends." Faye's eyes widened with embarrassment when she realized she was getting ahead of herself. Upon hearing what had come out of her mouth, it sounded as if someone else had said it.

"Where I come from the plan is to start out with a date first." He threw his greasy towel onto the backseat floor. "I thought the Northern sisters were supposed to be bold, but I see you Southern gals don't like wasting time."

Faye raised both hands to her face to contain her blush, bringing both elbows down hard on the steering wheel and accidentally setting off the horn. Both she and Harry jumped.

"You're dangerous behind the wheel, and the car isn't even moving," he said. Faye giggled, and Harry fiddled around with something else under the hood. "Okay now, turn the key and rev it up . . . slowly."

She turned the key in the ignition, and after hearing the V-8 engine roar, Harry was content.

"Okay, stop. That's enough."

She turned off the ignition and got out of the car. "Come on," she said. "We gotta split."

During the rally, Faye discovered that although Stokely Carmichael was even better looking than his pictures, what attracted her to him most was his message. She filled out the registration card to become a member of the Student Nonviolent Coordinating Committee.

That night, she and Harry danced at the afterparty until it got so hot in the basement they had to go out for

air. The couple walked until they found a private spot on the lawn next to an oak tree and sat down underneath it on a tiny patch of grass. Because the party had put him in a talking mood, Harry revealed what he wanted her to know about his life—that he was born and raised in Harlem, that he was twenty-seven years old, that he had no illegitimate children. He told her his father owned a dry-cleaning business, that he never knew his mother, and that he didn't know if he was the marrying type, but he'd like to give it a shot and settle down someday. After volunteering this background information, he lit up a cigarette and changed the subject.

"Anyway, like my man Stokely just said, black people need to 'define their own goals and create their own power bases.' That's why I plan to work as a mechanic until I make enough money to buy my own car repair shop." He put his hands behind his head, making a cradle, leaned back against the tree, and stretched out his legs. "Even though I already know a lot about cars, a degree from Booker T. would make me certified, because nowadays you need to have a piece of paper to go into business for yourself."

Faye sat on the ground with her legs folded one over the other, mesmerized by his words, anxious to hear more.

"Economic freedom is what'll lead black people to liberation and break the cycle of poverty in the ghettoes." He took a drag off his cigarette and blew out the smoke. "The community is where it all begins. We've got to beat the system, or create our own." He flicked his cigarette ashes on the ground and looked down to make sure the fire had gone out.

Faye had never heard anyone in Lemon City talk the way he was talking, and was impressed by his experience and his thinking; he spoke as if he had life all figured out, as if he knew exactly what he was doing and

where he was going. He seemed to share her belief that when the individual was strengthened, the group was strengthened, too. Even though their paths had just crossed, all the pieces were falling into place, and she knew this was just the beginning. Sitting right beside her was the man she needed, the ideal partner who would complete her most perfect plan. Harry would be her ticket into unknown Northern territory, her one-way pass to a new life on the topside of the Mason-Dixon Line. If she was going to get him to marry her, she had to work fast.

"That's exactly why I want to develop my own hair-care line," she said. "I'm calling it Nubian Silk—after the first people on the planet, who were Africans."

"Power to the people, my sister." Harry raised his arm and balled his fist in the Black Power sign. Then he scooped up his beer with the other hand and gestured a make-believe toast.

"It's not going to be greasy like those heavy pomades everyone's used to," Faye continued. "My product will be nongreasy and mostly natural."

"Here's to starting your own business." He downed the rest of his beer, crushing the can with his hands.

"The sad part is, I can't do what I want to do in Lemon City. I need to expand my thinking and be productive in a larger environment—one that's progressive, where there's an exchange of new ideas and high energy to make things happen."

While Harry was pulling up strands of grass, staring at the fullness of the moon, she was thinking how different he was from the guys in her hometown. Everyone there was in a routine. Even though she had everything she needed in Lemon City, it was predictable. Since it was the tradition that children take over the family business, or stay in the same line of family work, the notion of challenges was practically extinct. At least Harry had

ambition. The more he talked, the more charged she became. She was convinced they had good chemistry and compatibility.

"It's the same routine day after day, same conversation, same people," Faye added. "The only thing that changes in town are the traffic lights. But my folks will never understand why I have to leave Lemon City to pursue my goals. What they expect is for me to go home after graduation and do hair."

With his eyes still on the moon, Harry's only response was, "There's nothing wrong with doing hair." He stood and helped Faye off the ground and looked her in the eyes. "As long as there are sisters, there's always gonna be a need for someone to do their hair. Might as well be you."

When Harry walked her back to her dormitory room, he asked her for a date. They agreed to see the new movie downtown that everyone was talking about, *Shaft*. He leaned in to kiss her good night and she let him, then she sent him on his way across campus to where the male students lived.

The following Saturday after the movie, they wound up at Captain Jack's, the local fish-and-chips restaurant in town that not only had the best lobster tails and seafood in the area but also the lowest prices. The special menu written in bold capital letters on the chalkboard was unique in that it offered combination platters Southern-style: side orders such as peas and rice with chunks of hamhocks, dirty rice with pieces of chitlins, and succotash tossed with bacon.

A waiter placed a basket of warm cornbread muffins on the table and took a pad and pencil from his pocket, ready to take their order.

"I'll have the surf and turf special with clean dirty rice," said Harry. "The first time I had chitlins in my rice I couldn't eat them because I couldn't get past the smell.

Powerful things, those little chitlins. Even though I'd cut them up into bite-size pieces, the odor would still bring me to my knees, and I'm not the praying type. Ever since then, I've been getting my rice clean."

Faye noticed that Harry didn't gesture for her to order first, which would have been the proper thing to do, but she just let it slide.

"I'm not a big fan of chitlins either," Faye said to Harry, then she turned to the waiter. "I'll have the lobster tails with peas and rice mixed with hamhocks." Faye handed the menu to the waiter.

He wrote down their order and left as quickly as he had come.

"I don't think I've mentioned this, but my grandparents are my parents." Faye picked up a cornbread muffin and cut it in half. As the steam escaped, she smeared on some butter and watched it melt.

"That's biologically impossible." Harry took off his sunglasses and laid them on the table.

"My parents died in a car accident a long time ago, and my grandparents not only raised me and my brother and sister but adopted us."

"I certainly know what it's like to be abandoned." Harry leaned back, spread his arms across the back of the booth, and glanced over his shoulder to get a better look at an attractive sister sitting at another table, making out with her boyfriend.

"Did your daddy ever talk to you about your mother after she left?" Faye asked, as Harry returned his attention to her.

"No, not really. Pop's whole life revolves around his dry-cleaning shop and taking care of other people's dirty laundry. So one day, when his own dirty laundry showed up, he simply cleaned it, steamed out the troubles, ironed out whatever was wrong, and started life over,

brand-new, like a dress shirt starched on a hanger, ready for pickup."

"Like it never happened." Faye reached across the table and held Harry's hands. "Not even caring what effect it might have on you."

"Stuff like that doesn't affect me." Harry withdrew his hands and pulled them under the table.

"What gets me going is when my throttle doesn't work," Harry continued, hands resurfacing on the table to emphasize his point. "Or my gasket gets blown . . . or my water pump breaks."

Faye sensed Harry didn't want to talk about his pain so she focused on herself. "I was eight when my parents died, and it was hard for me to accept the fact that they'd never return."

"Whether someone's dead in your mind, or really dead, it all amounts to the same thing—gone like the hair that falls off your face and down the drain after a good shave."

Faye felt a little bit sorry for Harry, thinking he'd shut down his feelings so he wouldn't have to deal with his past.

"Nana became my mother and Ole Miss Johnson, the lady next door, looked out for me, too. She's an incredible woman who knows everything there is to know about herbs. Did you know that when you're tired, rosemary can actually rejuvenate you and give you energy?"

Harry shook his head.

"You just sprinkle a few drops of oil on a tissue and inhale it, or put it on your body so the warmth brings out the smell, and you feel brand-new."

"Never heard of that herb before, but I do know an awful lot about weed. I smoke a doobie on occasion, especially if it's that good shit coming out of Mexico these days."

Faye didn't want to appear to be shocked that Harry

smoked reefer. Not wanting him to think that she was from the backwoods and totally corny, she just played it off like she wasn't surprised and continued her conversation, ignoring how excited he became while talking about getting high. In fact, she thought she might try smoking reefer one day to see what all the fuss was about, since the only thing people smoked at home was tobacco. Without skipping a beat she continued, talking about geranium, telling Harry it was a good skin cleanser that also helped get rid of dandruff, and that she was planning to use the plant in one of her shampoos. She told him that eucalyptus was her favorite oil to put into bathwater, especially in the summertime because it was soothing and cooled her all over.

Somewhere in the middle of her conversation, she could see Harry become distracted again. To win back his attention, she pulled a few oil vials out of her handbag and asked if he wanted to try one out for himself. But the only thing she saw him reacting to was the fly sister with the Angela Davis Afro, who was built like a brick house, and making her way across the room to her seat. Faye cleared her throat to get Harry to refocus, but the only thing that brought him back to the table was the waiter, presenting them with their food.

"I just love my beautiful black sisters. All shapes, sizes, and colors . . . like picking honey fruit from a wide-variety tree." He picked up his knife and fork, ready to dig in.

Faye was glad when he finally bit into the turf part of his meal and kept his eyes on his plate. It was rude that Harry gawked at that woman in her presence, but she chalked it up to him not being used to having a girlfriend. All he needed was time, she thought, before he realized that that was what she considered herself to be.

Back at campus, she invited him into her room for wine when she discovered Lamona wasn't there. Boone's

Farm Apple flowed from the bottle, and when they finished their second glass, he kissed her good night. She parted her lips to welcome his taste. He lifted his hand to her breast and squeezed her nipple until he felt it harden between his fingers, and she gently pushed him away.

"Come on, baby. What's wrong?"

"I'm not ready yet."

"What you have to get ready to do? I'll wait. How long you gonna be . . . five, ten, fifteen minutes, max?"

She smiled at his impatience. "Soon" was all she could promise. As she watched him walk out the door he looked bowlegged, and she was glad to have made a good impression. When she climbed into bed, her chest was pounding, her heart was racing, and she found it hard to catch her breath. She hoped it wasn't indigestion—she hoped her body's responses to Harry meant that she was falling in love.

To celebrate the end of the school year, Harry took Faye to the Eddie Kendricks concert on campus. When he sang the finale, "Girl You Need a Change of Mind," Harry gave Faye a look she took to mean she needed to change her mind about sex and give up the panties real soon. At the end of the concert, he invited her back to his room, and Faye decided to part with her underwear. If Harry were going to become her husband, she'd have to get used to making herself available and detaching herself from her clothes in front of him.

He turned on the lava lamp. As she stared at the red glob pushing its way up through the thick yellow syrup, he put on the Dells' six-minute epic song, preferred music for couples who wanted to grind. As they slow danced to "Stay in My Corner," the reefer they had smoked at the concert and the music they were listening to helped put Faye in a sexy mood. Her mind relaxed, leaving her body in charge, and now it led the way. He

gently laid her down across his bed. When he removed her jeans, he slipped his fingers inside her, and then he licked the wetness between her legs, burying his face in the source. He told her she smelled like fresh hay, and when he finished exploring her field, she felt the force of his body come down on her.

It was Faye's first time surrendering herself completely to a man, and his careful entry deep between her bare welcoming thighs hurt so good. She didn't know whether to shout from the pain or to give in to the glory of ecstasy she had only imagined she'd feel before tonight. Once her body had adjusted to the size of his penis, she couldn't get enough of the stiffness that felt as hard as bedrock on a summit in the Blue Ridge Mountains. As their naked bodies rose and descended on the bed like waves cresting and folding in the ocean, their rhythm increased until they reached the height of intimacy, and when they came together, Faye had never felt so fulfilled and complete.

They made love again the following night without soft music and foreplay. They were two strangers who didn't waste any time sharing their secrets. From then on, they got along well enough to be a couple. Faye was convinced Harry was the right choice, and by the end of the second semester she was certain she was falling in love.

"You've been spending goo-gobs of time on the men's campus lately," Lamona said, looking at herself in the mirror. She took a comb, placed it dead center on the spot where her hairline met her forehead, and raked back, making a perfect part in the middle of her head. She brushed back the sides and collected what was left into a ponytail. "You don't want to flunk out or wind up like Yolanda Blakesly and have your stomach ulcer removed at the end of nine months."

Lamona was majoring in early childhood education, and suddenly Faye felt sorry for the kids. All she could

imagine was Lamona watching more of herself, caring more about her appearance, than looking after and teaching her young charges. "I'm acing all my classes," Faye said, sitting on the floor, leaning against big fluffy pillows, reading chapters in her American history book, and preparing to write an essay. "Everything's under control."

"Since you and Harry been doing y'all's thing this year, I guess you gonna introduce him to your folks this summer," Lamona said, examining her eyebrows in the mirror and then rummaging through her cosmetic bag for a pair of tweezers.

Faye shifted among the pillows, propping herself against the wall, in search of a comfortable position. "I already finished my portfolio for my final project this year," she said, changing the subject.

"Good for you. What did you finally wind up calling it?"

"Black Is Beautiful, of course. It's a scrapbook about young people like us—little-known profiles of college students who are destined to become leaders of tomorrow." As she was reading her textbook, she started jotting down some notes. "There's this sister down at Meharry Medical making great progress spearheading a cancer research program, and a brother in New York City who's being recognized as one of the country's top fashion designers. There's a young man out West, who just started his own trucking company, with a fleet traveling nationwide." She turned the page of her textbook, and continued writing in her notebook.

"Okay, I get the picture."

"It's not easy to find these news clippings; you gotta dig deep to uncover hidden treasures."

"I hear you, girl. I'm still working on my project. But getting the little kiddies to tell stories about themselves and then writing them all down so that they make sense

is a trip." Lamona finished plucking and began washing her face with oatmeal scrub.

"Ahem." Lamona pretended to clear her throat. "By the way, as your roommate, your ace boon coon, I can't believe you didn't use me as a model for any of your original hairstyles. What's up with that?"

"This was the year for natural styles. Next year's final project involves permed hair, so don't worry. You'll be my guinea pig then. That way, when I put you into my portfolio you can look at yourself all the time."

"Forgit you." Pretending to be insulted, Lamona turned off the running water and stormed out of the bathroom only to find Faye making fun of her, striking different poses, making various faces in front of an invisible camera.

"Okay, so I love myself. Now . . . what about you?"

Faye stared at her blankly.

"You didn't answer my question about Harry meeting your family."

Faye stopped laughing, grabbed a big pillow, and threw it at her roommate. "Between you and me, it's too soon for them to meet."

"What do you mean?"

"My folks are old-fashioned. They want me to marry someone from my hometown and live there forever, but I can't do that. It's not for me."

"But if you and Harry are serious, they've got to meet him sometime."

"The only way Harry is coming to my house is if he puts a ring on my finger, with the promise of moving up North."

Apparently that was enough information for Lamona. Faye was relieved that her roommate picked up her textbook, plopped down on her bed, stopped being nosy, and started studying for her exams.

When summer came, Faye knew that distance would

create a wedge between her and Harry. With him staying with his father in Harlem and her being confined to Lemon City, it was critical that they communicate in a way that didn't raise suspicion. As a result, the plan was to write to each other on the first and the fifteenth of each month; that way she could watch for the mail and intercept it before Granddaddy picked it up. The last thing she needed was for her grandfather to discover a return address from Harlem.

It was the middle of August when her sister, Louise, caught Faye going out to the mailbox and bringing in a single envelope, leaving the rest of the mail behind. Later, Faye could have kicked herself for being stupid enough to bring in just Harry's letter.

"What's that you got there?" Louise tried to grab the envelope from Faye's hand.

"Nothing. Just a letter from Lamona." Faye folded the envelope and stuffed it in her back pocket on her way into the house.

"Let me see it. If it's from your roommate, let me see." Louise tried taking the letter out of Faye's pocket. Faye swatted her sister's hand and slapped at her arm, trying to get her sister off her butt.

"I betchu it's from a boy. I bet you got a boyfriend and that's a love letter in your hand and y'all are talking about how much y'all are missing each other and want to kiss all up in the backseat of a car or something. I know that's what college kids think about and do. I'm telling Nana." Louise let Faye go and ran to the front door.

Faye ran in front of her and blocked the entrance. "Please don't tell Nana. He's just a friend."

"Then let me see it."

"No." Faye ran down Tuckahoe Road, waving the envelope in her hand, kicking up dust along the way,

laughing and screaming, staying as far in front of Louise as possible. Ole Miss Johnson pulled back her living-room curtain to see what all the commotion was about. She hadn't seen the girls acting silly since they were children and the tomfoolery brought a smile to her face. Faye could always run faster than Louise, and she kept on going until Louise got tuckered out and slumped over in the middle of the street, trying to catch her breath.

Faye wished she could tell Louise about Harry, but she was afraid her sister wouldn't understand. Then, toward the end of August, on the night before she was to return to Booker T., she mustered the courage to talk to her sister, deciding to give opening her heart and telling it like it is a chance. If Louise were going to explode after she revealed the truth about Harry, at least Faye would be leaving for school the next morning. With four hundred miles between her and the line of fire, at least she'd be out of harm's way.

It was Sunday night, and they were sitting on the sofa watching *Bonanza*. It was getting late, and Faye was nervous about bringing up the subject of Harry. To delay telling the truth, she found herself thinking that Ben Cartwright was a lot like Grandaddy, and she was a lot like the youngest child, Little Joe, except she wasn't pushed around by big brothers; her big sister was the person who bullied and intimidated her. When the commercial came on, she looked at Louise, seizing the opportunity to get her undivided attention because the show was almost over and she couldn't afford to procrastinate anymore.

"Louise, you know that letter I wouldn't let you read a few weeks back?"

"What about it?" Louise curled up her legs on the sofa and laid her head over the arm.

"It was from my boyfriend."

"Figures."

Faye was waiting for more of a reaction, at least some sign of excitement or interest, but when she didn't get either, she felt it was safe to continue. "His name is Harry."

"Don't sound familiar." Louise put her hand up to her mouth to cover her yawn.

"He's not from around here."

"Better not be an Outsider, is all I can say," Louise snapped before she closed her eyes, resting them, waiting for the show to come back on.

Faye decided not to say anything more. The hostility in Louise's voice convinced her she had already said enough, and she let her conversation trail off into the sunset. When *Bonanza* returned, Faye was relieved that her sister wasn't expecting a response to her comment and continued to be absorbed by the Cartwrights on the Ponderosa.

When Faye returned to campus in September 1971, she rarely ran into Harry. There were sporadic phone calls, occasional chance meetings after classes, and dinner here and there at Captain Jack's. Although they dated once or twice a month, he claimed the reason for his absence was the mandatory senior project, which required that he assemble a V-6 engine from scratch, a monumental task that he professed was extremely time consuming. Faye had a senior project, too, and still managed time for love and friends. She didn't fully understand Harry's reason for creating the distance between them, but she felt she had no choice but to be patient. Then something happened that made her reconsider her position. When winter break rolled around, Harry drove her to the train station. But after the break ended, Harry forgot to pick her up.

"What were you thinking?" Faye was so upset from having to wait for over an hour at the train station that she practically yelled in his ear.

"I'm sorry, baby, I just lost track of time."

"Track? Please, don't speak to me about tracks. I've had enough of tracks. I'm tired of tracks. I don't care if I never see another track again. I just want to go to my dorm room, thank you." She was so angry that they barely spoke during the rest of the ride to campus.

Over the next several weeks, Faye spent her time at the beauty center called "The Madam Building," named after Madam C. J. Walker. She was creating hairstyles for her "Black Is Beautiful II" portfolio, and admiring Lamona's patience in the chair almost as much as she was enjoying her work. Lamona's hair was long, thick, and coarse all at the same time, which lent itself to great versatility in styling. After giving her a touch-up, Faye spent the afternoon arranging Lamona's hair in a variety of ways: poofed up, parted in the middle with hair that fell on either side and swooped around her ears, parted on the side with a back flip, tight curls that drooped down into loose corkscrews, a French twist, a teased-up bouffant, piled on top of her head and hung with soft curls, hair with tapered back and sides, and a bob cut with and without bangs. After creating nine unique styles she was happy with, she took a picture of each one with her Kodak Pocket Instamatic camera, in addition to taking a Polaroid as a backup.

"You've been spending a lot more time in the room lately," said Lamona, as she sat in the salon chair watching Faye hit the button on the camera and being still until after hearing it click. "What's going on with you and Harry?"

"He's as busy as I am, I expect." Faye tried to sound unaffected by Harry's noticeable disconnect from her life. "We're all trying to graduate this year."

"Between you and me, I don't think he's working as hard as we are."

"What do you mean by that?"

"Come here." Lamona beckoned Faye with her finger to come closer as if she didn't want to run the risk of someone overhearing them, but Faye ignored her, intent on getting her shot. "I hear he may be seeing someone else," Lamona whispered loudly.

Faye jarred the camera and accidentally snapped the picture before she was ready. "I guess we're finished here for today." She didn't want to talk about Harry anymore, and she didn't want Lamona to see how upset she really was. She put her cameras back into their cases and added, "Thanks for being my model this afternoon."

"I had fun." Lamona kept her eye on Faye, watching her as she paced the room waiting for the last Polaroid to develop.

"Where you going?" Lamona stood up, taking off the plastic cape, draping it across the chair.

"Across campus."

Faye didn't call before she went up to Harry's room, and she didn't yield when the front-desk monitor tried to stop her. She went straight up to the second floor. Standing in front of his room, hearing muffled sounds that reeked of sexual activity, she pounded on the door. When he didn't respond, she began kicking it, becoming even more frustrated when she attracted everyone's attention on the floor—except Harry's.

A weary male student appeared down the hall and shouted at Harry, "Come on out, you coward. Deal with the sister. I can't study with all this racket."

On the opposite end of the hallway, another student checked out the scene. " I can't believe this," he said, making the connection. "Man, this is wrong . . . this is so wrong. Where's the respect?" The young man shook his head and slammed and locked the door behind him.

A student with a towel wrapped around his waist came out of the bathroom when he heard the commotion. "You're busted, brother. Might as well get your be-

hind dressed, come on out, then turn it 'round and get it kicked."

Faye hit the door so hard she thought her foot might go through it.

Finally, Harry appeared. She pushed back the door and barged into the room, knocking him off balance, catching the sister who barely had enough time to zip up her jeans.

"Is this what you call working on your fucking V-6 engine?" Faye screamed. "Are you gonna tell me this is a part you need for your senior project?" Faye pointed at the young woman's crotch, and Harry ducked, thinking Faye was going to hit him. In the heat of the moment, it was the only thing she could think of saying, the only words that could prevent her from punching him in the face. She looked into his eyes and saw nothing. He attempted an apology but she was already back in the hallway, making her way down the stairs and out the front door.

Later that afternoon, Faye's phone rang. She picked up the receiver and dropped it down on the cradle. By the end of the day she had pulled the phone jack out of the wall. All Lamona did for the next month was collect the letters, cards, candy, flowers, and stuffed animals that Harry sent over to redeem himself. She put each item in a corner on the floor, and within days, a pile of guilt began to form. Each time she added a new contribution to the mound, Lamona shook her head and said "Um, um, um." Faye didn't know if the disgruntled sounds were meant for her or for Harry, and she didn't ask.

After looking at Harry's shrine in the corner for more than a month, Faye's anger was beginning to dwindle. She missed him but, more than that, she didn't want to punish him forever. After all, with three months left until graduation, she had a life-changing decision to make.

The deciding factor came six weeks after the incident,

on a warm day in March, when a handful of pebbles came through her open window and landed on the shag area rug on the floor. When she leaned over the windowsill and looked down, she saw Harry.

"What the heck are you doing? Have you completely lost your mind?" Faye was annoyed, but pleasantly surprised to see him.

"You won't return my phone calls. You won't answer my letters. You won't acknowledge my gifts or even see me. I have to depend on rocks to give me a chance to look at your beautiful face."

He lowered his head in a way that made Faye think of a homesick puppy in a pound. Then he looked back at her and said, "I'm so sorry. I was wrong. Please forgive me. I wasn't thinking. That girl means nothing to me. It will never happen again."

"Get down on your knees," Faye shouted, as if she were a commander at the Norfolk Naval Base.

Harry got down on one knee.

"Both knees. I want two knees. I want you down on the ground."

He got down on both knees and added, "Please, baby. Please. I'm sorry. You're the one I love."

It was early in the morning and several students were on their way to classes.

"How will I know for sure you won't cheat on me again?" Faye leaned out the window, anxious to get an answer to her question.

"I give you my word."

One student shouted, "His word probably ain't worth a dime for a local phone call."

"Give the brother another chance," another student said in passing, forming a V with two fingers, giving her the peace sign.

"Forget the brother, sister." A female student gave her the thumbs-down. "Don't go for the okey-doke."

"We all make mistakes," said a male student as if he had been in Harry's position before.

"Shirley Chisholm just announced she's running for president. *All* sisters should follow her lead and be strong and independent women." The men expressed shock and the women cheered.

Faye looked down at Harry, who was wearing a scoop-neck dashiki that revealed the hairs on his chest and a pair of tight jeans that showed off his ass—one of her favorite parts of his body. In the midst of all the passersby below, he suddenly looked small, harmless, and manageable, and since the Lord teaches people to forgive and forget, she looked into his eyes and decided to give him another chance.

Being back together was like being back in love the first time they met. If Harry wasn't her soul mate, he was close enough. He invited her to every party, concert, and event on campus and when they weren't studying together, they were making love. Every time she and Harry had sex, he blew her mind, which convinced her that he was destined to become her husband.

The closer they got to graduation, the more she became obsessed with marriage. The big day was coming soon. She had to act quickly. She was content with the way their relationship was going, and she had to get him to propose to her now. She could easily picture herself walking across the auditorium stage in her cap and gown, but walking down the aisle in her bridal gown and train was still a blur in her mind that hadn't quite come into focus.

In early April, when he still hadn't popped the question, the thought crossed her mind to propose to him herself, but she wasn't that bold. They were eating lunch in the school cafeteria when she brought up the topic of marriage. The only response she got from Harry was him choking on his food, and she figured her timing

wasn't right since she'd caught him off guard. Not being the least bit offended, she thought the best thing to do was to give it a rest and bring up the subject again some other time. She did—the following week. After a few days had passed she came up with another strategy. Thinking that Harry was reluctant to propose because, like all men just getting started in life, he might be worried about lacking the proper resources to support a new wife, she thought she'd put his fears to rest. The next time they were in the cafeteria, she told him about her family's land, reassured him of Granddaddy's wealth and the chances that they wouldn't have to worry about money. Not only was Lemon City rich in history, it was rich, period. The only source of concern might be how long it would take Granddaddy to give them his blessing after getting used to the idea of them moving up North to join the Black Power movement, like they'd discussed. She watched Harry as he held his cheeseburger in midair, halfway between the table and his mouth, giving serious thought to this new notion of financial stability. When she mentioned her family's wealth, his eyes widened and his lips pulled back taut as if he didn't want too big a smile to form on his face. She was glad he was relieved that money wasn't going to be an issue. She sensed that he'd feel more comfortable asking for her hand in marriage now that the pressure to begin a new life wasn't a hardship put entirely upon him. She didn't have to mention the subject to Harry again; her intuition proved to be right. By the middle of April, two weeks before graduation, he finally agreed to elope.

CHAPTER FOUR

In Nana's daydream, the gurgling sound of someone drowning, releasing their final breaths underwater, became louder and louder until she realized it was a pot boiling on the stove. How Faye had fallen in love and married the Outsider was still beyond her. At this point, it wasn't up to her to try to understand. It was too late for that—now she had to try to accept. She could still hear her family gathered in the living room, mumbling about how Faye and Harry had first met. Nana was glad that she wasn't in there to listen to the tale, that her job was a solitary one in the kitchen. She picked up the electric mixer and beat the egg whites in a large, round, plastic bowl until their peaks were stiff and looked like snowcapped mountains. She slowly poured hot syrup into the egg whites and added the grated lemon peel, lemon juice, and yellow food coloring. As she waited for the frosting to cool, she sat wiping the sweat from her hands on her apron, but no matter how often she wiped them, perspiration seemed to seep through her skin like water forcing through cracks in a dam. Every time she slid her hands against her apron, she became more obsessed with the idea that what had brought this unexpected intrusion into her family was the smell of money. Sniffing around her granddaughter, Harry must have figured that a woman from Lemon City—a town with a rich heritage and people—was prosperous.

When the frosting had finally cooled, she poured

the yellow cream into the cylinder-shaped tube and squeezed, adding to the words "Congratulations Graduate" the words "And New Bride" on the cake. She considered writing "and Groom," but she wasn't used to thinking in pairs and it was already too late—she didn't have room for a whole new word.

Nana pushed open the swinging kitchen door with her elbow and set the cake down on the dining room table. Since the French doors separating the living room from the dining room were always kept open, she had a clear view of the men in front of the fireplace. Granddaddy and Billy were sitting next to each other, with Harry sitting across from them as if he were on the receiving end of a police interrogation. Nana smiled at Harry when he looked up at her as she entered the dining room, but as soon as he looked away she sucked her teeth and shook her head. She caught Louise staring at her as if the child could read her mind.

"Go'ne and make yourself useful." Nana shooed Louise into the kitchen, resenting her granddaughter's efforts to eavesdrop on her thinking. "Get out the good china and bring out some sun tea. We got company." Nana added, "Mind your manners and quit staring."

"Harry's not company," Faye said. She and Elvira were sitting at the dining room table, looking through a scrapbook of pictures Faye had taken at college of her original hairstyles and designs. "He's family."

Nana smiled. "It's the first time he's here, baby. That makes him company. Besides, he shouldn't mind being a novelty for now, 'cause being a guest in this house never lasts long." She smiled in Harry's direction and wondered if her face was going to crack from all this grinning. "You've gotta forgive my grown grandchildren, Mr. Thompson," she said politely.

"Harry . . . please. Please call me Harry," he said in

an effort to be a gentleman, taking off his suit jacket, resting it on the back of the chair.

Faye picked up on the tension in the room. "And you may call her Nana," she said, using her finger as a shovel to scoop up some frosting and put it into her mouth—but not before Nana slapped her hand. "Ow!" Faye rubbed the sting out of her grandmother's attack. Nana knew she had overreacted, hitting Faye's hand a little harder than she should. She didn't know how it happened; she must have just slipped.

"He can call me, 'Ma'am' if he wants to," she said to Faye, "or Mrs. Dunlap will be just fine." It was too soon for that Outsider to be calling her by her family name. "Y'all go'ne, now; git away from here," she said to the girls. "You sit down at the table and think you gotta eat. Take another swipe at my cake and I'll swat y'all right on outta here." She waved her hand toward the door with such force that if someone had been standing there, they'd have been knocked upside the head. "Well, I ain't ready to serve ya yet, so go'ne out on the porch. Git." She shooed them out of the dining room. Elvira, who was starting to get hungry, grabbed a bag of Cheez Doodles off the table.

Nana had gone into the kitchen, and when she walked back into the living room with three drinking glasses on a serving tray she suddenly saw the irony: As she stared at the three men sitting before her, then at the pictures of the trio, John F. Kennedy, Martin Luther King Jr., and Robert Kennedy, which hung above her mantel on the fireplace, she was struck by the incongruity—the image of the peacemakers hanging on her wall and below them, the vision of chaos that sat in her living room. For sure, they'd have to get through a long, tough transition time that would test their last nerves and try what was left of their patience.

"So you say your folks are from Harlem . . . you got

any people here in the South?" asked Granddaddy. Harry shook his head.

"I can't remember the last time we've been in the presence of an Outsider, never mind having one in the house," Nana offered while pouring sun tea into their glasses and trying to figure out if Harry identified with the phrase. "You, Granddaddy?"

"Cain't say I remember none." As Granddaddy answered the question, his tone seemed to make Harry tug on his sideburns and shift uncomfortably in his seat.

When Nana finished filling their glasses, she retreated to the kitchen. She wished she could sit with the men to learn more about the Outsider, but everyone was hungry and she had to serve brunch. To resolve her dilemma, she propped the kitchen door open with a flatiron doorstop so she could eavesdrop whenever something caught her attention.

"I know you just finished school and all, Harry, but what is it that you want to do exactly?" Granddaddy pushed back against the arms of the La-Z-Boy and put his feet up on the footrest. Billy took a toothpick out of his pocket and began picking at his teeth, more for effect than for hygiene. He'd seen cops do the same thing on TV shows like *Mod Squad*, and if cool worked for them, he thought, it would look good on him, too.

"I plan on working at a car repair shop and saving money until I can afford to buy my own place . . . that's what I really want to do."

"Come again?" said Granddaddy, who sometimes had selective hearing when he wanted people to repeat themselves.

"My dream is to own my own car repair shop . . . back up North," Harry added.

"Say, what?" said Nana from the kitchen. As she burst through the door to get closer to the conversation, she remembered to start grinning again. "What'chu say,

Harry?" She said it sweetly, wiping her hands on her apron.

Billy had never seen that expression on his grandmother's face before. Her mouth was locked into a smile that pushed her chubby cheeks up so high it made her eyes disappear. She looked so uncomfortable grinning that hard, he thought it must be painful. Nana was not a small woman and her presence, as tense as she was, amplified the uneasiness in the room.

"Aw, Nana, the young man said something about going back up North . . . he didn't mean nothing by it." Granddaddy deliberately made light of the comment since the Outsider would only be taking his granddaughter up North over his dead body. Immediately, Nana started choking on her sun tea. She had taken a sip and forgotten where her mouth was, and some of the liquid dribbled down her chin. She wiped it off with the back of her hand.

"Now that he'll be living in Lemon City, he probably means he's going up North just for an occasional visit. Ain't that right, son? That's what you meant to say, isn't it?"

"I suppose I could do that, too," said Harry.

As she retreated back into the kitchen, Nana was so relieved that she started grinning for real.

But Granddaddy wasn't fooled. He knew what Harry was thinking, and it was up to him to prevent it from happening. He thought about the old car repair shop on Old Dominion Road that had been vacant for at least a year. This would be the perfect wedding gift for his new grandson-in-law. Granddaddy was confident the man wouldn't turn him down. So what if it was in the South instead of in the North? If Harry had asked his permission in advance to marry his granddaughter, Granddaddy would have pretended to have taken time to think it over. He wouldn't have considered an Outsider as a

suitable match. But Faye had taken that privilege from him, and it would take time to get used to it. Granddaddy knew he had to accept their union for the good of the family. What's done was done. That wasn't a rule; just common sense.

After checking out Harry with as much scrutiny as the sports section of the Sunday newspaper, Billy decided Harry was not to be trusted. He just didn't look right in his tacky green suit, plus he didn't smell right, covering his own scent with too much Old Spice aftershave as if he might have something to hide. Billy also didn't like the way his eyes shifted back and forth without his head moving, looking from right to left at him and his grandfather as they asked him questions. He thought it was rude the way Harry stared at the pack of Kools in his shirt pocket every time there was a pause in the conversation like he couldn't wait to get outside and have a smoke. It was the manner in which Harry nervously crossed and uncrossed his legs when he finished a sentence, waiting for him or Granddaddy to react before he proceeded to tell his story, that bugged Billy the most. Even though Billy had only four years under his belt as the Lemon City Sheriff, he felt he was just as good as any detective in getting a vibe on people's characters. He concluded that Harry was as crooked as the lines on a road map, and he bet that time would prove him right. But when he looked through the window onto the porch and saw how happy his sister was, he decided to lighten up on the dude and give the chump some slack.

The midday sun cast a shadow on the Dunlap house. Faye, sitting beside Louise on the porch swing, was showing her sister the rest of her college hairstyle-and-design scrapbook, but all Louise kept saying was "Umhm . . . umhm . . . umhm" every time she turned the page, and her sister's form of communication was driving Faye crazy. If Louise had something on her

mind, Faye wished she'd get it out of her mouth and get it over with.

Elvira, perched on the porch railing across from the sisters, sensed the attitude building up between them and took it upon herself to create a distraction. "Check it out . . . ," she said, licking the orange powder from the Cheez Doodles off her fingers and peeking through the window. "Just look at 'em . . . Billy and Granddaddy in there for over an hour giving Harry the third degree, just drilling him like a Texas oil well." She pointed at the men, still talking in front of the fireplace.

"What do you expect when you bring home a total stranger and announce to your family you're married to him?" Louise made no effort to keep her voice down. "It's not the sort of thing that happens every day . . ."

"Shh," whispered Elvira.

"Don't shush me," Louise said, then finished what she had to say to Faye, ". . . especially around here."

Louise's chest was heaving, her breath becoming deep and loud to the point that Elvira thought she was going to punch her baby sister.

"Take it easy, Louise." Elvira shoved the bag of Cheez Doodles between them as though she believed the intrusion of a snack would head off any arguments. Louise shoved her arm inside the bag, pulling out a handful of orange crunchy things as if she were yanking out someone's heart.

"We should be happy for Faye." Elvira grabbed her sister-in-law and hugged her, as though demonstrating to Louise what to do.

"How long you been knowing this dude?" Louise asked, making a face that looked like she had just sucked on a lemon.

"Almost two years," Faye said.

"Then how come we're just finding out about him now?"

"I tried to tell you last summer." She put her hands on her hips. "But you weren't ready to hear it."

"You're not with him 'cause you're pregnant, are you?"

Elvira looked mortified, her face half-hidden behind the bag of Cheez Doodles.

"Gone are the days when you have to be with a man 'cause you're carrying his child." Louise folded her arms across her chest and leaned her head to one side, smug in her feminist position.

Faye rolled her eyes and responded from the other side of the Cheez Doodles bag. "I'm with him because I love him." Then she turned to Elvira. "I just didn't want to make a big deal out of getting married."

"A husband is a big deal. An Outsider is a bigger deal. Your family needs to know about your long-term plans before they become permanent."

Faye took a deep breath and leaned against the wooden railing before deciding to continue on to the second part of her confession. "If that's the case, then my family needs to know this, too." She braced herself, folding her arms across her chest, taking the same defensive posture as her sister. "Harry and I are just passing through. We're moving up North to join the Black Power movement so we can upgrade the development of *all* brothers and sisters. You know what they say, 'the need for the hour, is Black Power.'"

Louise put her hands to her mouth, doing everything she could to prevent herself from laughing. "You can't join the Black Power movement like it's a YMCA membership. Besides, you ain't never been north of Lemon City. If I didn't know any better, I'd ask you what you been smokin' or what pills you been poppin'. I know all about those reefer parties y'all have at those colleges."

Elvira dropped the bag of Cheez Doodles on her lap

and looked at Louise. "You mean . . . you think . . . Faye is tripping?"

"If y'all want to make fun of what I'm saying, then forget it." Faye was so upset that spit flew out of her mouth. Something wet landed on Louise's blouse, and she could no longer contain her laughter.

"I can't expect y'all to understand anything, anyway. What I'm saying is way over your heads." Faye stomped her foot, clenching both fists, regressing back into the battle stance she used to take with her sister in childhood.

One look at Faye and Louise laughed even harder. Faye looked at her sister like she was a fool and started smirking, too, which triggered Elvira into a fit.

When the sisters settled down from their giggling, Faye returned to being serious and continued her confession. "Okay, I'm busted. The real reason I need to move is because I've already started developing my own hair-care line. I'm calling it Nubian Silk. When I go up North, I'm not going to be just a beautician—I'm going to be an entrepreneur and have a whole chain of hair salons. Harry's not just going to be a mechanic; one day he's going to be the proprietor of his own auto shop. Maybe he'll have a chain of auto shops, too."

The thought of her sister leaving Lemon City made Louise shake her head. Faye gave up talking about herself, realizing that no matter what she said, her sisters still wouldn't understand how she felt. The saddest part was that with all they'd been through together, her happiness was something she'd never be able to share with them. However, this was supposed to be a joyous occasion and she didn't want to bring herself down. After having the laughter clear the air, it made room for them to slip into easy conversations and reminisce about old times and catch up as best they could on what was going on in each other's lives. It was the neutral subjects that

kept them in comfortable territory, the telling of favorite stories that gave them common ground and made them best friends again.

"Remember when you were about ten years old and Nana told you not to pick those wild blackberries in your Sunday-school clothes after church, and you went out into that blackberry field and picked them anyway?"

Faye knew where the story was going—she had heard it a hundred times, and so had Elvira, and it always managed to get a laugh. With every telling of the story there seemed to be slight variations and new embellishments. Sometimes Louise would spend more time building up the Sunday-school part, sometimes she'd play up the role of the blackberries or exaggerate Faye's stubborn refusal to listen to Nana. And if Louise really felt like embarrassing her baby sister, she'd jump up and down and dramatize all the hollering and carrying on Faye did when Nana found her and her church clothes smeared with purple. If Faye becoming the object of a joke put Louise in a good mood for the moment, so be it.

"You came home and Nana asked you where you were and you said, 'Nowhere.' Nana knew you were lying 'cause you had blackberry stains all over your mouth, on your hands, and cute little dress—you even had the nerve to stash some in your pockets and your pink patent-leather pocketbook. Talk about a whuppin' . . ." Louise turned to Elvira. "Nana tore her up. Not so much for the blackberries as for the lying."

"And all you did was laugh," inserted Faye, "just like you doing now."

"Wasn't nothing else I could do," continued Louise. "You should have known better than to cross Nana."

Louise's words hung in the air. "That's kids for you," Elvira added nervously, hoping the sisters would keep their truce.

"Speaking of kids, Vi. What's happening with you?" Faye was more than willing to change the subject.

"Those kids at that elementary school 'bout to drive me crazy. By now, you'd think I'd be used to 'em being so rambunctious. But they're great practice though, 'cause me and Billy are still trying to have our own."

Nana called them inside before Elvira could elaborate. When they entered the dining room, fried chicken, potato salad, biscuits, and the newly redecorated graduation-wedding cake greeted them.

Faye headed straight for Harry to give him a hug, thinking he'd need one after putting up with her family on his own, but before she could reach him, Nana called her into the kitchen. Having contained herself with politeness all afternoon, Nana finally let go of the feelings that were about to make her burst.

"How come you didn't say nothing about this?" Nana swung her head in Harry's direction.

"Because you would have made me come back home." Faye was careful to sound humble, but not apologetic.

"You got that right. Would've been the best thing for you. Now you done got yourself into a mess." After piling the steaming-hot corn onto the cob onto the platter, Nana shoved the platter into her granddaughter's hands.

"Give him a chance, Nana."

"Young lady, The Rules aren't made to be broken."

Nana walked through the kitchen door into the dining room forcing a smile on her face and Faye followed, feeling like she was getting a facial from the steam rising from the corn.

As everyone took their places around the dining room table, Granddaddy was studying the honeymooners. He'd had a couple of hours to think long and hard about how he would handle the situation.

He hadn't planned on doling out any more cash. He

had bought the town's hair salon, Hair Today, Gone Be Beautiful Tomorrow, for Faye as a graduation present. The original owner had become bored with cutting hair and had gotten a real estate license, later putting the salon up for sale as her first exclusive property. The more Granddaddy thought about it, the more he knew that buying another establishment, The Shop, the vacant car-repair and service station down on Old Dominion Road, was a good idea. Money was no object when it came to keeping his family together. Besides, Lemon City hadn't seen a good mechanic since Theolus Weaver passed away last year. The Shop came equipped with existing pumps, so if the repair part of the business was slow, the gas part could pick up the slack. That settled it. Hair Today, Gone Be Beautiful Tomorrow would be Faye's graduation present, and The Shop would be the couple's wedding gift.

At the last minute, Granddaddy decided to attach some strings to the proposition to give his grandson-in-law an opportunity to prove himself worthy of his gift. Instead of buying the repair service station outright, he would make it a business arrangement, which would give him a chance to see what kind of man Harry was. Granddaddy felt no guilt behind his spur-of-the-moment plan, and most important, he saw himself abiding by Rule Number Eight: DO BUSINESS AT HOME FIRST, THEN WITH OUTSIDERS YOU CAN INVITE INTO YOUR HOME, AS A LAST RESORT. In his mind, he was doing business at home with an Outsider as a last resort. Even though the caveat was that business would be conducted with an Outsider his granddaughter, not he, had invited into his home, he exempted himself from that part of the rule. Besides, he didn't want to get too technical about it during an emergency like this. He'd just take out a bank loan and cosign it, and then he and Harry would split the monthly note. That would give Harry half the finan-

cial responsibility for The Shop, without him thinking he could get something without having to work for it in this town. He didn't think his new grandson-in-law would have a problem with the negotiation, or with accepting his benevolent offer. Judging by their conversation, he seemed real anxious to have something to call his own.

It was awkward having an Outsider in their midst. Now that everyone was facing each other around the dining room table, the reality of having a total stranger forced into the family had rendered them mute. Granddaddy broke the silence and turned to Faye.

"Now that you have graduated from community college, tell us what they taught you up there in cosmetology school that you couldn't learn here at home." Granddaddy grinned through his teeth.

Faye recognized the expression—more like a sting—which usually meant he was angry and would circle before he was ready to attack.

"First off," Faye started, carefully choosing her words, "I learned more about the kinds of ingredients that promote healthy hair, chemicals as well as natural herbs, and got a chance to experiment with them. Most importantly, I was able to begin work on my own line of hair-care products."

"That's nice," said Nana, looking at her husband and nodding her head in approval, hoping he would agree.

"I also learned a lot about the Black Power movement." Faye thought it was best to sneak in that bit of information while everyone was still proud of her accomplishments.

"Is that right?" Granddaddy raised his eyebrow, which sent a signal to his ears to perk up. He didn't think he'd

ever get used to the fact that Negroes were preferring to call themselves "black."

"Does that mean you've got a French beret and a leather jacket and gone militant on us or somethin', like one of them cougars?" asked Billy, who looked sideways at Harry, suspecting the Outsider had put these thoughts into his sister's head.

"It's not cougars, Billy." Faye sighed, knowing he was trying to make a joke. "It's panthers. Black Panthers. And all it means is that I'm now thinking about how I can make a difference in the fight for black people and equality."

Louise lifted a spoonful of potato salad from the bowl to put on her plate, but suddenly changed her mind about having seconds. What she had to say was more important than eating. "According to the literature—and you know I read everything that comes into the library on the subject—Black Power is about solidarity, not about individuals. Only the group, only the community can make political and economic changes."

Before Granddaddy knew it, he was shaking more hot sauce onto his fried chicken than he should have. All this talk about Black Power was giving his arm a mind of its own. As he finally gained control of himself and took a bite out of the breast, he couldn't decide which was making him hotter, the meat or Harry, who had obviously corrupted his granddaughter's thinking.

"Well, being a mechanic and owning my own place is one way of making a contribution to the struggle," said Harry. Granddaddy almost choked.

"And how's that?" asked Billy, applying butter to his biscuit, careful to make sure that Harry noticed his skill in handling a knife.

Faye jumped in, pointing her drumstick at Billy. "The more individuals that take responsibility for their own

destiny, the more it adds up to economic independence. The ultimate result is social and economic freedom."

Louise cleared her throat. "In case you didn't hear me, I repeat: Black Power is a group thang. Not an individual thang. That's how brother Stokely came up with the phrase, 'Power to the people' in the first place! Right on," she said, proud of making her point, raising her fist at the table.

"It seems like Black Power can be anything you want it to be, as long as it's about lifting up the race," said Elvira, trying to get into the conversation and, as usual, attempting to keep the peace.

Nana decided it was her turn to speak up on the subject. "If that's the case, I say we got plenty of Black Power right here in Lemon City." She didn't like talking about "movement," she liked it when people stayed put. But Faye was clutching onto the idea of a movement with such passion that Nana was afraid she wouldn't let it go. Because she knew that once her granddaughter latched onto ideas they usually stuck, the whole conversation was making Nana restless and uncomfortable. She shifted from one side of her hefty buttocks to the other.

"You make Black Power happen any way you can," Faye said, shrugging her shoulders in response to Louise.

Granddaddy watched Faye, sitting smugly at the far side of the dining room table. He felt his blood pressure climb, seeing his granddaughter rising up high and mighty, and talking down to her family.

"What do you know about the races?" He pounded his fist on the table with such force it caused everyone to jump. It was his job to bring his granddaughter back down to earth. She was making herself out to be a big shot just because she had spent two years in college, but

now that she was back home, he had to remind her of her place in the family.

Faye took a deep breath and braced herself, knowing she'd reached the point where she'd have to be quiet and still and let the storm that was raging toward her pass through.

"What do you know about discrimination?" Granddaddy looked directly at his granddaughter, greeting confrontation head-on.

"Just what I read and hear and see on TV." Faye lowered her eyes and spoke to her plate, then looked back at Granddaddy again.

"You were born and raised in Lemon City, where none of that stuff exists." A piece of what he was chewing on almost came out of his mouth, and he shoved it back in with his finger.

Before Faye realized it, her hands had gripped the arms of the chair and she was leaning forward. "But that doesn't mean we should ignore it and deny that it happens to other people."

"Young lady, if Negroes didn't have segregation, then the floodgates to hell would open." He flagged his arms through the air. "Negroes everywhere would abandon their own banks, schools, hotels, hospitals, resorts, and stores and lose everything they worked so hard to have."

Nana got up to start clearing off the table. Once her husband got going on an argument, he didn't stop until he finished it, and she didn't feel like sitting through this one. It was a shame that all this bickering had to occur on Faye's first day back home, but her granddaughter had brought it on herself when she decided to go to college and return with an Outsider.

"Who do you think are gonna patronize Negro businesses?" Granddaddy didn't wait for Faye to answer. "Negroes. That's who."

"Granddaddy, separatism as a strategy for equality has never worked, and it never will." By the time Faye said it, she realized she sounded more like a whiner than an advocate for the revolution.

At this point, the debate was between Faye and Granddaddy, and the rest of the family knew better than to interfere. If anyone had any doubts, Billy gave Harry a look that told him not to butt in. This had nothing to do with him. It was family business.

"I got equality, and I got separatism." Granddaddy pounded his fist on the table, causing everyone to jump again. "I got the best of both worlds, right here." His eyes locked onto Faye as if they had strapped her into her chair. She couldn't move, and he didn't blink. "All I want is peace of mind and my own shit. As soon as Negroes give up their own shit, they'll be begging other folks for theirs." Granddaddy paused to let everyone in the room digest his words, and added, "Plus, y'all know what I told you happened to Easely, right?"

Everyone except Harry looked at each other, recognizing Granddaddy's pain.

"He was my best friend. Y'all remember me talking about that, don't you?" He looked around the room as they nodded solemnly in their sadness.

"That oughta tell you something about the outside world." Granddaddy focused again on Faye. "It's one thing for your Nana to let you go across the state, but heading outta state is outta the question."

Nana saw the redness glaze over her husband's eyes as he bowed his head before anyone else could see. Then she saw him fight back the memory that was clouding his vision.

"Granddaddy, I'm not Easely, and that was a long time ago, and don't worry, that's not going to happen to me."

"'Twas like yesterday to me, young lady. The outside

world is full of all kinds of dangers, and you don't get no warnings. Things just happen out there, they just sneak up on you and *blam*." Granddaddy dropped his knife and fork on the table and hit one hand against the other, startling everyone. "Things will never be the same."

Faye slumped back into her seat, feeling as though the wind had been knocked out of her. She couldn't allow her grandfather to use an example from the past as an excuse for her not to take a chance on a different kind of future. She was taking a risk, but she had no choice other than to stand up for herself. "Harry and I are leaving Lemon City," she announced. "We're moving up North the first week of June." She hadn't meant to blurt out her statement that way, but it was too late to take it back. She knew how much her leaving would hurt her grandfather, but it would kill her if she stayed and didn't follow her heart.

All eyes in the room focused on Granddaddy. As he spoke, he looked directly at Harry. "I hate to be the bearer of good news, but I've got a surprise for you two lovebirds." He smiled, but something about the way the corners of his mouth didn't turn up all the way made Faye nervous, as did his tone and the way he said the word "lovebirds."

He reached into his pants pocket. "As a graduation present, here are the keys to Hair Today, Gone Be Beautiful Tomorrow. I've been planning this surprise ever since you went away to college." He handed the keys to Faye, who was speechless. "The beauty parlor is all yours," he added. "I know, it's a dream come true, but you deserve the best. It's what you've always wanted, ever since you were a little girl. Remember?" Granddaddy smiled as he locked eyes with Harry, a signal that meant his granddaughter was staying in Virginia. Granddaddy directed his attention back to Faye.

"Don't feel obligated to say 'thank you.'"

"I never expected . . . I don't know what to say . . ." Faye was trying not to look or sound defeated, but she knew the attempt was unsuccessful. ". . . a simple gold necklace or a watch would have been fine . . . Granddaddy, please. You don't have to . . ."

"I did."

"I couldn't possibly accept . . ."

"Yes, you could. Consider it already done."

"Thank you," said Faye, trying to sound appreciative. She wouldn't dare decline Granddaddy's offer, especially not after their argument, particularly not in public. The more she pretended to be grateful, the bigger the knot in the pit of her stomach and the lump in her throat grew.

"And you," he turned back to Harry, "you will be the proud owner of the vacant car-repair shop and gas station down on Old Dominion Road. I don't have keys for you right at this moment, but I'm going to the bank first thing Monday morning to get the paperwork in order."

Harry knew he'd get something out of the marriage deal, but he had never suspected anything as big as this. He sat frozen in his seat, with eyes as wide as chestnuts, his face going into tiny convulsions trying to suppress a smile.

"Don't feel obligated to say 'thank you,' either." Granddaddy thought the man must have forgotten his manners.

"Thank you, Mr. Dunlap," said Harry, getting up from the table, recovering from the shock, and shaking his in-law's hand. Faye looked on in horror. It was bad enough she had to figure a way out of this mess, but now she had to come up with a way to bail Harry out, too.

"There now," Granddaddy said, a gleam of victory in his eye. "You and Faye will have everything it takes to live right here in Lemon City. I just gave you all the Black Power you'll ever need." He paused and looked

Harry square in the eyes. "So, Harry. What do you think about that?"

Harry cleared his throat and put one elbow on the table. He was still trying to process the great news that was swimming around in his head. "I guess we could get used to it, all right," he said, avoiding eye contact with his wife.

"Okay, Granddaddy," Faye said, slumping into her chair and sinking into defeat. "We'll stay for a while." She had almost gotten up the courage to say "no" to him, to turn down his generous gift, excuse herself from the table, and go speeding up the interstate highway north. But without talking to Nana beforehand and getting her support in advance, she couldn't go that route. Having Nana on her side about going to college was one thing, getting her grandmother's support on leaving Lemon City permanently was quite another. Now that she was stuck in the harbor with this anchor of a hair salon holding her down, it would take time to figure out a way to sail free.

Resigning herself to extend her visit until she could modify her plan, she looked up from her plate and said, "At some point we've got to get on with our lives. More than likely, we'll settle down in New York." She spoke directly to her grandfather, and then looked at Harry for confirmation, but he didn't look back.

CHAPTER SIX

Even though Harry was dead, there was more food than usual on the table this Thanksgiving Day. Everyone was helping himself to seconds, eating as if this meal would be their last supper together for a very long time.

"Why're you looking at me?" Granddaddy asked Nana, who was squinting her eyes, stretching her neck, and peering in his direction. "It's Thanksgiving. I'm supposed to be eating like this."

"I'm not looking at you." She gestured for Faye to pass her the candied yams.

"You staring right at me . . . I can see that. My vision ain't as bad as yours. Ain't she staring at me, Billy?"

"Looks that way to me," he said. "Maybe she's rediscovering how good-looking you really are. Or maybe she's trying to see if there's a piece of food stuck between your teeth." Granddaddy took a finger and wiped it across his teeth, and then scrubbed them with a napkin.

"Just kidding, Granddaddy."

"I'm looking past you, trying to see if I missed a spot of tarnish on my good silver gravy bowl," said Nana. "I cleaned every piece in the set the other day, but I still see a smidgen of a fingerprint on my bowl."

Directly behind Granddaddy was the cherrywood china closet, where Nana kept her best silver, porcelain, and clay figurines of colored people and angels that had been passed down to her or given as gifts over the years.

The brown figures, ranging from the color of heavy

cream to the darkness of Blue Ridge Mountain High-
land coffee, were a reminder of Nana's family tree, me-
mentos from generations of Lemon City's 100-year
history. Each piece had been donated by a Crawford
woman and had its own story of how it came into the
collection. Every now and then, when she needed
strength from her ancestors, Nana would gaze upon the
little people in the china closet for support or share a
quiet moment with the angels.

What had come out of the silence today hadn't been
surprising. When she'd made herself still, she heard a
distant voice tell her that Harry's death could not have
been avoided. He was an evil man, like poison to the
town, and it had been in everyone's best interest for him
to die.

Faye looked at Nana, who was staring into the china
closet, and wondered where her mind was drifting off
to. Ever since Harry's death, her grandmother was act-
ing stranger by the day. Faye couldn't figure out if it was
due to nerves or to something she was hiding. In the past
few days, she had spent more time on housework than
she normally did, as if cooking would consume the truth
and cleaning would purge it from her family. Nana got
up from the table, scrubbed the gravy bowl with a soft
cloth and silver polish, washed her hands, and sat back
down.

Saint started playing with her food bowl in the
kitchen. The constant thumping against the baseboard
was getting on Nana's nerves, so she called the cat into
the dining room, telling her to quiet down and to sit next
to her. Upon hearing her mistress's voice, Saint imme-
diately followed orders, curling herself around Nana's
ankle. Saint was truly obedient, just like an old, faithful
dog.

Faye looked at the cat on the floor and wondered why

Harry couldn't have been as loyal to her as Saint was to Nana.

"Losing a husband, no matter how troubled the marriage was, is still awful sad," said Nana, attempting to console her granddaughter. She took a bite of her turkey and looked up at the ceiling, perhaps hoping that staring at the peach-painted plaster would help her find the appropriate words. "It's like those raccoons 'round here. Everyone knows they're a menace. Always getting into folks' trash cans, transmitting germs and diseases. Yet on the other hand, it still pains me to see 'em lying all sprawled out in the middle of the road with their guts hanging out." Nana patted her mouth with her napkin. "No matter how much I dislike those varmints, I don't like to see 'em dead. 'Cause 'coons are still God's creatures, just like your husband was one of God's creatures, too." Everyone at the table gasped at the analogy Nana made between Harry and roadkill.

"All I know is Sheriff Taylor is coming first thing in the morning." Billy couldn't let Harry's humanity go too far before reminding his family that he was still the cause of one of them going to jail. "We'll all have to sleep here tonight to keep an eye on each other and make sure nobody gets the urge to escape."

"Don't be ridiculous." Louise tugged on the onyx Black Power fist dangling from her necklace. She hated it when Billy did his job by the book. "None of us is crazy enough to leave town."

Billy leaned across the table, into her face. "Then why do you have a one-way train ticket to leave town first thing tomorrow morning?"

"Nana, he's lying." Louise stood up from the table and her chair fell back on the floor. "He's trying to set me up."

Billy started to laugh. "You should have seen the look

on your face, Lou. Gawd, it was priceless. Do that again."

"That's not funny." Elvira punched her husband on the arm.

"That train ticket belongs to me," said Faye. The room fell silent. Even Saint lifted her head and perked up her ears to listen. "But the train isn't scheduled to leave tomorrow. It departs in four days—on Monday morning."

She had thought long and hard about buying that one-way ticket. She was hoping that Harry would finally take her seriously; see her side of things and decide to come with her. In any event, it had been a whole year and way past time for him to make up his mind. She had to be prepared to fulfill her plan, even if she had to leave Harry behind. Up until the last minute, Harry had called her bluff. But by that time, the conflict in her mind had ended and, no longer requiring the company of her husband, she would have tractor-plowed through anything that got in the way of her leaving Lemon City. But now, it didn't matter anymore that Harry wouldn't go with her. For one, she no longer cared. For two, he was dead.

(handwritten margin note: Faye planned to leave Lemon City w/o wanting Harry)

The morning after Faye returned from college, she and Harry had moved into the family's cottage, which was completely furnished, making shopping for furniture and appliances the least of their worries.

The cottage down the street from Granddaddy's house was barely visible from Tuckahoe Road. The sycamores' overhanging branches, the white and chestnut oaks, the pitch pines and spruce-firs, the purple bushy rhododendrons, and the buckeyes with their beautiful yellow flowers hid the cottage from passersby, while shielding it from the sun. A gravel driveway alongside the house stopped short at the point where it met the thick of the woods bordered by trumpet-shaped bluebells and clusters of small white flowers blooming on wild mountain ash. A bald patch of dirt emerged as a pathway, the results of being stepped on regularly over the years. The trail had a slight curve in it, winding around to the front door.

The cottage smelled like a musty old closet that had been sealed shut since last summer. Faye pried open the windows to release the stuffy dampness, only to have the sweltering May humidity rush in. The heat weighed heavily on her, like Granddaddy's generous gifts. As quickly as he had given them the hair salon and auto shop, she would try her best to return them, sell them, or exchange the unused presents for something more prac-

tical. But before she could focus on that, she had to clean up the dust and disinfect her temporary residence.

The first thing Harry did was set up the stereo and put the Delfonics eight-track cartridge into the tape player. Once the volume was adjusted to an appropriate level, the newlyweds began to sweep away the cobwebs and scrub the house from top to bottom, starting in the main room, which served as the living and dining rooms. After that, they'd scour the kitchen and bedroom.

Faye was on her knees, scrubbing the hardwood floor, and then realized that all she had been doing was moving the hand brush around and around in the same circle, creating one spot noticeably lighter than the floorboards in the rest of the room.

"Harry. We're about in as much mess as this cottage." She sat back on her knees and wiped the perspiration from her forehead with the back of her yellow Playtex rubber glove. "Now what are we gonna do?"

"What do you mean?" asked Harry.

"Don't pretend like you don't know what I'm talking about." Faye picked the next area on the floor and started scrubbing. "Granddaddy's so-called wedding and graduation presents—those aren't gifts. They're bribes to keep us here."

"That's an awful way to talk about your grandfather. He seems like a decent man to me."

"That's not the point. The question is, how do we gracefully back out of this without hurting Granddaddy's feelings?" Faye threw the washrag into the bucket of dirty water like a beat-down boxer throwing his towel into the ring.

"Come, on, baby. We'll think of something." He slowly lifted her chin, then looked into her eyes before he pressed his lips against her mouth. When he felt her soften, he moved in for the kind of kiss that made him want more.

"Come on, baby," he said into her cheek. "Let's do it right here."

"We have to finish cleaning first." She leaned against his chest with one arm positioned to push him away.

"We're almost done." He grabbed her closer.

"It's hot in here." She knew that if they stopped now, they wouldn't get done until the wee hours of the morning, and she was already exhausted from the events of yesterday. "Later, baby. Let's just keep working."

Harry turned up the volume on the stereo. The song "Somebody Loves You" was playing so loud it made it difficult for them to talk, but Faye could tell by the bulge in Harry's pants that he wasn't interested in talking, that conversation was the last thing on his mind.

When they finished cleaning the bedroom, Faye felt she could finally relax. She found a brand-new set of sheets inside the dresser, tore open the plastic, and proceeded to make up the bed. As she leaned across the mattress to smooth out the creases, Harry walked into the room. From his point of view, her backside looked inviting, and he took advantage of the opportunity to be intimate with his wife. She turned around to face him, but he wanted to feel her ass against his groin and grabbed her shoulders to hold her firmly into place. Their lovemaking sucked out what little air was left in the room, and afterward they collapsed from the heat and from exhaustion. Harry fell asleep. As Faye lay there thinking about what he had said to Granddaddy yesterday afternoon and his refusal to acknowledge her presence, she pushed her husband's arm from around her waist and shoved him over onto his side of the bed.

The telephone rang as she was dozing off. "Hello."

"Quit bumpin' and grindin', you honeymoonin' hussy, and get your butt outta bed."

"Excuse me?" she said to Louise. "I'm whipped. You have no idea how dirty this place was." She fluffed out

the section of her hair that had been made flat by the pillow. "I just finished cleaning. I was taking a nap."

"Well, it's time to get up."

She looked at Harry, who was sound asleep. "For what?"

"'Cause me, you, and Vi are going to find Nana a cat."

"You must be kidding. That can wait until tomorrow." She cuffed her hand around her mouth so she wouldn't wake her husband. "I just came home from college. I just unpacked. I just cleaned up this funky old cottage. And I'm dead tired," she added in a loud whisper.

"We don't care. You have to come with us because it was *your* graduation cake the rat chewed up."

"Rat? Did you say rat?"

"Well, it was a field mouse, at least one, maybe two."

"There was nothing wrong with my cake. You're getting to be as bad as Vi with all your exaggerating."

"I'm talking about the first graduation cake. You didn't see that one because it had a hole in it and Nana had to put it in the trash. Yesterday, we were eating graduation cake number two. Now Nana is bugging out about rodents taking over her kitchen and the house. So me and Vi decided to get her a cat, and you're coming with us. And that's that." Before Faye had a chance to respond, Louise hung up the phone.

An hour later, Louise pulled up in her powder blue 1968 Ford Fairlane 500, six-cylinder, two-door hardtop coupe, and they headed down Route 23 looking for kittens. They didn't have to travel far before they saw a bucket on the side of the highway with the words FREE KITTENS written on it. They turned left into the long, winding driveway that led to another narrow dirt road through the woods, parked the car in front of the only visible house for miles, and rang the doorbell.

A young boy answered the door, and when they told him why they were there, he called for his mother, who led them to an unfinished basement, cool as a cave, where they saw four full-grown cats in a box. The lady explained that the kittens were two years old and the only reason she kept the bucket with the sign on Route 23 was so that they'd still have a good chance of finding a decent home. There were too many for her to continue to feed. The cats were different colors and, despite their age, they were all still huggable and cute. Louise looked to Faye to make the decision since it was her cake that had gotten all chewed up.

"I wish we could take them all home," Elvira said.

"Now what would Nana do with four cats? She doesn't do *that* much baking." Even though Elvira and Billy were desperate to have children, the idea of returning home with a litter was more than Faye could handle.

"Each of us could take one so there'd be one in each household," said Elvira, stroking the red tabby, who arched its back and hissed, making her retract her arm quickly.

"That just made things easy. One down, three to go." Faye winced, having just been reminded of how unpredictable cats could be. Come to think of it, Harry was a little like a cat. She was thinking of his surprise announcement to Granddaddy that they could get used to living in Lemon City.

"Are we doing this through process of elimination?" asked Louise, tapping her fingers along the rim of the box. "If that's the case, go 'head Elvira. Stick your arm in there again."

"Very funny," said Elvira.

"Y'all don't take this long shopping at the Five & Dime." Louise was getting impatient. "These cats are free. Just take one."

Faye continued watching the cats, refusing to allow

Louise to break her concentration. She didn't know exactly what she was looking for, but she knew that when she found the right cat personality, she'd recognize it and bring that cat home to Nana.

Elvira turned to Faye. "Let's flip a coin or try eenie, meenie, mynie . . ."

Just then two of the cats sat on their hind legs and started a chorus of meows as another one backed into a corner and curled into a ball.

"Since I'm really not a cat person, let's see if this works." Faye called, "Here kitty, kitty. Here kitty, kitty." Remarkably, one of them, the gray-and-white striped cat, stopped meowing and strutted over to her. As she picked up the tabby, the first thing she noticed was its deep blue eyes and the diamond-shaped patch at the base of its neck and two white front paws, which made the cat look like he had stepped into a bag of flour. After closer inspection, she noticed that the cat was a girl. Out of curiosity, the cat leaned over to sniff her and to Faye's surprise she pushed her nose forward to touch the cool wetness. When the cat didn't take a swat at her, she felt it was safe enough to rub her face in its fur. Purring like the low-grade speed on an electric blender, the cat returned the gesture of affection by lifting a white paw and placing it on her shoulder, keeping its claws sheathed. This assured Faye that the cat was good-tempered and smart to boot. "This is the one we want," she said when the inspection was complete. They thanked the lady for the free bag of litter and the litter box as they walked out the door.

Once outside, Faye did a little test. Since the cat had come to her when she called it, Faye wanted to see if it had other canine characteristics. She put her down on the ground and just as she suspected, the cat trailed behind her, slowly wagging her tail, all the way to the car.

On the drive back to Nana's, they considered various

names. After Spot, Fido, and Cleopatra Jones didn't work, the only one they could all agree upon, which Faye came up with, was Saint—since Nana needed protection from potential rodents that could ruin her cakes in the future.

Nana was thrilled when they presented her with Saint. She had been sitting in her cane rocking chair on the porch, listening to gospel music on the radio. When Faye took Saint out of the litter box and placed the feline into Nana's arms, she embraced her new pet as if it were a brand-new baby just born into the family, deserving to be wrapped in one of her handmade knitted blankets. Assuming it must be hungry, she carried the cat into the kitchen and took two small bowls out of the cupboard. One she filled with water, the other she filled with pieces of fried catfish left over from last night's dinner.

The smell of fish made Saint leap down to the floor. Nana sat in the chair, folding her arms over her ample bosom, watching Saint to make sure she enjoyed the meal just like she was a guest. When she finished eating, Nana introduced her to the litter box on the back porch and then returned to her granddaughters on the front porch. When Faye told her the story behind the acquisition, how Saint had just acted like a dog, Nana went back into the house, searching for the cat so she could teach it to beg and go fetch and to sit.

She was so excited about having the animal that she immediately wanted to show it off. It was the kind of news she would have shared with her neighbor Ole Miss Johnson, way back when they used to be friends.

When they were young, Nana and Granddaddy and Easely and Lurleen had had all kinds of fun. As inseparable as the Indian and his buffalo on a five-cent nickel, they stayed at each other's houses so much that they teased each other about who lived where. They went to

dances, benefit dinners, plays, and fashion shows together. They played Pokeno and Yahtzee and teamed up on Scrabble and Bid Whist. Drinking various versions of Johnnie Walker Red Scotch became their routine and they always had a laughing good time. One day after Nana had saved enough S&H green stamps to buy an electric mixer, the first thing she did was show it off to Lurleen and invite her over for a trial run.

Nana threw all the ingredients into her baking bowl, plugged in the electric mixer, and watched it work.

"Ain't that something," said Lurleen, staring into the bowl. "It's about time they made an appliance as easy as that to simplify the baking process. I get tired of cramping up my arm doing it manually."

"I hope the cake turns out the same," Nana said, examining the texture of the contents in the bowl.

"We'll find out soon enough. In the meantime, check on those other speed functions. I wonder if they're really different."

Nana looked at the "low," "blend," "whip," and "high" buttons on the electric mixer. While she meant to slide the button to "low," her thumb accidentally moved it to "high."

Lurleen screamed and hopped back from the table as the batter jumped out of the bowl. Nana let go of the mixer, raising both arms to block the splatter from attacking her face. The mixer took on a life of its own, vibrating on the table until it knocked the bowl on the floor and created an even bigger mess. The women just looked at themselves, laughed, and began licking the sweet batter off their skin.

A few weeks after that, Nana discovered she was pregnant, and she and Granddaddy and Easley and Lurleen began to spend less time together. By the time their baby daughter, Aurelia, was born, the Dunlaps hardly ever went out socializing with their best friends anymore. As

Nana became more focused on her infant, Lurleen took raising her tomatoes more seriously. But it wasn't until after Easely died that the real bad blood came between them—the reason she had barely spoken to her neighbor in over twenty years.

As if Nana's falling out with Ole Miss Johnson wasn't bad enough, the animosity she felt toward her new grandson-in-law was starting to grow, and she felt it might get worse. However, she couldn't use the silent treatment with Harry. For the sake of her granddaughter, Nana had to be civilized and make conversation and a concerted effort to get along. Pretending was never her strong suit, and she wasn't known to be a quitter. Tomorrow morning would be as good as any to get a better sense of what the Outsider was all about. She'd invite the newlywed honeymooners to church.

On Sunday morning, Faye and Harry were in the middle of making love, nearing what would have been a great climax if the phone hadn't rung.

It was several seconds before Faye's hand finally found the phone. "Hello," she said.

"Sounds like y'all are still sleeping over there," said Nana.

"Well, sort of."

"Get up," Nana ordered. "It's time to get up."

"How come?" Faye looked at Harry, who groaned and pulled the covers over his head.

"It's Sunday morning, chile. We all going to church."

Until the very last minute, Harry tried everything imaginable to get out of going to Sunday service. He faked illness, pretended to be asleep, claimed he had wrenched his back while cleaning the day before, swore he couldn't walk because he stubbed his toe, said he couldn't wake up without coffee, and verified there was

none in the kitchen, but Faye convinced him church was a family obligation, something he had to do.

The Dunlap family walked down the aisle, taking their seats in their usual pew. At their first glimpse of the Outsider, the Ladies of Mt. Zion Baptist Church, who were sprinkled throughout the sanctuary, shook their heads and sucked their teeth, which amounted to a wave of clucking that rippled across the stained-glass windows in the room. Pastor Lucas T. Walker sensed the overwhelming tension among the group, thick as a wet towel sagging on a clothesline, and wasted no time in beginning his sermon.

Nana watched as Harry clapped in rhythm with the choir, followed the Bible when the scriptures were read, paid the offering, paid attention to the community announcements, and waited patiently for the Holy Ghost to pass through parishioners randomly seized by the spirit. From her point of view, all was going along fine until they got to the part in the service where it was time for everyone to recite the Lord's Prayer. She noticed Harry's lips were moving, but he was saying the wrong words. With his mouth out of sync with the congregation, Nana realized the Outsider didn't know the Lord's Prayer. *Lord have mercy on our souls,* she thought, and then she raised her head to the high ceiling for a private chat. That's when she heard the crash. She grabbed her heart and thought lightning had come down and struck Harry, but it wasn't as dramatic as that. A section of plaster loosened by dampness and rain over the years had finally freed itself and fallen from the ceiling, letting gravity take its course. Fortunately this happened in the back of the church, and no one was hurt. But the timing was uncanny, and as Nana looked at Harry, she wasn't completely convinced it was a coincidence.

* * *

In Lemon City, word traveled faster than a frog sucking down a fly. It was hard to keep a secret and harder still to keep your business to yourself. It seemed words were picked up by the trees and tossed along their branches until they rolled off and drifted onto someone else's porch. By the time word got out that Harry was a mechanic, cars had lined up in his and Faye's driveway like white on rice. What else could he do but steer his customers down to Old Dominion Road and open up The Shop? He worked with old tools he had left over from college for about a week until he made enough money to buy new ones. Then he called the gasoline truck company from Jefferson County to fill up his pumps, and after whacking the weeds that were coming up through the pavement so his customers wouldn't have to drive through a concrete forest to get to him, he was in business.

Faye was in Hair Today, Gone Be Beautiful Tomorrow, shaping up an Afro with an electric razor when Granddaddy called her. "He what?" she said into the phone. "You what?" she said in the same tone. "He's lost his mind, and I'ma have to help him go find it," she said after she hung up.

Everyone who heard her conversation shook their heads. That's what you get for marrying an Outsider. When she finished her last customer for the day, she put the CLOSED sign on the door and drove to The Shop to get some answers.

Faye's car came to a screeching halt when she reached the garage. She made enough noise when she slammed the car door, scuffed up enough dirt with her shoes as she approached, made as much racket as she could to announce her arrival, but not once did her husband look up.

"Harry, we need to talk."

"Baby, can't you see I'm busy?" He was fiddling with something underneath the hood of a car.

"This is important. We need to talk."

"Look at this 1969 chartreuse convertible Mustang with a 289 high-performance V-8 engine. Isn't she a beaut?" Harry stood up long enough for Faye to see the joy on his face, the satisfaction he experienced when working on a car. Then he ducked back under the hood as quickly as he appeared, as if he'd been away from the object of his affection too long.

"Don't change the subject. Why did you sign such a long-term bank loan?" She started pacing alongside the sporty-looking car because she couldn't stand still.

"The payments were low." His head was still buried underneath the hood.

He stood and picked up a towel that was already dirty and wiped more grease on it from his hands. She could tell he was stalling for time when he used the same soiled towel to remove the sweat from his face. She started to tell him about the black mark he'd streaked across his forehead, but she was so mad she changed her mind.

"Your grandfather . . . he was the one who kept bugging me about signing that damn piece of paper, so I went on ahead and signed it."

"Granddaddy? Don't drag him into this. You're grown. No one can make you do anything you don't want to do."

"Baby, you know how pushy he can be. Like you told me back at school, he's the kind of man who's used to having his own way and will do anything to get it."

Half of what Harry was saying was right. Knowing the kind of pressure Granddaddy could put on someone, she knew he was partly telling the truth. The part of the story she didn't understand was why he agreed to go along with it.

"Harry, what are you doing?" She raised one eyebrow as if that would give her a better chance to see the truth.

"I'm trying to figure out what's wrong with this carburetor."

She was talking to his back while he hunched over the engine. If that wasn't bad enough, she realized that after all this time, he wasn't paying attention to her, or worse, not taking her seriously. Either way, the outcome wasn't good.

"No. I mean, first you tell Granddaddy that we'll stay for a while, and now this. We made an agreement. We said that we'd only stay one week."

When he lowered his eyes to the floor and fidgeted with his sideburns, it occurred to her that Harry might not want to leave Lemon City at all. Between the heat from the sun, the stuffiness inside the garage, and the intensity of their conversation, Faye was starting to feel faint and had to steady herself against the Mustang. Marriage was supposed to be her ticket to freedom; instead it was about to make her pass out.

"You know, there were a lot more cars in here this morning," Harry continued. "I actually need to start keeping a calendar now and scheduling appointments, I'm so busy."

Faye leaned against the wall to regain her balance, then remembered all the dirt, grease, and grime around her, and straightened up on her own.

"Wait until the word gets out 'round town that The Shop is back in business. I could use someone part-time to help me get organized. Are you interested?"

Before she could respond, she heard the sound of the toilet flushing off the tiny adjacent office. It not only startled her, but the fact that someone might be eavesdropping on their conversation made her angry.

Without thinking, she banged her fist on the hood of the car much harder than she'd intended to and felt

numb from the pain. She didn't like that he was acting as if she were less important than the high-performance vehicle he was working on. When he glanced at the imprint she left on the Mustang, he gave her a look that could kill and she thought she saw the devil.

Realizing she might have pushed Harry too far, she softened her tone. "Let's talk about this tonight," was all she could say for fear of saying something she'd later regret. Faye sped off in her 1968 beige Volkswagen Beetle, leaving behind a trail of dust and possibly a lifelong dream that would never materialize.

A beautiful woman, the color of semisweet dark chocolate, came out of the bathroom and stepped down into the garage. When she was sure the disturbance was gone, she tightened the yellow chiffon scarf around the bun in her hair and adjusted her skirt. Harry offered to take her for a test-drive, but she insisted he give her the bill and her keys. He watched her hips sway like wildflowers caught in a light summer breeze and then slide into the driver's seat until it looked as if she were levitating over black leather. He stood frozen as she backed out of the garage and didn't take his eyes off her chartreuse Mustang convertible, which seemed to glide down the street.

By the time Harry got home, it was six o'clock and dinner was on the table. All afternoon Faye had told herself to stay calm and to work things out, to have a discussion and not an argument with her husband, but when they finally sat down to eat, she blurted out, "How could you sign that bank loan knowing how much I want to leave?" She had never been good at beating around the bush.

He picked up his fried pork chop, took a bite, and waited until he finished chewing before answering the question. "Why don't we just stay put for a while." He

narrowed his eyes like a weasel at her from across the table.

"You've got to be kidding." Faye looked at him as if he had completely missed the boat and fallen into the river. "I want to leave now."

"You like working at Hair Today, Gone Be Beautiful Tomorrow, don't you? And I like working at The Shop. So what's the problem? I'm just talking about staying in town for the rest of the summer. We might like it. Let's give it a shot."

Harry's words were casual, and Faye felt that if she didn't stand her ground she could be tricked.

He took a swig of his beer and wiped his mouth with the back of his hand. "Look at it as getting some real work experience. You know, like building up our credentials."

Even though she didn't like what he was saying, she tried to grab on to his logic and follow.

"In the meantime, I'll work something out with your grandfather to get us out of the bank contract. There may be some clause or loophole that we can get out of within a certain period of time, which could take a couple of months." He was ready to close the deal. "So how's that sound?"

It sounded as if Harry had everything all figured out. That seemed to be the way with Harry. He could be a real smooth talker when he wanted to be and had a way of twisting words like a rubber band around a rock on a slingshot. When he fired them out, you never knew how something was going to hit you.

On one hand, what he was saying made some sense—the part about getting experience. On the other hand, she hoped this wasn't an attempt to renege on their agreement altogether. After all, the last thing she wanted to admit to herself was that she had married Harry for no good reason. Even though she was ready to leave

Lemon City now, she didn't want to put up too much of a fuss, because the plan was for them to leave together, and she wanted Harry to be happy. Harry's happiness was important to her. So what if they stayed until the end of the summer? After living in Lemon City for twenty years, three more months wasn't going to be the worst thing that could happen. Besides, people's plans changed all the time, and she didn't want to be so set in her ways that she didn't have the flexibility to go with the flow. By early September for sure, they'd be headed up North, right after the Annual County Fair.

"You know I really don't want to stay . . ." Faye lowered her voice, then looked down at her shoes. The fight that was in her was beginning to fade like a photograph that had been left out in the sun.

He sat back in his seat, folding his arms across his chest as if the man of the house had spoken and he had the last word.

"If we leave at the end of the summer, that sounds fair enough." She shook her fork in his direction as a warning. "But I have to tell you, the next time there's a major decision to be made, you have to include me in it. That's what married life is all about."

Harry got up from the table, mumbling something underneath his breath, on his way to the refrigerator for another can of beer. As Faye watched him guzzle it down, she wished that life with her husband would flow that easily.

The Annual County Fair was the third-largest event to hit Lemon City since Lincoln freed the slaves and the governor gave them the two thousand acres of land to do with as they pleased. It took place during the first weekend in September and was celebrated with as much fun and force as fireworks exploding into the evening sky.

The Fair also sparked a thirty-year rivalry between Nana and Ole Miss Johnson. The open contest over who had the biggest and best tomatoes started out as a friendly competition between the neighbors. But an incident occurred after Ole Miss Johnson's husband, Easely, died. It involved Granddaddy and had necessitated intervention by the Ladies of Mt. Zion Baptist Church.

Granddaddy and Easely had been friends since childhood. They were inseparable, best friends. When they came of age, Granddaddy took his rightful place as heir to protect the town as the Lemon City sheriff, and Easely perpetuated his family lineage by becoming one of the most successful and profitable farmers around. When they got married, they built houses next door to each other and their wives became best friends. Then, one day in the summer of 1937, Easely left home early in the morning with bushels of freshly picked vegetables from his garden, loaded up his brand-new 1937 Chevy truck GC series black pickup, and headed out to Route 23 and across the city limits to sell the best of his harvest. It was the last time Mrs. Johnson or anyone in Lemon City ever

saw Easely alive. They found him two days later with a
noose tied around his neck, hanging from a poplar tree
about ten miles outside of town, off the highway in the
woods in Jefferson County. It was one of those "no rea-
son" killings—no reason for killing other than the color
of his skin. Granddaddy hadn't seen a rope wrapped
around anyone's neck since he was nine years old, and
the sight of his dead best friend tore him apart. He held
himself together long enough to cut Easely down with a
pocketknife. After laying his stiff body on the ground,
Granddaddy sank to his knees and pounded the earth for
every wrong he felt had been committed because of skin
color. He didn't stop until his fist bled and his eyes were
drained of tears and his body went limp like Easely's
probably did when his neck broke. Easely's death was a
gruesome reminder of how dangerous life outside Lemon
City could be, and Granddaddy prayed that all his im-
mediate kin and all his kin to come would never be fool-
ish enough to leave their home.

Granddaddy turned his head as he heard an engine
approach, and Jefferson County sheriff Jethro Taylor
pulled up in his patrol car to the heart-wrenching site.
The Lemon City sheriff noticed Jethro's young son,
Beauregard, sitting in the front passenger seat. Beaure-
gard took one look at Easely's brown, dried-up,
hunched-over body engulfed by his fatal pain, and he
turned his head and vomited out the window.

For over twenty years, Granddaddy never forgave
himself for not going out with Easely that morning
when he'd called over to the house. He couldn't help
thinking that if he had been with his friend, with his hol-
ster and his gun, this never would have happened. To
compensate for his absence and alleviate his guilt, he de-
cided to look after his friend's wife. Poor Mrs. Johnson
was devastated, and some folks thought she'd never
fully recover. In fact, some still believed that she lost not

only her heart that day, but she'd also lost her mind. She let down the curtains in her house in mourning. Years had passed before she pulled back the barriers and invited the sun to come in again.

Granddaddy spent as much time as he could with Mrs. Johnson, hoping that in some small way he could help fill the void and pay back his friend for not being there when he needed him most. For the next several months, he looked after her. Taking out her garbage, repairing whatever needed to be fixed, watering her garden, making sure she had food in the refrigerator, and picking up around the house gave him some relief from his own grief.

Nana also volunteered to help out her longtime friend, but the newly widowed woman seemed to miss having a man around the house, only wanting Granddaddy at her beck and call. Whenever Nana offered to wash the dishes that were starting to pile up in the sink, the widow waved her away, claiming she'd do it herself. But when Granddaddy made the same offer, she gladly accepted. Nana soon figured out that her assistance wasn't needed and she let her friend Lurleen have her way.

After three months of watching Granddaddy work through his guilt, Nana decided he had paid off his debt. She began to feel he was spending way too much time with Easely's widow. Enough was enough. He was neglecting his own chores and, more important, he was neglecting her. What was worse, Aurelia, their seven-year-old, kept asking why her daddy was spending so much time away from home.

Nana's suspicions were intensified by the fact that her husband began to reek of the lemon oil Lurleen used to clean her house; a sweet smell that stuck to his skin like bitter, stale perfume. Besides that, the curtains were always drawn, and she couldn't see through to the other side to know how her neighbor was showing her appre-

ciation. While she trusted her husband, she didn't trust the loneliness of dead men's wives as far as she could throw a stick.

One afternoon while Aurelia was taking a nap, everything came to a head. As most people thought, Lurleen Johnson was out of her mind, but now it also seemed she was intoxicated by Nana's jealousy. After standing on her front porch in her white satin slip, Lurleen sashayed up to Granddaddy, who was tending the petunias in the wooden planter boxes that decorated his front yard. She looked at Nana, who was standing across from him pruning the rhododendrons, but she paid Nana no mind. When she requested the other woman's husband's assistance with her laundry, acting as if the other woman were invisible, Granddaddy told her he was busy. Even though he knew his neighbor could see for herself that he was preoccupied, she didn't care. Repeating that she had no clean clothes to wear, she demanded Granddaddy's help.

Granddaddy didn't mind helping her when she needed it, but it occurred to him that this situation wasn't about help, but about asking for trouble. When her insistence failed, Mrs. Johnson proceeded to flirt with him, ignoring Nana's presence. It was at that moment that Nana decided Lurleen wasn't as crazy as other folks believed. She stopped feeling sorry for her neighbor. She wanted to slap the hussy right then and there, but she caught herself. After all, she was a good Christian woman. So she did what any good Christian woman would do. She headed straight for the phone in the kitchen and called the Ladies of Mt. Zion Baptist Church. One conversation was all it took to round up a group of volunteers to relieve Granddaddy of what he felt was his moral obligation. After that, Mrs. Johnson had someone from the church visiting her every day to take care of her needs. Mrs. Johnson didn't speak to Nana for a very long time.

After Easely's death, Nana took the threat of her neighbor's liberties seriously and carried it through to include not only keeping her hands off her husband but also staying away from her daughter. The more Nana's heart wreaked vengeance, the more she transferred that feeling onto everything that had to do with her and her neighbor. As a result, she became more determined than ever to win the grand prize at the Annual County Fair. She would see through the jealousy to find a way to plant a superior fruit. With her neighbor out of commission, she'd use this opportunity to crank up her green thumb to get her competition to finally step down. Nana turned the friendly competition into a fierce one that would entangle the women with each other and occupy much of their time for years to come.

During this rivalrous period, Aurelia was growing up, evolving into a smart and beautiful young woman. When she turned seventeen, she became an elementary school teacher just like her mother and married a tax attorney who was also a member of the Town Council. Granddaddy built them a two-family house diagonally across the street from the big house where he and Nana lived, and a cottage down the street for those occasions when they wanted more privacy and a change of scenery.

Granddaddy was committed to his family and wanted to keep them close, especially his grandchildren. Having them live across the street instead of in another part of town guaranteed he'd see them every day and be an integral part of their lives. Eventually, Aurelia had three children and he was blessed each time. William was named after him, although his parents called him Billy. Two years later came Louise, and four years after that came Faye, the one who looked just like her mother, and she was the one he held closest to his heart.

Then death struck again on Route 23. One dark, stormy night he received a phone call about a fatal car

accident. He never saw his daughter and son-in-law again. Granddaddy and Nana were devastated. It was the only time they had ever stopped speaking to each other because they couldn't find the words to provide comfort to one another. When they first got the news from a county sheriff, Nana went into Aurelia's old room, flung herself on her bed, and cried until she started kicking at the mattress, pulling up the sheets and shredding them to pieces. When Granddaddy heard the ruckus, he ran upstairs and held his wife until all the anger left her body and only the sadness remained. Granddaddy knew that between the two of them he had to be the one to stay strong. When he felt his wife's emotions were a little more under control, he'd go outside at night in the backyard behind the shed and sob until his reservoir was empty, or use the rocking chair on the porch until the rhythm calmed and consoled him.

After a week had passed and they were able to go down to the courthouse and make it official, they adopted their three grandchildren, vowing to raise them as their own. Both were determined not to lose any more members of their family. Nana became like a sheepdog rounding up the herd, making sure it stayed together, and Granddaddy became a rancher with a double-barreled shotgun, protecting his property and living assets against all intruders.

It might have been simply a coincidence or some kind of small miracle, but around this time, Mrs. Johnson pulled back her curtains and seemed to collect some of her senses. In an effort to return the kindness that had been given to her, she took care of the Dunlaps during their time of grief. She cooked for them, washed their laundry, cleaned their house, watched the children, and helped them with their homework as best she could, and did a fair share of hair-braiding between Louise and Faye until Nana and Granddaddy were back on their feet.

They hadn't had any contact with their next-door neighbor in over twenty years, since the Ladies of Mt. Zion Baptist Church started their home visits. The Dunlaps were astounded by Lurleen's appearance. The lack of sunlight had caused her skin to age, and living in darkness had caused her eyes to bulge slightly, which made her look a bit insane. When the grandchildren first laid eyes on her, she gave them a scare, but eventually curiosity brought them out of hiding from around Nana's wide skirt and they came forward. In time, the stranger who lived next door grew on them. They nicknamed her Ole Miss Johnson, a title she didn't mind—that was who she had become.

A few months later, when Nana and Granddaddy were able to manage on their own, Faye chose to follow the lady with the unusually sweet smell back to her home. Some days she smelled like lavender and lemon. Other days she smelled of peppermint and pine. Faye wanted to know all about these new scents; where they originated and what made them linger as long as they did. The fragrance that Ole Miss Johnson carried with her was soothing and Faye clung close to every dress her new friend wore, holding as much of the tranquilizing fabric as she could to her nose. Even though she was only eight years old, Faye found comfort in being close to this unusual woman. While she didn't have as many soft places to lie on as Nana did, Faye enjoyed her company nonetheless, since she no longer had access to her mama.

One day, Faye stepped onto Ole Miss Johnson's veranda. When she opened the door, a hundred scents greeted her. Little brown bottles filled with scented oils lined the mantel over the fireplace and the faded, floral wallpapered shelves in her kitchen. Scented candles, aromatic incense and oils, potpourri, and dried herbs were situated in various arrangements around the house, in

places where most people would have had fresh-cut flowers or knickknacks on display. As the lady took her through a tour of her house, she told Faye that she hardly ever visited a doctor because she had remedies that cured everything from insomnia to indigestion either outside in her backyard or inside under her roof.

It wasn't long before Faye learned that not everything smelled like heaven in her neighbor's house. One day when she had a cold, a temperature, and a terrible cough, Ole Miss Johnson gave her a cup of elderberry tea with garlic and honey. The smell was so bad she had to pinch her nose to drink it. When she did, her eyes rolled back into her head and her face twisted into a knot. It not only tasted vile, but as the day went on, it made her smell awful, too. She tried sucking on the cherry sour balls that Ole Miss Johnson kept especially for her in a glass candy dish on the coffee table, but that didn't get rid of the garlic taste in her mouth or the pungent odor that seemed to come from her body. She swigged down some grape soda, but all that did was make her belch and give her gas, which made her feel even worse. When she went to ask Ole Miss Johnson what to do, she didn't even have to open her mouth. The old lady smelled her coming through the door. As she approached, her neighbor waved her hand in the air, scrunched up her nose, and told her to sit down while she made her a cup of a different kind of tea. She brewed some peppermint leaves to sweeten her breath back to its normal state and ran her a bath with lavender oil so she could smell like herself again.

When Faye had finished soaking in the tub, Ole Miss Johnson directed her to a large oak-framed canopy bed. The bed was so high that Faye needed a stepladder to climb into it. Ole Miss Johnson said she'd feel better if she took a nap, and that there was one other thing that would help her sleep. After that, the older woman lay

down next to her and started to sing. Faye liked the "Go Tell Aunt Rhody" song, despite the fact that she sang it off-key. "Go tell Aunt Rhody, go tell Aunt Rhody, go tell Aunt Rhody the old gray goose is dead." Faye had heard the song a hundred times, but now she was curious. As she began to drift into sleep, she wondered who Aunt Rhody was, but she was too tired to ask. Then she thought about the old gray goose being dead like her parents, and that made her sad, but she refused to cry. When she awoke hours later that afternoon, her cough and fever had disappeared and she felt so much better, she went outside to play.

During the period that Nana was in mourning, she worried about Faye spending too much time at Ole Miss Johnson's, wondering if avoiding home was her grandchild's way of distancing herself from memories and the source of pain. While Nana was trying to deal with her loss, she saw how grief was affecting her other grandchildren. When Billy came home from school, she'd see him sneaking in old, broken things and pieces of junk that he'd find outside on the road, surrounding himself with clutter as a distraction because he didn't want to be alone. Louise, who was always a tomboy, became even more aggressive. Determined to beat all the boys in every sport, she released her anger by kicking the ball the hardest, let go of her frustration by running the dirt-carved bases the fastest, and rejected sympathy from others by being the meanest when any opposition got in her way. It was a long process, and after a few years the Dunlap family was finally able to get back to normal.

Part of that routine would include Nana's renewed interest in the Tomato Competition at the Annual County Fair. In the more than thirty years since Easely had died and Nana had rebounded from her own tragedy, she had not won a single Tomato Competition. She'd come in a close second a few times, but she always missed by a few

points with the judges saying her tomato had a blemish, or it was too small for the variety, or the taste was too tart, or the flesh was too tough, or the tomato had too much pink, or the fruit wasn't meaty enough. There was always something that made her well-attended produce slightly less than perfect. Most people would have given up trying to win the competition by now, but not Nana. Absolutely unwilling to accept defeat, she intensified her mission to do everything she could to get her hands on that ribbon and her head underneath that crown. Vowing to make the Dunlap family tomatoes extraordinary enough to surpass her neighbor's, and fueled by the hope that this year her time would come, she was ready to launch an all-out campaign to win the grand prize at this year's Annual County Fair.

Nana had no influence over Faye's decision to bring home an Outsider, but she did have some control over her garden. Since she chose not to take her anger out on her granddaughter, she directed the emotion toward her neighbor, making her more determined than ever to obtain victory in the Annual County Fair.

Faye bringing home an Outsider made Nana even more focused on achieving her vegetable objectives. Every Saturday morning, Nana even strolled through the lush vegetation, walking up and down the rows of her garden, inspecting the leaves and stalks, looking for any signs of disease, making sure that everything was growing healthily. The two months before the County Fair were the most important. She was pleased with the way her plants were maturing and getting stronger every day under the nurturing sun. By giving them as much care as a mother hen about to hatch a chick from an egg, she was hoping to have a good shot at winning the Tomato Competition.

At the same time Nana was hauling a fresh bag of manure from the shed, Ole Miss Johnson was looking out her back window, watching Nana's every move. Obviously not wanting her rival to get an edge on the competition, she came outside with a bag of fertilizer. When Nana kicked up the mulch around her plants and rearranged the chips to absorb the moisture, Ole Miss Johnson sneaked a look over her shoulder to see what

Nana was doing, and did the same. When Nana put down a layer of manure, Ole Miss Johnson put on her garden gloves and spread all her wealth around, too. When Nana pruned the suckers from the plants, Ole Miss Johnson copied her. And when she got out her hose and watered, Ole Miss Johnson was like a shadow, just two steps behind, giving her bounteous crop a drink in case it was thirsty, too. Being spied on and imitated didn't bother Nana at all. Quite the contrary—it gave her an overwhelming sense of satisfaction to be considered a threat by the incumbent.

Having established herself as a force to be reckoned with, Nana dragged her stool underneath the shade tree. Nana was glad for decent weather and good company with her in the backyard, even if it was four-legged and furry. Just as she kept track of Saint, she didn't let Ole Miss Johnson too far out of her sight. She followed Ole Miss Johnson with her eyes as the old lady retreated back into her house. Her neighbor slammed the screen door behind her so hard it sounded like one of those gunshots signaling the games to begin.

Saint took off, squeezing through the picket fence, sneaking into Ole Miss Johnson's yard and getting herself into mischief. She proceeded to play with a tomato that had fallen on the ground, grabbing it with her claws and taking bites out of it as if it were a giant catnip treat.

The cat, who never touched Nana's tomatoes, seemed to enjoy the taste of her neighbor's. Nana's first thought was that maybe there was something about the beefsteak variety that made them tastier than the tomatoes she was growing. Before she could draw any conclusions, she was startled by a quick scampering sound that made her knees rise off the ground, prompting her to lift up her skirt. For no apparent reason, as if she had backed into a sucker bush, Saint took off suddenly, making a mad dash through a path in Ole Miss Johnson's

garden and trampling down several tomato plants along the way. When Nana realized Saint was actually chasing a mouse, she didn't bother calling her back home since it was a natural excuse for trespassing. But Ole Miss Johnson, who had been looking out the back window, didn't see it that way.

"Ernestine Dunlap. Git that cat away from my tomatoes lessen you want me to skin it."

"Cool your furnace, Lurleen. She's just helping you with your field-mice problem."

"Looks like you charged her with tearing up my garden. I wouldn't put it past you, no sirree. I'm getting me a dog, ya hear? A hungry dog that'll rip that cat to shreds just like it's doing to my tomatoes." She disappeared through the window and within seconds popped her head back out again. "Think you can rob me of my crown? You need more 'n a cat to do that. You need a doggone army and a cat-a . . . a cat-a . . ." Her eyes shifted to the side then rolled up in her head as if searching for the right word in her brain. "A cat-aclysmic cannon to ruin my crop and defeat me." She slammed the window shut.

As usual, Nana didn't pay her any mind. But the sound of her neighbor's raging voice was enough to propel Saint back through the fence and into Nana's lap.

August arrived as fast as the soft blue haze comes and goes each morning over the Blue Ridge Mountains. During the summer, morning was the only time of day when the air was fresh and it was easy to get along. As soon as the sun showed its face in the sky, the air turned heavy, hot, and humid, discomforting every living creature in Lemon City. It hadn't rained for weeks and wells were beginning to dry, which made the gardeners' jobs more challenging. Then, one day the temperature dropped, and that's when Nana knew she was in trouble.

The hot spell broke suddenly, and the mercury plunged into the fifties. When Nana went outside to inspect her garden first thing in the morning, she panicked. The leathery-looking scars on the bottoms of her fruit revealed the truth and made her throw her hands up to her face. Blossom-end rot, an unforgiving disease, had invaded her yard during the darkness, ravaging and killing her tomatoes. From the shock of cold air, her plants had begun to wither and die. All her hard work had fallen with the temperature and had been stolen away by the night. The Fair was only weeks away, and there was nothing she could do to save her crop—her tomatoes had been slaughtered. Maybe she pruned the plants back too far, perhaps she hadn't added enough calcium to the soil. It was too late now. The damage had already been done. It was total annihilation. After the gruesome discovery, her first reaction was, Why in God's name did this have to happen to her? Her second reaction was to see if it had happened to her neighbor.

She peeked into Ole Miss Johnson's garden. As far as she could tell, her neighbor's tomatoes were fine. They looked normal and healthy. Immediately, Nana became suspicious. Sabotage was the third thing that came to Nana's mind, which made her so angry that all the rage seemed to flow through her hands. Furious, she got down on her knees like a dog frantically scratching up the dirt searching for a bone, but she was looking for something entirely different. When she found the silver trail buried underneath a rock, she threw the fat slimy land snail over the fence. She knew it wasn't right, but she hoped the slug would feast on her neighbor's plants and cause damage to them, too. After looking toward the heavens and mumbling something to the sky about forgiveness, she wiped the dirt from her hands and walked away.

Ole Miss Johnson had been watching Nana from her

back window. "Ernestine Dunlap, git that slug out of my yard before I git you with my shovel!" she yelled. Nana urged Saint to slip through the hole in the fence and take a bite out of one of Ole Miss Johnson's beefsteaks just for spite. As if she understood her mission, Saint grabbed a tomato and took a bite. Ole Miss Johnson ran out of the house, ranting and waving a pitchfork because she couldn't locate her shovel, and Saint took off like a spitball in the wind.

Nana wasn't a hateful woman, but that night she picked up a rock and hurled it through Ole Miss Johnson's open window. She wasn't really thinking about what she was doing. She felt frustrated and helpless about her crop. She heard something break and saw Ole Miss Johnson poke her head out the window. Nana leaned back against her house, closer into the shadows.

"Who's there?" yelled the lady next door.

When Nana's hands could no longer contain the sounds she was smothering in her mouth, she ran into the house, threw back her head, and let out a laugh that sounded like the gaggle of a chicken. Ole Miss Johnson sucked her teeth. "Ernestine Dunlap, you're one stupid mule." She slammed the window shut.

Since Nana was no longer in the running for this year's competition, it was her final stab at getting back at her neighbor.

She had nothing left to lose.

Just as summer was passing as quickly as mayflies buzzing over a mountain creek, business at Hair Today, Gone Be Beautiful Tomorrow was growing faster than Virginia creepers along an old dirt trail. Women were coming and going to the hair salon with such frequency that Faye decided to hire another beautician and install another chair. Hair dryers were blowing, hot combs were steaming, scissors and shears were cutting, and the

women who were getting perms were still complaining that the chemicals that had their scalps burning were left in their hair too long. It was the first Friday in August, the night of the church jamboree, and the women wanted to make sure their "do's" were coifed just right.

It seemed the women had gotten over the initial shock of Faye bringing home an Outsider. But every now and then she'd hear whispers behind her back, get a look of pity delivered to her face, or feel a slight coolness that would make her button up her smock to her neck because someone had left a small chill in the room. The women might not agree with Faye's choice for a spouse or admonish her because she broke the First Rule, but deep down in her soul she felt their patience. They didn't need to chastise her with words, because sometimes talking around a subject and not mentioning it at all was punishment enough. Regardless, she was still a Dunlap. That name carried a lot of weight and good wishes in the town, and despite the people's disapproval, she knew they still loved and supported her and cared about what happened next.

No matter how busy Faye became at the hair salon, it was her habit to close by six o'clock to go home to make dinner for her husband. Some days Harry would show up on time. Other days, he'd arrive late and Faye would wind up having dinner by herself. Sometimes, she'd cover his plate with aluminum foil and keep it warm in the oven, so his food would be ready when he got home. Nevertheless, she had to cook, because Harry made it clear that TV dinners were absolutely out of the question, despite the fact that he usually ate his dinner in front of the TV. Harry was working at The Shop just as hard as she was working at the beauty parlor, but unlike her, he preferred and seemingly enjoyed the overtime. She didn't mind him coming home late every now and then, especially since he promised he was saving his

money so they wouldn't have to rely on Granddaddy for help when they moved.

Faye felt that she and Harry had been getting along much better lately. He came home early that night to go to the church jamboree because he had claimed he didn't mind going to the House of the Lord when it was fun and didn't have anything to do with religion. While he was trying hard to please her, she was making an effort not to drop constant reminders about leaving town after the Annual County Fair. Even though things were going well, a little voice in her head kept warning her not to get too comfortable in Lemon City, because the town had a way of sneaking up behind a person and ambushing their thoughts.

The jamboree, which always took place on the first Friday night of every month, was held in three different areas: two social rooms of the church, and a huge outside portable tent.

In Fellowship Hall, the Pursuit of Happiness Glee Club was performing Aretha Franklin songs, a cappella style. Faye waved and Harry threw up his hand at Bootsie, one of Granddaddy's best friends, who was a tenor singing backup vocals on the stage. Down the corridor, the Washington Room was buzzing with the chatter of mostly older folks who were hard of hearing and only comfortable communicating in an environment absent high-volume noise. The outside tent was where the majority of folks were having a good time, dancing, laughing, catching up with family and friends, or hoping to meet that someone special. It was the end of the week and the start of a new month, and the Lemonites celebrated life, blessings, and the fruits of their labor with exuberance.

Underneath the tent outside, Faye and Harry arrived just in time to hear the finale from The Highlands Trio. With banjo, fiddle, and harmonica, the three men got

the crowd jumping, with the guys swinging the gals to the sounds of traditional mountain music. The dance floor was packed and whoever didn't have a partner was standing around the fringes, bobbing their heads and tapping their feet. When the band stopped playing, the record player started spinning, and the dance-hall songs of Ella Fitzgerald, the local girl from Newport News, filled the tent. Everyone let out a cheer, and more people got up to move to the beat or stood on the sidelines, grinning, clapping to the music.

The canopied tent was crowded, and the heat from the sweaty bodies made the Lemonites easily forget that the night was cool and as dry as the needles on an eastern white pine. Since Nana was at home, sick from the massacre of her beloved tomatoes, Granddaddy and Louise had stepped out to the jamboree together.

Faye and Harry spotted Granddaddy and Louise on the dance floor, then they found Billy and Elvira with their heads bobbing up and down in the crowd. Then Faye looked up and practically in front of her was Ole Miss Johnson and Clement, Granddaddy's other best friend, making their best effort at dancing a two-step. She pointed out the strange couple to her husband.

Faye swore that Clement had a crush on Ole Miss Johnson, but she always sensed that he was too afraid, or too shy, to take their friendship to the next level. In a way, Faye didn't blame him. She noticed that whenever Clement smiled in the old lady's direction, Ole Miss Johnson seemed to put up a frown or create some excuse for distance, as if being nice to him was taking her miles out of her way—which was why Faye was surprised to see them dancing. But there was something else about the two of them that Faye couldn't figure out, some kind of chemistry between them that they didn't care to share.

"Will you stop holding me so tight," Ole Miss Johnson complained to Clement. Faye, standing close to

them, couldn't help but overhear their conversation. "You're 'bout to crack my rib cage."

Clement loosened his grip to make his partner feel more comfortable.

"Can you stop breathing on my neck?" asked Ole Miss Johnson.

Clement rolled his eyes and tried to please his partner.

Faye pursed her lips to prevent herself from laughing and squeezed Harry's hand so he could get in on the fun.

"Turn your head the other way, where you can get more space for your nose and more room for air," Ole Miss Johnson added.

"Why you so cantankerous tonight, Lurleen?" asked Clement, dressed in a new Montgomery Ward suit and a pair of nice lace-up dress shoes.

Clement was wiry, and his sharp features were enhanced by the few wrinkles that came with age. He was a handsome man who still had most of his hair and all of his charm, and he moved with a youthful step uncommon for a man in his late sixties. Unfortunately he wasn't coordinated, and he accidentally stepped on Ole Miss Johnson's foot.

"Ouch!" Ole Miss Johnson yelled. "Stop stepping on my dern foot!" and then she kicked him.

"Ouch!" he yelled back, as he watched his partner storm off into the crowd. Then Clement, who'd noticed a few witnesses giggling in the crowd—including his best friend's granddaughter—said to Faye, "That old woman. I think the only person she's nice to is you. I think she better start taking some of her own dern 'calming herbs,' something to help her get through the change of life without meanness. Something that'll help her take the pressure off, you know . . . not having a good man around when she needs one." Clement rubbed his shin and disappeared into the crowd.

Faye laughed at Clement, then she grabbed Harry and

led him onto the dance floor when a slow song came on, throwing her arms around his neck. She noticed he was looking preoccupied and asked, "So what are you thinking about?"

"I hope we never become as cranky as that," Harry said, watching Clement sidle up to Miss Sadie, another good-looking woman his age.

"Not if we keep making love, which by the way, we haven't done in a while." Faye leaned against Harry's chest and buried her face in his neck, inhaling his scent. Usually when they slow danced she felt some movement in his pants, but tonight he had very little to give her.

"You know I've been busy," he said coolly, and Faye swore she felt his body stiffen slightly.

"So what?" she said softly, and lifted her head to look at him. "Work never stopped you from taking care of business at home before." She didn't want to argue. She only wanted him to know she missed him.

"Well, I'm home early tonight, so you may get lucky." Faye didn't care for his arrogance but she decided to take what she could get.

"Guess what?" She changed the subject.

"What?"

"I've been marking off the days on the calendar and we have almost one month to go. Practically four weeks left, and then we can say good-bye to this place," she said, jumping up and down with childish anticipation. Harry didn't seem excited by her joy.

"Not now, Faye. You're destroying the mood." Her husband released her, letting her go. "Can't you stop obsessing about this?" They stopped dancing and it was an awkward moment, but they tried to play it off by dancing together, separately. The slow song was still playing, and the honeymooners looked even more stressed trying to move to the music in slow motion.

Her husband's outburst and the unnecessary attention

he caused them embarrassed Faye. She danced opposite her husband with no expression on her face, wondering what she had said to create this provocation, thinking about what to do to fix things and make them right. She watched as her husband did a "spot check" around the tent. She let her eyes do their own wandering and they landed on Granddaddy, who was looking straight at her, obviously upset at having been one of many spectators to witness their disheartening scene.

Ole Miss Johnson, leaning against the refreshment counter with a cup of lemonade, took in the scene from across the room. She knew Faye wasn't going to be happy from the moment she saw the young woman come home with the Outsider. The old lady felt sorry for her young friend, sorry that she didn't trust how the town had raised her, and sorry that she didn't listen to what her family had taught her. She wished she could hold the young lady like she used to when she was a girl and rock some sense into her, but of course she was way too grown for that. Unfortunately, there was nothing she or anyone else could do except sit back and let the consequences run their course. She wondered if Faye would still be adamant about her spousal preferences if the girl's mama were still alive.

However, the one thing Ole Miss Johnson wouldn't have to worry about anymore was the girl's grandmother being in this year's Tomato Competition. Now that disease had demolished her enemy's ammunition, she had regained her lead in the race for her crown. This year, the only thing she might have to battle, if it came down to it, was the cat.

Granddaddy wished Nana had felt well enough to attend the jamboree. He watched as Harry pulled away from Faye as if she had stepped in organic fertilizer, and he had to dance as far away from her as possible to avoid the stench. It made him mad when he saw the dis-

appointment and frustration on his granddaughter's face. He wished he had the ability to protect his baby girl from harm's way, but because she'd made her decision, the situation was out of his hands. Or maybe that wasn't entirely the case. If things continued the way they were going, he'd be left with no choice but to rectify the situation. Maybe he'd have to talk to Billy and figure out a way to make the necessary adjustments to his grandson-in-law to get him to act right, or find a way to get him out of town—dispose of him for good. Granddaddy knew that Harry should count his lucky stars that Billy hadn't seen the incident, because if he had, Harry wouldn't have two good legs to stand on.

Even though Granddaddy had made the loan arrangement, he was half expecting his grandson-in-law to talk to him during the grace period and break the contract he'd negotiated out of love for his wife and respect for her wishes. But now it was too late for Harry to get out of the deal without legal complications and fines. Granddaddy was conflicted. There was no denying that he wanted his granddaughter to stay in town, but not because of deceit. He was beginning to question if Harry really cared for his granddaughter, or if he was just in love with his granddaughter's money. Based on his experience, dishonesty had a way of exposing itself. It was only a matter of time.

It was almost midnight when "Blueberry Hill" by Fats Domino transitioned into "Love Train" by the O'Jays, and the older folks who couldn't keep up with the faster tempo left the dance floor, making room for the younger generation to move in. Granddaddy was trying as best as he could to keep up, dancing with Louise. When the O'Jays sang the chorus and he spun his granddaughter around, she must have seen something in the room that disturbed her because her eyes came back as if she had just seen a ghost. The next thing Granddaddy saw was a

kindly looking, well-built gentleman approaching, dressed in jeans and a casual short-sleeved shirt, and smiling as he made his way over to them. As the man got closer, Granddaddy recognized Medford, Clement's son. When Medford tapped Louise on her shoulder, she hesitated before she stopped dancing and turned around to look him in the face.

"Excuse me, Mr. Dunlap." Medford smiled at Granddaddy.

Granddaddy returned the greeting and stopped dancing, relieved to catch his breath. Out of respect, he politely nodded his head to give the young folk their space, but as he attempted to leave them alone, Louise wouldn't let go of his hand.

"Hello, Louise," Medford said with a smile in his baritone voice.

"Hello, Medford," said Louise, trying to smile back.

There was an awkward pause, then Medford spoke to Granddaddy. "Sorry for interrupting, Mr. Dunlap."

"No. No interruption at all," said Granddaddy sincerely, gesturing for Medford to take over his dance. Granddaddy hadn't seen Medford in years. He was almost old enough to be Louise's father's age if he were still living, God rest his soul.

"Oh, no, Granddaddy. We're not finished. I'm sure you've got a few more dances left in you." Louise grabbed her grandfather's arm.

"If that's what you're thinking, you know more about me than I know about myself." Granddaddy chuckled as he tried to wrangle his arm away from Louise. When he saw Ole Miss Johnson at the refreshment counter and set out to join her, Louise wasn't having it.

"I've been selfish with you all night long, sugar. I don't mind sharing you with Medford." Granddaddy smiled at the man, then looked at his granddaughter. She was

gripping his arm so tight, he could tell she wasn't letting him go.

"The song is almost over," said Louise. "Let's just finish this one out."

"Oh well, son," Granddaddy said to Medford. "I guess you'll have to come back later. Nice seeing you again." Granddaddy waved good-bye to Medford with his free hand.

"I look forward to seeing you at the Annual County Fair, Louise," Medford called to his friend. "I'll be on the auction block again this year. I hope you've been saving your pennies."

Louise smiled, sincerely this time, and Granddaddy could tell that Clement's son had just made his granddaughter blush.

Louise was a junior in high school when she first fell in love. She'd made the transition from tomboy to young lady, and although everybody thought the change had happened overnight, for Louise it was a long time coming. It was hard giving up the status and the respect she had earned by playing with the neighborhood boys. Throughout her childhood and adolescence, she had been considered an equal to her male counterparts and now she felt forced to lower her standards. She thought being someone's "girlfriend" meant she had to be subservient. It seemed she certainly had a greater sacrifice to make than the boys did, which meant she probably had more to lose. From what she saw at school, there were girls everywhere losing themselves—some deliberately acting stupid in class, others wearing tight clothes that made them look like they couldn't breathe, still others who would even turn against their friends—like they were under a spell cast by the domineering boys and were absorbed by their demands every day. What happened to girls when they acquired boyfriends made Louise fight the unavoidable for as long as she could.

But when Louise turned sixteen, Carter Lightbrook walked into her life and became the first boy she surrendered to. It was love at first sight, although at the time, Louise was unwilling to commit to that high level of emotion. After six months of sharing their lunches, doing their homework together, writing love notes, and riding the bus to and from school, Carter finally convinced Louise that he was truly her boyfriend. It took him almost a whole school year to prove his love to her, and when he passed the test, she cautiously gave him her heart.

Even though Louise was sixteen, she had a hard time persuading Nana that she was old enough to have a boyfriend. After many arguments with her grandmother, and the various occasions when she cornered Granddaddy to win his support, Nana finally gave in and let Carter Lightbrook come courting on Saturdays after Louise did all her homework. When Louise and Carter finally finished their junior year, he presented her with a ten-karat gold friendship ring and made it official that they were going steady. By now, Louise was beside herself. She walked around with dreamy eyes and became forgetful about things. She only wanted to spend time with her boyfriend, neglecting her friends and everybody else, and her heart raced whenever she was with him, which made her come to believe that being "absorbed" and under a "spell" wasn't such a bad thing.

Then one morning Louise woke up with a temperature and a few red, blotchy pimples on her face, and went to school on the same day that Carter decided to kiss her for the first time in public. The next day, Louise woke up with the chicken pox, and Carter never called her again. She spent a week out of school due to the childhood illness and two more weeks in bed due to healing a broken heart.

She had heard that when Carter had gone to school the

following day, the pox had gotten him so bad that it spread to his eyes, inside his mouth, underneath his fingernails, and all over his private parts. The attack was so brutal he had to be rushed to the hospital and quarantined, and Louise heard that he almost died, but he didn't. After that, Carter didn't want to have anything to do with Louise. He accused her of withholding information, claiming she knew she had chicken pox, and intentionally wanted to get him sick, maybe even wanted to kill him. When the disease had attacked his private parts as ferociously as it did, Carter wondered if he could get venereal disease from kissing, and started spreading rumors about his ex-girlfriend through the school's express gossip pipeline. When Carter's doctor announced he'd have to live with permanent scars covering more than 80 percent of his body, Carter lost his mind and the rumors about his ex-girlfriend became even more rampant. Calling Louise names like "Black Widow" because she'd administered the "kiss of death" mortified Louise and she couldn't understand how the love of her life could be so cruel. As it turned out, Carter was incorrigible.

Granddaddy felt helpless to assist his older granddaughter during this difficult time and wished he had the power to take away the pain so she could finally get out of bed. When he got wind of how this young man was tarnishing his granddaughter's reputation, however, it was time to take matters into his own hands. He asked Nana to accompany him and together they paid a visit to Mr. and Mrs. Lightbrook, who lived several blocks away, on Piedmont Road. The Lightbrooks were kind enough to let the Dunlaps into their home, although Granddaddy could tell they were extremely upset by their visit. Granddaddy asked to see the boy, but Carter, too self-conscious or afraid to face the parents of the tormented, refused to come downstairs. Granddaddy addressed the Lightbrooks, saying there was nothing he

could do to erase what had been done. Nana added that she would pray for a quick recovery for the stricken boy. Then Granddaddy continued, talking about how chicken pox would run its course, but the lies and the foulness coming out of the boy's mouth could cause permanent and irreparable damage to his granddaughter, and that he couldn't allow that to happen. He added that while the boy was too young to bring up on charges of slander and defamation of character, he had a grandson who was training to be a sheriff. At some point, he reminded the Lightbrooks that one day Carter would be grown, and that later in life their son might mistakenly be accused of a crime or suffer some terrible accident, and come up against the law and need a favor from him or the sheriff. He warned them that if that ever happened, he'd have to deny them that favor if this nonsense didn't stop. When Mr. Lightbrook asked Granddaddy if he was being threatened, Granddaddy calmly and politely said no. The elder Dunlap confirmed and assured him that he was a rule-abiding citizen, and was simply adhering to Rule Number Nine: MIND YOUR BUSINESS PERSONALLY AND PROFESSIONALLY. And as far as he was concerned, his granddaughter was his personal business. After that, Granddaddy tipped his hat to his hosts, thanked them for their time, and wished them a nice day. Nana and Granddaddy left the Lightbrook home and there was never another unkind word spoken about Louise again. In fact, the family moved to the other side of town and into a different school district.

"Love Train" had ended and Granddaddy and Louise stopped dancing and called it a night. After thinking about the way Louise had acted around Medford, he realized that he hadn't seen his granddaughter interact with another man since that Carter fellow, way back when. Well aware that his granddaughter didn't pattern her life after the Virgin Mary and had flesh-and-blood

boyfriends every now and then, he was hoping that one day she'd get over her case of the jitters, get together with a nice guy like Medford, and settle down. The fact that Medford was old enough to be her daddy didn't bother him at all. In fact, he felt a daddy might be the kind of person his granddaughter needed because she had missed having one around in her life.

The night of the jamboree was the first night that Harry had been home at a decent hour in weeks and Faye didn't want their time together to go to waste, despite what had happened between them earlier in the evening. It was a long day and when they arrived at the cottage, they went straight to bed. Faye walked to her closet and began to undress. Harry stood at the foot of the bed and let his pants fall to the floor. Faye pulled her top over her head, threw it into the clothes hamper, then walked over to her husband. She began lifting his T-shirt along the sides of his body, feeling his skin against hers, allowing her hands to climb up slowly to his arms. When she reached the top of his torso, she gently slid his shirt over his head. She wrapped her arms around him and he hugged her. She placed her nose along his neck and was excited by the smell the sweat had left there at the end of a hard day. She leaned against Harry and together they collapsed on the bed. Her body followed his as he turned off the lamp on the night table. She reached over his shoulder and turned the lamp back on. She wanted to see the love in his eyes when he entered her wetness. As he slowly eased his way into her warmth until he was completely inside her, he teased her slightly, before releasing himself too quickly, leaving her appetite unfulfilled. Without any regard for her needs or her feelings, he turned off the lamp and said, "Good night, baby. I'm exhausted. Time to go to sleep. You need to get some rest, too." Harry turned over. Shortly after that, he began to snore.

Faye felt as if he had walked away from her in the middle of a sentence, while she was still in the process of finishing a thought. Lying in the dark, unable to move from her state of disbelief, she decided to give herself some attention. Not once did her hands moving against her hips on the mattress disturb her husband; not once did her moans startle his rest. She didn't like being neglected and wondered if there was another reason besides work that was making Harry so tired.

She was still wide awake in the darkness, and it was quiet enough outside to hear a whippoorwill's shrill song in the woods in the distance, a woodpecker drumming its chisel-like beak against a tree, and the sounds of crickets chirping in their syncopated chorus. The night sounds of the repetitious harmonies transitioned Faye's thoughts to chants of "We Shall Overcome" on freedom rides and in street marches.

She thought about the way Harry seemed to have lost his enthusiasm tonight; she had hoped his attitude wouldn't spread to the life they had planned together, that his mood was only temporary. She pulled the top sheet over her head and felt lonely sleeping with her husband, back-to-back, with enough space to put a pillow between them.

Louise had volunteered herself along with Faye and Elvira to bake pies for the Annual County Fair. But she forgot to tell them about it until two days before the pies were due. Two days before the Fair, they found themselves standing in the produce section of the Piggly Wiggly just minutes after it opened, mulling over slim pickings for sweet-potato and apple pies. It seemed everyone else who'd planned on making pies that weekend had been more organized and gotten there first.

Elvira pushed the shopping cart and said to Louise, "I can't believe you promised we'd bake three extra sweet-potato pies for the pie-eating contest, on top of the five apple and five sweet-potato pies for the bake sale." She turned to Faye. "Should we kill her now or later?"

"Let's keep her alive until she bakes her share of the pies."

Ignoring the insults, Louise went back to examining the sweet potatoes, testing the ones that were the firmest in search of the perfect spuds. She forgot to tell her sisters about the bake sale because she had been thinking about Medford. The last time she had seen him was at last year's Annual County Fair. She'd known him all her life. Since his daddy, Clement, was her granddaddy's best friend, on occasion he'd bring Medford over to the house. Usually, he'd get bored, being too old to play with her and Faye or Billy, and too young to get involved with grown folks' conversations. As a result, she didn't

get to see him that often. As time went by and she grew older, she began noticing Medford a little bit more. There was something about the way he matured and filled out, the way he walked, and always seemed to have something on his mind, which made him appear to be smart, that made her take a second look. When they had gotten together last summer, he did more than turn her head. But Louise's policy about being attracted to a man made her prefer to do it at a distance. Since she had resisted thinking about him all year, she was now about to burst with a heated excitement that she hid behind a cool façade.

"What are you thinking about?" Elvira asked Louise. "You been feeling up those same sweet potatoes over and over again for the last two minutes."

"Thinking about poor Nana," she lied. "It's a shame what happened to her tomatoes. I asked her to make three green-tomato pies, or fry up some green tomatoes to serve and sell at the Fair to give her something to do to keep her busy."

"When I was there this afternoon, all she did was stare into the TV and provide advice to the people in her soap operas." Faye was inspecting the apples, checking their skins for brown puncture marks, making sure they were worm-free.

"You'd be depressed, too, if you was planning half your life to do something that didn't work out," said Elvira.

"You can say that again." Faye gave up on picking over individual apples and grabbed a prepackaged bag filled with Galas. "I'm gonna be depressed if Harry doesn't want to leave town after the Fair."

"We're just glad you stayed all summer." Satisfied with her selection, Louise put three bags of sweet potatoes into the shopping cart. She could have told her sis-

ter how wonderful it was to spend all this time with her, but she didn't want to get mushy.

"We really want you to stay with us forever." Elvira put two more bags of sweet potatoes into the cart.

Faye nearly gagged at the prospect of a life sentence in Lemon City. "As much as I love y'all, forever is an awfully long time for me to be locked up in this town."

"When did you start hating it so much?" asked Elvira.

"I don't hate it." Faye put two more plastic bags filled with apples into the cart. "It's just that the things I want to do I can't do here, is all. It's like I need room to breathe, and there just isn't enough air space in Lemon City."

"You choking, Louise?" Elvira said as she turned to her sister-in-law.

"Nope. Not me. I ain't gagging."

"Me, neither." Elvira moved her mouth to one side, which turned up her cheek, gesturing to Faye that Lemon City was okay and she was the one with the problem.

Faye realized that her family would never get it. So why bother trying to explain herself to them?

After hauling the bags of groceries up the flight of stairs to Louise's house, the three women rolled out dough and peeled and baked until late evening. Exhausted, Faye couldn't wait to get home and climb into bed. Despite what had happened the other night between her and Harry, including his bad timing, she was still anxious to see him. When the last pie finally came out of the oven, she rushed home to the cottage. She fantasized that she would find him packed and ready to leave. He'd greet her with open arms so she could fall right into them and he would make love to her all night long with a hunger she'd never seen. And after making love, Harry's leg would extend and wind around corners like

a rubber band, so he'd have one foot already out the front door in preparation for their trip up North.

But when she opened the door and called out his name, no one answered. Her heart sank as she felt let down again, and whatever thoughts she had about great sex dried right up. She imagined him at work at this hour, but the more she thought about it, the more common sense told her that there were only three things a man could be doing at this time of night in Lemon City: either he was at home, at a bar alone, or at a bar with another woman. She could easily envision him at The Tap by himself, but her imagination did not stretch far enough to see her husband at that grungy bar with another woman.

In need of company, she turned on the TV. The picture was fuzzy, so she hit the console hard with her fist. This served a double purpose. The TV image cleared up, and Faye felt less frustrated, angry, and hurt. When all the blurry lines finally came together, a sea of black faces came into focus. The news was covering a black political convention in Gary, Indiana. Faye became absorbed in the scene. For the moment, she forgot all about Harry and concentrated on what was happening. Folks walking outside the convention center were carrying signs, chanting "Nationtime, Nationtime. Nationtime." A woman spoke into the reporter's microphone, telling him that they were protesting to help get black officials elected as mayors and as representatives to Congress. Then the reporter said to the people watching TV that this was the first time that black members of the House of Representatives had formed a Black Caucus to develop a strategy to pass laws on health, black enterprise, and education. Hundreds of people were gathered in front of the steps and along the sidewalk, and Faye wished she could jump through the RCA to be right there shouting and uniting with them. Then the camera showed what was going on

inside the convention center, and Faye could hardly believe her eyes. She had never seen that many black people gathered in one place in her life. It looked like every black person and black leader in America was there. The reporter was saying that twelve thousand people were at the convention, and Faye was searching for anyone who looked familiar. Sure enough, she spotted Jesse Jackson from People United to Save Humanity, Dorothy Height from the National Council of Negro Women, Imamu Imiri Baraka from the Congress of African People, and Coretta Scott King from the Southern Christian Leadership Council. The story ended, and the TV went to a commercial. The people's strong sense of pride reached Faye right there in her living room. She just hoped the passion of the times would keep rolling and growing until she could get to where the action was and join in with the people in the movement.

She looked at her watch. It was eleven fifteen and Harry still wasn't home. He must be busy at The Shop. She forced herself to think about something else. He was working many hours lately. Soon The Shop would be behind them. Who knew how far Harry would advance once they went up North, where black people were changing the world?

That same night, Nana was in the kitchen listening to gospel music on the radio, hoping to lift her spirits. She smiled, shaking her head, thinking about how Louise wouldn't let her leave the house until she promised to bake green-tomato pies for the Annual County Fair with the few usable tomatoes left in her garden. It was a rare moment when Louise's caring qualities came out. It wasn't often that she'd let down the wall and let the sweetness shine through. But of all her grandchildren, she could count on Louise concerning herself with the family. She was amazed that Faye had gone in the opposite direction—turning her back on the family. Then

there was Billy, who just flowed with everyone like a strong current on a river and was the kind of male child that every mother wished for.

Thinking about her grandchildren provided Nana with a temporary diversion from the disappointment of losing the Tomato Competition before she'd even had a chance to enter it. As Sister Rosetta Tharpe sang "God Leads Us Along" on the radio, Nana hummed along with the chorus, pouring herself a sip of dandelion wine to calm her nerves and ease the pain. Every year she lost was another year that made it harder for her to get up her energy to start all over again. Even though quitting wasn't in her blood, she was beginning to see that sometimes a dignified surrender was best, that the knowledge that some things were best left to those folks who knew more about them was the truth she'd have to swallow.

She rinsed off a few dozen green tomatoes and placed them on the counter in a porcelain bowl. After drying her hands on the dish towel, she got out the rolling pin and the flour to get started on making the crust. Nana hummed along with Mahalia, as she looked out her kitchen window into the house next door and happened to glimpse the moving shadow of her neighbor. *Life would be so much different,* she thought, *if Easely were still alive.* Competition for the Tomato Crown might not be as fierce if the witch next door still had her husband, and Nana had to admit that sometimes she missed her former best friend.

∾

CHAPTER ELEVEN

∾

At the Thanksgiving table, Faye put a piece of ham in her mouth and accidentally bit down on a clove, which left behind a nasty taste that made her think about her sister. Faye had first sensed a bad vibe between her sister and her husband after last year's Annual County Fair. Come to think of it, it seemed Elvira got real turned off to Harry at the same time, too. There had been a mysterious plumbing problem at The Shop soon after the Fair and Harry's toilet had suddenly backed up and waste spilled out on the floor. He had to shut the place down for a day, and then a week later, he left The Shop to find all four of his car tires flat.

Whenever she confronted her sisters about the friction, they assured her there was nothing to worry about, that everything would turn out fine. Now, as she glanced at Louise pacing herself with her meal and Elvira helping herself to thirds as if it were just another Thanksgiving Day, she wondered if everything turning out fine had anything to do with her husband turning up dead.

With the tension in the room getting thick enough to cut with Granddaddy's electric carving knife, Louise felt it was time for the truth to set them free. "Okay. Let's get everything straight. The Jefferson County sheriff is coming in the morning, so we might as well go around the table and say where we were at the time of the murder. Just spit it out and get it over with so we can enjoy

the rest of our meal." She paused and looked at each member of her family. "Billy, you go first."

"Why me? You go first." Billy helped himself to a second round of candied yams, then went back to the casserole dish to scoop some extra syrup.

"All right." Louise tapped her fork on her glass to get everyone's attention and used it as a pointer to address the table. "Supposedly, the murder happened around midday Monday afternoon. I was at the library. It closes at four thirty, and I left at around five. That's late afternoon. That's where I was." She twirled her fork, then banged it on the table like it was a courtroom mallet and pointed it toward Billy. "Now it's your turn."

Billy cleared his throat, then sat back to a more relaxed position in his chair. "I was at the police station. I picked up the phone when the call came in. Y'all know that already." Billy gulped down the rest of his iced tea, then crunched on the remaining ice cubes so loudly that Louise paused before moving her pointer to Elvira.

"Elvira."

"Wait a minute," Faye interrupted. "*I* called you."

"Yes. That's right," said Billy, trying to figure out where Faye was going with this. "So, what does that make you, Sherlock Holmes?"

"But how do I know you didn't do it—sneak away from the office to commit the crime, then sneak back to work like you had been there all along? Was there anyone else at the station?"

"No." Billy shifted in his seat. "No. Everyone was on patrol. It was my turn to man the desk."

"Aha!" shouted Louise, to what seemed to everyone to be at the top of her lungs.

"Oh, go screw yourself," Billy said to Louise.

"Watch your language at the table, young man," Nana chimed in.

"Excuse me." Billy apologized to Nana, then dealt

with Faye. "I was in my office, minding my own business. How do I know that you didn't kill him, then make the call?"

"It's not my nature to kill."

"Desperate women will do anything." Billy punctuated the sentence by nodding his head.

"That's a perfect segue to Elvira." Louise looked at her sister-in-law and smiled.

"What do you mean, me?" Elvira was fidgeting with her napkin like she was nervous.

"It's your turn," said Louise.

Elvira placed both hands on her lap and concentrated. "I was taking the kids home on the school bus, dropping them off, which is my usual routine . . ." She looked at her watch and hesitated. "I finished making the rounds at about two thirty."

Everyone turned to face Elvira, including Billy.

"Stop staring at me like that. I was driving the bus. I was with the kids. Then I went home. I got there a little before three. I do that every day." She picked up her fork, but it fell to the floor. When she cleaned it off with a napkin everyone noticed the slight tremor in her hand.

"So what did you do after three o'clock?" asked Louise.

"I was at home, like I said, cleaning out the hallway closet, trying to get rid of some of Billy's junk . . ."

"Eh!" said Billy. "Whadaya mean 'junk'?"

". . . watching *Match Game* at the same time," Elvira continued, ignoring her husband.

"Did you have any witnesses?" asked Louise.

"Of course not." Elvira became indignant. "Who would be watching me at home when it's just me and Billy?"

"Aha!" said Louise. "So Billy was there!"

"No, he was at the police station, like he said." Elvira was getting tired of being the object of interrogation.

"Well don't get your story confused," said Louise. "I'm just trying to help."

"You know what I mean." Elvira was frustrated that what she said didn't come out right. "Only Billy and me live in the house, so cain't no one be there watching me when he's not around—no. There were no witnesses. You just have to trust that I'm telling you the truth."

"Faye, where were you?" Glad that her sister-in-law had finally gotten that off her chest, Louise continued to make her way around the table.

"I was leaving the hair salon, heading home."

"What time did you get there?"

"I don't know; I wasn't wearing my watch."

"Billy, what time did she call?"

"I don't know. The clock in the office was broke."

"Another piece of junk," added Elvira. "He found it in the trash can at the secondhand store, and it ain't worked in months. He just has it for show."

"I was already at home," said Nana, "watching my soap opera."

"I was playing checkers with Clement and Bootsie downtown at the general store, and that's all I have to say about it." Granddaddy was tired of all this mess. He was so mad at Harry and the predicament that he had caused his family to be in, that if Harry walked through that door, he'd make sure that no-good son of a gun died again.

When they finished sharing their alibis, Faye looked around the table and thought their stories sounded as plucked as the bird on the platter—bits and pieces of the truth scattered here and there, impossible to get to the whole of it. From what she gathered, there were three people at home or at work who didn't have witnesses, and three people in public places around the time of Harry's death. It seemed to narrow the list of suspects, but in reality any one of them could have taken a detour on that fateful day—any one of them could be lying.

Faye was tired. She had been making pies with her sisters all evening. After she watched the news, she crawled into bed without taking a shower. In the middle of the night, she rolled onto her back with her eyes still closed, using her arm along the sheet like a windshield wiper, feeling around for Harry, but he still wasn't there. Being left alone, she was beginning to feel as worthless as a jar filled with air. Now that it was morning, she dragged herself out of bed to percolate some coffee and make herself useful. There was a note taped to the refrigerator door. *Had to go to The Shop. See you at the Fair around 3—love, Harry.* Her spirits lifted a bit knowing that her husband had at some point come home in the middle of the night. She had been hoping they'd go to the Fair together so they'd have a chance to finalize their plans, but at least he cared enough to leave the note. Faye dialed Louise and told her she wanted to go with her and Elvira.

The cacophony of the Annual County Fair consisted of cheers from the Ferris wheel, screams from the roller coaster, and laughter from the merry-go-round. Music, chatter, and all the sounds of a good time ricocheted off the hills, through high peaks and narrow ravines, disappearing deep into the Blue Ridge Mountains. The clear blue sky was dotted with colorful hot-air balloons, and the smell of roasted peanuts made the air salty-sweet. At the entrance to the fairgrounds, a ragtime band per-

formed at the base of the twenty-foot-tall brass metal statue of the founding fathers. The elements had taken their toll on the statue, which ironically came to reflect a more accurate picture of the town today. Over the past one hundred years, the high yellow cast had rusted so that it was brown in places, and in others it was burnished by rain and sun and turned to cast-iron black. The old founding fathers now represented the color spectrum of the faces in Lemon City, from high yellow to blue black, with shades of rust brown in between.

Inside the fairgrounds was a world of magic and make-believe that could convert even the oldest patron into thinking that for a day, age was only a state of mind. There were arts and crafts and antiques booths; canned fruits, jam, and vegetable booths; and canopied tables for baskets and pottery. There were farm equipment and talent shows, a beauty pageant, a parade, and a full-fledged circus. There were platforms erected in various locations hosting drama, comedy, and musical events, attracting spectators by the droves who applauded the entertainment. There were horses, pony-and-buggy rides, a petting zoo with pigs, cows, wild turkeys, goats, deer, groundhogs, foxes, and a black bear. Food stations with hot dogs, corn dogs, fried whiting, barbecued ribs, trout, apple fritters, cotton candy, and candied apples were readily available, making sure everyone had enough to eat to keep up their stamina and endure the fun of the day.

The Dunlaps arrived in two separate cars at the dirt field that served as a temporary parking lot. When they walked through the gate, Nana and Granddaddy veered to the right to the Ladies of Mt. Zion tent, where they were serving homemade dinners to raise money for the church. After Nana and Granddaddy ate lunch, they took a short walk to the amusement area, where they found the Clown-Over-the-Tub game. A clown was sit-

ting on a wooden plank over a tub of water, waiting for someone with good aim to make him fall in. Nana looked at the clown and what she saw instead of a clown face was the face of Ole Miss Johnson, sitting on top of a clown body. She paid twenty-five cents, which gave her five shots at the clown, and immediately she started throwing. Granddaddy was trying to coach Nana with her pitches, but she kept hurling wild balls, aiming at the clown's face instead of at the target over his head. While the clown kept ducking, throwing up his hands, Nana was yelling, "Take that, and take that," and things like, "I'll get you yet, with your big nose looking like a tomato." And on the fifth try, Nana finally dropped the clown into the water, winning a Raggedy Ann doll as a prize. The clown was relieved when Nana walked away.

Then Nana and Granddaddy came upon a shooting gallery. It was Granddaddy's turn to fantasize. Watching the little ducks trail behind each other in a row, Granddaddy crouched down to the level of the single-gauge rifle and started shooting. Five quacking ducks went by, and he knocked all five of them down. As he was aiming at the yellow-beaked targets, Harry crossed his mind. He was angry that the Outsider was making his granddaughter unhappy and firing BB after BB gave him satisfaction. When he finished firing off his frustration, he let Nana pick the prize, and she selected a blow-up doll that was actually a stand-up punching bag. She said it reminded her of what she wanted to do to Ole Miss Johnson. Then Nana and Granddaddy went over to the ringtoss game. When they finished tossing hoops over bottle necks, they took a break and relaxed on a horse-and-buggy ride.

Billy was on regular duty along with a few other officers from the auxiliary police force. He'd signed up for the morning shift on purpose so he could spend the af-

ternoon with his wife. His deputy was scheduled to take over around midday and he could hardly wait to be relieved. He hadn't taken time off in a while, and this break would do him good.

Faye, Elvira, and Louise arrived at the Fair shortly after noontime as well, and took their posts at the bake sale booth. They divided the time so at least one person would be at the booth while the other two could go off and enjoy the Fair. Faye volunteered to take the first shift, and Elvira and Louise waved good-bye. Their first stop was to watch Elvira's fifth-grade class participate in the performance of the traditional Cultural Heritage play, a reenactment of Lemon City's founding fathers and its honorary citizens. The play was a source of pride for the townspeople and served as a tribute as well as an annual reminder to new generations of the original settlers and the sacrifices they made.

Elvira clapped so long after each child successfully delivered his line, Louise missed hearing parts of the performance. Devoted parents didn't share all of Elvira's enthusiasm, and stared in her direction until she stopped. After that, Elvira saved her clapping for the end of each scene.

Faye was selling slices of cake and pie to everyone, and they were all showing up like she was giving them away for free. When Elvira and Louise returned to the booth and saw what was left, they were pleased, and when Faye showed them the cash box, they were even more thrilled. Satisfied that she had met her sisters' expectations, Faye grabbed Louise's hand and off they went to the merry-go-round.

"So, where's your husband?" asked Louise as she stood in line buying tickets.

"He'll be here around three o'clock. He had to work." Faye looked at her watch; it was half past two.

"I . . . see," said Louise. At first she looked concerned,

then she put a smile on her face. "Let's go." She grabbed her sister's hand once she had the tickets, and started running. "We can have fun without him."

They went straight to the merry-go-round, passing several children carrying colorful balloons along the way. Louise handed the attendant two tickets and they jumped on two horses. They were giddier than the little kids on the carousel, kicking the wooden horses, pulling on their reins, pretending they could make them go faster.

The next stop was the Ferris wheel. Around and around they went, until Faye felt herself getting sick when the attendant stopped their bucket at the top of the ride. Having just finished spinning on the merry-go-round and now stuck in what seemed like a hundred feet in the air—the height of the bucket competing with the Blue Ridge Mountains—Faye looked down at the ground and could no longer hold it in. She vomited, and watched as her lunch barely missed landing on some-one's head. Thinking about Harry and their lack of inti-macy lately had completely turned her stomach, and the possibility that he might be seeing another woman was the real thing that was making her sick.

When the attendant finally let them down, they went back to the bake sale booth and the first thing Faye did was pour a cup of water from the cooler. After drinking the water slowly, she poured more water over a napkin and dabbed it against her forehead and the back of her neck to cool down from the heat, and to cool the thoughts of infidelity she had been resisting in her head.

In the picnic area, where the shade from oak, hickory, and sycamore trees kept the tables cool, Granddaddy had found his buddies Clement and Bootsie, and rounded up a fourth player to start a game of Bid Whist.

"I heard that Joe Frazier wants to fight George Fore-man," said Granddaddy, dealing out cards.

"Who you think is gonna win?" asked Bootsie, studying his cards, sorting them in his hand.

"I'm not a betting man, but that boy, George, is taller, younger, and bigger than Smokin' Joe," said Granddaddy. "He looks strong as a farm mule, too," he added.

"Strong don't necessarily mean fast," said Bootsie, putting down a card and collecting a book he had just made, starting his pile.

"If you ask me," said Clement, "Smokin' Joe will scramble his brains and serve 'em up with bacon for breakfast."

"I'm rootin' for the underdog," said Bootsie. "I know George is gonna make the champ work hard for his money."

"I guess we'll just have to wait and see," said Granddaddy, slamming down an ace on the picnic table and winning the first hand for him and his partner.

Louise was at the bake sale booth, cutting a slice of apple pie for a customer. As she handed the teenage boy the paper plate, she looked at her watch and realized it was almost 3:00 PM. Harry should be arriving now, she thought, but more important, the Soul Mate auction was about to take place. Louise's breath suddenly became shallow as the butterflies began moving in her stomach. She was uncomfortable meeting Medford's eyes at the jamboree because he'd shown up a month early and she wasn't ready to deal with him out of context. For the moment, she was only willing to be free with him as it related to the Annual County Fair.

In 1968, the Soul Mate auction replaced the Sadie Hawkins dance. One of the members of Mt. Zion Baptist Church decided the auction would be a better benefit fundraiser for the town because services could be bought by the highest bidder and be sold at a premium. Most of the members were skeptical at first, because the idea of an auction block had implications of the days of

slavery, but at the time, the community chest was low and when the members took a vote, money became the deciding factor. If this recommendation hadn't come from an organization under the aegis of the church, it would have been considered too daring, but since the Ladies of Mt. Zion gave their stamp of approval, the auction was instituted. And it paid off.

Louise scanned the lineup for the auction block and spotted Medford instantly. He was wearing a pair of bib overalls absent a T-shirt underneath, allowing her to focus on the details of his body. The hot sun made the sweat glisten on his broad shoulders and the tight ringlets of hair shine on his muscular chest. She was afraid to get involved with the beautiful brown man with the big strong arms because he might crush her with rejection. But the auction was different. Their time together lasted only a few days and it happened only once a year. Last year he'd paid for her. This year she had come to reciprocate. Keeping it businesslike and all things equal made it easier for her to justify her plan to continue where they'd left off. She saw him searching the crowd and when his eyes finally met hers, he locked on to them and smiled.

All it took was eighty-five bucks—one week's pay— and she and her manservant were on their way. She had the day all planned. As they walked around the Fair she gave him the list of things he had to do. A section of the fence in her backyard needed repair, she needed trellises built for her roses, shingles replaced on the roof, her linoleum floors could use a new coat of wax, and while he was at it, she'd ask him to chop wood so she'd have a few cords for winter. All this work she knew would take him at least one day—maybe two or three—and she would enjoy every minute of it.

"With all those chores you have lined up, I should

have started working for you at six o'clock this morning, Miss Louise." She smiled at this truth.

"Just do what you can," she teased. "I have to get my money's worth." Her hair was pulled up into a big Afro puff that looked like a chrysanthemum had been planted on her head. Wearing a tie-dyed Jimi Hendrix T-shirt and Land Lubber jeans, she bounced alongside Medford as light as a leaf falling from a tree, taking its time to hit the ground.

"As you know, I aim to please. You won't be disappointed."

The memory of their naked bodies wrapped in heat made her glance down at her feet, trying to hide her embarrassment. Not until she collected herself did she look into his face.

"Don't worry. You'll get a meal out of this." She put her hands inside her pockets as if they had gotten in the way and she didn't know what to do with them.

"Food? What I was thinking was more along the lines of dessert."

In the middle of her giggle she stopped. Something that wasn't funny caught her attention.

"What's the matter?"

"I thought I saw something." Then she corrected herself. "I mean, someone." Her eyes followed the figure as she walked through the crowd to get a closer look, dragging Medford behind her. She thought the figure saw her, too. He looked right at her, then stopped dead in his tracks as if he had been caught with his hand in someone else's pocket, then he started walking quickly in the opposite direction. The more aggressively Louise pursued him, the more he backed away. She thought maybe his eyesight was poor and he was mistaking her for someone else, but when she got within fifty feet of her brother-in-law, close enough for positive identification,

he acted as if he were backed into a corner, and didn't know which way to go.

"Harry!" she called out from the crowd. "Harry! Over here!" Louise beckoned him with a sweeping arm motion to join her. She knew it was Harry, and she knew he had heard her, but when she called his name again his brisk gait turned into a canter. "Harry, where are you going?" She dropped Medford's hand and ran after him. But he was already way ahead of her, pretending not to hear. The next thing she knew, Harry had jumped into the driver's seat of a chartreuse green Mustang convertible. As it revved up and sped off, what caught her attention was the back of a woman's head with a pink chiffon scarf tied around a ponytail that was blowing in the wind. *That cheating dog*, Louise thought to herself, and she kicked the dirt so hard she made a hole in the ground. She couldn't believe he was trying to sneak into the Fair and make an appearance just to let her sister know that he'd shown up. He was planning on frontin' for his wife, then splitting with that two-bit ho. Ain't that a blip.

"Come on, Medford," she said, returning to the vicinity of the Ferris wheel where she'd left him. "Let's go get us some hot dogs." She grabbed him by the hand, leading him through the crowd. He figured that when she cooled off and was ready to tell him, she'd explain what had just occurred.

By coincidence, Faye just happened to be at the hot dog stand. Taking a break from the bake sale booth, she was sipping ginger ale through a straw when Louise and a big country-looking brother who reminded her of Li'l Abner sat down next to her. "Hey," she said. "I've been looking all over for Harry." She glanced at her watch. "It's almost four o'clock. Have you seen him?" Faye looked Medford up and down, thinking he looked familiar and that her sister could do much better.

Louise had only lied to her sister about little things, like denying that she borrowed a sweater or swiped a lipstick or used up the last of the tooth powder, but this was a big one. She couldn't bring herself to tell Faye the truth. "No," she finally said. "I just came from the auction, buying Medford, here, for a day. You remember Medford, don't you? He's Clement's son." Faye nodded her head in recognition, but still didn't think he was much to look at.

At the other end of the park, Nana was enjoying herself as best she could. Fanning herself to keep cool in the late afternoon heat, she stuck around long enough to see Ole Miss Johnson claim her crown for the twentieth consecutive year in a row. Nana was beyond disappointment when she looked on to see the bright red-and-gold crown planted on her neighbor's head and the red velvet cape draped across her shoulders, but she forced herself to smile at royalty once again.

It was then that Nana had an epiphany. Inspired by injustice, she decided to petition the Ladies of Mt. Zion Baptist Church to institute a term limit for wearing the crown. If the president of the United States could have one imposed upon him, so should the Tomato Queen. After she mustered up a congratulations to her neighbor as proof that she wasn't a sore loser, she collected her husband from his card game and they made their way to the parking lot to head back home.

Billy's deputy had called him on the CB radio earlier in the afternoon to say he had come down with the flu and was running a high fever and couldn't get out of bed. Dreading the overtime he was about to begin, Billy paid ten cents for a regular cup of coffee to give himself a boost, and for a change of scenery he took a break and a ride down Route 23. As he was cruising along the highway, he honked and waved at Nana and Granddaddy in their 1962 four-door nine-passenger Ford Country

Squire station wagon with brown side panels. Shortly after that, he passed Sheriff Beauregard Taylor driving a 1970 white Chevrolet Nova two-door coupe patrol car. He was all grown up, having taken over his daddy's job and being appointed sheriff around the same time as Billy. Unlike his daddy, Billy always thought Beau seemed unhappy about the work. The younger Sheriff Taylor tipped the front of his beige Stetson as he nodded. Billy honked his horn, lifted a few fingers off the steering wheel, and waved. Then something peculiar about the next car approaching caught Billy's attention: A green Mustang convertible drove past him on the other side of the highway, and the driver looked a lot like Harry. He would have had a clear view of the man because the top was down, but at the exact moment they passed each other, the driver ducked. *Must have dropped a lit cigarette or was looking for something on the floor*, Billy thought. *Drivers today should be more careful, especially when they're carrying precious cargo.* Billy caught himself staring after the passenger with the pretty face from his rearview mirror. He thought he knew all the good-looking women in Lemon City, but he'd never seen this one before.

When Faye got home, Harry was making his version of a BLT sandwich, with fried bologna, lettuce, and tomato. She kissed him and smelled beer on his breath. Determined not to argue, she said, "You missed a great time at the Fair today. And the pies . . . we sold all of them."

"I was there," he said, grabbing his sandwich, turning on the television, "but I couldn't find you." He mumbled the words while crunching with his mouth full.

She looked at her watch. "About what time was that?" She sat down on the orange crushed-velvet love seat against the wall, adjacent to the chair where Harry sat, directly facing the TV.

"Around three o'clock, like I said." He spoke without taking his eyes off the TV.

She didn't like the tone of his voice, or the fact that he made her feel invisible. After all, he shouldn't be the one with the attitude—she was the one who had been stood up. "Harry. We're supposed to be moving this week. The Fair is now over. Which day are we going?" If they were going to fight, it would be about something important, something like moving up North and getting out of Lemon City, not about missing each other at the Annual County Fair.

"Will you stop bugging me about this moving thing?" It was the first time he'd looked at her. His eyes cut like a knife. She had never seen his face so distorted. She tried to make her words as smooth as water, but the fire within him raged and the flames only got bigger. He moved from the living room and sat at the kitchen table. It was an action so simple, one that he did every day, yet this time it had such an unexpected force behind it that it scared her.

"What do you mean?" Faye's voice cracked, then she felt it shake as she followed him into the kitchen.

"I mean, give it a rest—let it go. You're starting to sound like a broken record."

"Harry. What's the matter? What happened to you? What's happening to us?"

He intended to pound his fist on the table, but it landed on the other half of his sandwich instead. "Ain't nothing wrong with us. We're married, that's all. Isn't that what you wanted?"

"Isn't that what *I* wanted?" She sat down in disbelief across from him at the other end of the kitchen table.

"Yeah, you got what you wanted. Now what *I* want is to stay."

"You can't be serious."

"As a heart attack, and you know what? You'll get

over it." He got up, threw his empty beer can into the trash, grabbed his jacket, and headed for the door.

"Where are you going?"

"Out," he said, " to get some peace. I can't get none here."

She waited for the door to close before she dropped her head into her arms on the table and cried, wondering if he meant some piece of ass or some peace of mind. She might have trapped Harry into marriage in order to leave Lemon City, but now she was beginning to wonder if he had trapped her so that he might stay.

There's a Rule in Lemon City: AIRING YOUR DIRTY LAUNDRY OUT IN THE STREET WILL SMELL UP THE NEIGH-BORHOOD. Faye didn't want to pollute the environment. She had no choice but to sort things out on her own.

~❧~

CHAPTER THIRTEEN

~❧~

To show appreciation for the work that Medford had done around the house, Louise cooked him an elaborate meal, complete with peach cobbler and homemade vanilla ice cream. After dinner, she drew a bubble bath to relax the muscles he used to replace the shingles, chop wood, repair her fence, and build five beautiful, handcrafted wood-carved trellises. Tomorrow he would wax the floors. She took out her Isaac Hayes *Hot Buttered Soul* album and put the needle down on the sultry four-minute song "I Stand Accused" to serve as background music for the rhythm they were about to create on their own.

She searched her linen closet, looking for a matching washcloth and towel. The bathroom door was cracked open, with just enough room to see his reflection in the medicine cabinet mirror. She watched him as he began to peel off his clothes. She didn't move until he was totally naked. Beautiful, absolutely beautiful.

The problem was that Medford desired her heart, but she was reluctant to let him cross over into the private places of her soul. Good sex was all she wanted with him. She didn't have the courage for anything else. That little sneaky scene with Harry at the Fair was confirmation that she should keep her distance from men. And while the event was still fresh on her mind, she thought it best to call Elvira with the news. What happened today with Harry was way too important to put off until morning.

She placed the washcloth and towel on the wall rack in the bathroom and told Medford she had to make a quick phone call to her sister-in-law before it got too late. *Harry*

His eyes followed her as she turned and walked away. No woman had ever been as open and as carefree about sex as Louise. She wanted it with no strings attached, and something about that kind of independence appealed to him and made him want her more. But he recognized that he could go only so far with her. With Louise, he knew he had to be patient. From what little he knew about her, she was the kind of woman who had to believe she was in control, doing things when she was ready, in her own time. He didn't mind giving up his power, knowing eventually she'd make a move to let him know she had decided to open her heart. A woman like Louise was worth waiting for. Just as though they were dancing, he'd follow her lead. She'd get to feel more comfortable with him and never let another brother cut in. *Louise*

Louise was thankful that it was Elvira and not Billy who picked up the phone. She didn't think she could bear making small talk with her brother right now. She was sure it would be a bad idea to tell Billy what she'd seen. Her brother had a temper that could snap just like his knee, and he had learned from Granddaddy to be protective of all members of the family. He was liable to arrest Harry for some trumped-up charge or even worse—to kill him.

"Girl, you won't believe what I saw at the County Fair."

"Who? What?" Elvira sat up in bed and adjusted her back into the pillows.

"It's a *who*. Listen, is Billy there?"

"No."

"Good. I saw Harry leaving the Fair with a woman."

Elvira nearly dropped the phone. "Quit jivin' me."

"No. I ain't jivin'. I'm square business. He was there with another woman. I called him. He didn't even stop or turn around or wave or nothing. He just ran away from me and then got into this green convertible Mustang with some ho wearing a pink scarf and drove off."

"Dag . . . Who was she?" She pulled back the covers and folded her knees into her chest.

"Heck if I know. I didn't get a good look at her. Musta been an Outsider."

"Did you get a license plate number?"

"I didn't get that close."

"What are we gonna do?" Elvira placed the palm of her hand against her forehead as if that would help answer her question. "You know the Rule," she added.

Louise recited it like she had when she was in grade school. "Cheating Makes You Lower than a Dog Scratching Up a Worm in the Dirt."

"Mr. Low has got to go." Louise peeked around her bedroom doorway to make sure Medford couldn't hear her conversation. "I know we have to do something," she added, "but whatever it is, we'll have to do it later. 'Cause right now I got Medford right here where I want him, naked and in the tub."

"Don't worry. I'll think of something."

"Keep it from Billy 'til we come up with a plan."

"I'll try." She hung up.

Elvira could hardly wait for Billy to get home to tell him all about Harry. Whenever she got worked up, she had a hard time recalling details, so she began scribbling notes on her conversation with Louise. When Billy arrived, she ignored Louise's advice.

"Baby, you will not believe what happened today."

"Try me." Billy sat down in his favorite chair and began taking off his boots.

"Sugar," she said before she took a deep breath,

"Louise saw Harry with another woman." She pronounced each word as if Billy could only read lips, pausing long enough for the information to register.

Billy's ears began to burn, but he said nothing, just looked at his wife and listened to her as she continued. Elvira referred to her notes. "Louise said he was in a convertible with the woman, but I don't remember the color or the kind—I forgot to write it down."

"What else she say?"

"Said the woman had a pink or a red, or a fuchsia-colored scarf . . . or maybe it was a green scarf that blew in her hair as they flew down the road. Or maybe green was the color of the car . . . anyway, Louise couldn't get the plate number and didn't recognize the woman. She assumed she was an Outsider, too."

"I saw a green convertible headed toward The Tap on Route 23 this afternoon." Billy began to put his boots back on. "I'm gonna check it out." He was calm. Knowing how excited his wife could get, he didn't want to upset her, didn't want to let on that the blood shooting to his head was because he hadn't initiated a good, old-fashioned ass whuppin' in a very long time, and the anticipation was enough to make him burst.

Route 23 was the only road in and out of Lemon City, and The Tap was just over its border, outside the city limits. It was a juke joint where fallen Lemonites and locals from Jefferson County went to keep their secrets. The Ladies of Mt. Zion Baptist Church called The Tap the "devil's back pocket" because it attracted the lint—the part of the main fabric of society that was left over and needed to be brushed away.

Despite the fact that Billy was still in uniform, none of the dissolutes paid him any mind when he walked into The Tap. Even a sheriff wasn't above debauchery. As he walked through the strands of love beads overhanging the door leading into the smoke-filled room, he made his

way to the back, where he thought he'd find the slimiest of the sleaze obscured in darkness. Sure enough, his hunch was right. There was his brother-in-law in a booth, slugging down a shot of cheap brandy. He had his arm around a woman with a pink chiffon scarf in her hair.

The bar was so crowded and noisy that when he stopped at the booth, he had to rap twice on the hardwood table to get Harry's attention. Finally, Harry looked up, perturbed at the interruption, until he saw Billy. Harry immediately pushed away his lady friend to put some space between them, but it was too late. He was busted. Harry began rambling about dropping off a car for his customer, but Billy wasn't buying it. He politely asked his brother-in-law to step outside for a minute, because there was a message that needed to be delivered. Reluctantly, Harry followed Billy through the bar. When they reached the lighted parking lot, Billy stepped into the shadows and snatched Harry by the collar. All he said was, "If I catch you cheating on my sister again, I'll hurt you worse than this." Then he punched Harry dead in the face.

Harry could have punched him back, maybe kicked him in his trick knee, but he wasn't that big a fool. He was living in a mighty nice house, not paying much on the mortgage, plus he had his own business. Life couldn't be better. As he walked away with his hand holding his throbbing eye, Billy added, "If there is a next time, you'll be kissing your ass good-bye instead of your girlfriend. Now git on home to your wife where you belong."

As soon as darkness turned into dawn, Faye got up and started cooking breakfast. She didn't want her being upset with Harry to carry over into a new day. It was a scary feeling when your husband was unavailable to you. As she lowered the flame under the catfish and the apples she was frying so they would turn a perfect

brown, she took the time to think through how she could improve their relationship and make things right. _Faye_ She refused to feel sorry for herself, because she wasn't a victim, but all her life she felt something pulling her, like a string had attached itself to her belly button and she had no choice but to move with the tug and obey. The Rules came first, her family second, a husband third, and then her children, if she had any, would follow fourth. After that, it was presumed she'd pull up the rear, falling back to the end of the line. Now Granddaddy had given her Hair Today, Gone Be Beautiful Tomorrow, and that was an obstacle, an additional burden to carry. The fact that Harry loved The Shop added more weight to the difficult process of leaving. Faye was tired of fighting and driving herself against the norm. After all, it wasn't uncommon for women who loved their husbands to give up their dreams for them. Lots of women made sacrifices. It happened all the time. Maybe Harry was right. Maybe they shouldn't rush into leaving Lemon City. Maybe working in The Shop would provide him with the hands-on experience he needed to be successful up North. And while he was getting his act together, she could pursue her goal of developing Nubian Silk. As long as she could stay on track, maybe it wouldn't be so bad if they stayed in Lemon City just a little while longer, especially if it would make Harry happy. She hadn't thought about Harry's happiness in a while, and she was starting to suspect that might be part of their problem.

When he entered the kitchen, she turned around to hug him, but instead she backed away in horror. Seeing his black eye, she immediately grabbed a handful of ice cubes from the freezer, put them into a plastic bag, and placed it against his head. The ice might do something to reduce the swelling, but it would do nothing to help Harry's bruised ego.

"What in the world happened to you?" she asked.

"I tripped over a gas hose and fell into the pump."

"You've gotta be more careful." Faye was glad Harry let her tend to him, but was confused because his story didn't make any sense.

"Yeah, I know."

She held the bag of ice over his eye, taking advantage of the opportunity of having Harry's full attention, using the situation to suggest they make a brand new start. "I've had a chance to do some thinking."

"I'm sorry about yesterday." Harry looked up at Faye and placed his hand over the ice bag, relieving his wife of her duty.

"Maybe we can agree to some kind of compromise."

"What do you have in mind?"

She began setting the table. "What if we stay in Lemon City for another year? That'll give us some time to save money and figure out where we're gonna go."

"I'd like to stay." He attempted a smile, but Faye could see that it hurt.

"Just before we leave, you can sell your half of The Shop back to Granddaddy or someone else, and Granddaddy can give the salon back to its original owner, or maybe some other young woman in town is dreaming about having her own salon."

"Sounds like a plan," said Harry, peering at her through the plastic bag with his one good eye.

"So that settles it." She sat a pitcher of orange juice on the table. "Let's agree to leave next year around this time right after the Annual County Fair. No excuses."

Faye exhaled as she sat down. While he was busy eating, she studied his face. There was no expression. It was as cold as the ice pack that had just covered his eye, and despite their conversation, the thought that crossed her mind was that she might have to leave town by herself.

It wouldn't be the first time Faye felt this overwhelm-

ing sense of loneliness. When she was four years old, just tall enough to peek over the kitchen table and count the crumbs that Nana missed while sponging down the vinyl place mats, she had a recurring dream. It always came in the middle of the night, often disturbing her so much that she'd lay awake until dawn. She would see herself falling through darkness, arms and legs flailing, like a ladybug on its back desperately trying to flip over before it got in harm's way. Down, down, down she fell through the pitch-black tunnel. No sound did she hear, no noise could she make as gravity pulled her through the hollow darkness. At the end of infinity was a plush feather mattress, waiting to catch her. When she landed on it, she was catapulted back up through the darkness, back to the top of nowhere, only to begin her spiral journey downward again. The experience made her feel much like a yo-yo, and she would wake up dizzy and so afraid that she would remain curled into a little ball until the sun came up.

(handwritten margin note: Faye's Dream)

She hadn't thought about that bouncing dream since she was a child, but something about its repetitive nature was beginning to feel familiar as she sat in the kitchen eating breakfast with her husband. It reminded her of her life with him. Up and down, both places empty, up and down, the scary sense of going nowhere. Married life was turning out to be similar to her nightmare.

As they ate breakfast in silence, Faye slumped into her chair, giving herself a chance to get used to the idea of living in Lemon City for another year. In an effort to relax, she felt the energy drain from her body, as she prepared for the routine that was about to settle in.

Billy had carved only half the turkey, giving Faye a clear view to its cavity. The baked apple had shriveled up and fallen deep into its belly, and Faye imagined that was where the tomato had ended up in Harry. She dabbed the creases of her mouth with her napkin before making the announcement. "You know, I don't think I'll ever get married again."

"Don't say that," said Elvira. "Right now your husband's dead and lying on a slab in the county morgue, but give it some time, and before you know it you'll be jumping the broom again."

Faye looked at Elvira sitting next to Billy and noticed they were both kinda chubby, except that Billy was much taller and more muscular and you couldn't tell with him as much. As they sat there grinning at each other, still very much in love, it made Faye wonder if eating more was the secret to being content.

"I can't imagine spending the rest of my life with someone else," said Louise. "With the same person, no less."

"What's wrong with that?" asked Billy.

"We're doing it," said Billy and Elvira, and Nana and Granddaddy, like a chorus.

Louise reached over the table to help herself to some candied yams as if she were stockpiling ammunition to help win her philosophical debate. "Check it out. Nowadays people are fulfilling their sexual needs with-

out getting married. Everybody's doing their own thing. More and more women are having babies without husbands."

"First of all, young lady, whoever said that marriage was all about sex?" Granddaddy's eyebrow raised up over his right eye as it usually did when he was annoyed. "Marriage is about building a life with someone, like me and your grandmother here. It's about laying down a foundation for a family and planting the seeds for generations to come."

"See? Planting seeds. Now that's what I'm talking about," said Billy, nudging and winking at Elvira.

Nana couldn't wait to have great-grandchildren. She had trained herself not to interfere with Billy and Elvira's personal lives, but since he'd brought up the subject, she figured that gave her permission to ask her standard question. "So when're you two gonna start your family? I can't wait to see my great-grands runnin' around the house."

"Believe me, Nana. We work on it every chance we get," Elvira said, making it sound like she was exhausted from trying.

"See? What did I tell you," said Louise. "Sex. That's what it's all about." Proud that she had made her point, she elbowed Faye so hard that her macaroni and cheese flew off her fork and landed in front of Granddaddy's plate. Letting nothing go to waste, he picked up the cheesy clump and popped it into his mouth without skipping a beat.

"In their case, it's about making babies," Granddaddy corrected. "That's what sex is supposed to be for, young lady." He had a lot to say on the subject, but he was also hungry, which resulted in his talking with his mouth full.

"You mean to tell me that you and Nana only had sex to make babies, and not for your own enjoyment?"

The way Granddaddy sat up in his chair and made it

scrape across the floor, Louise could tell he was getting riled up and ready to preach. "Don't you worry 'bout what me and your grandmother do," he said, pointing his fork at Louise. "You just listen to what I say. You young people keep messing around, and you're gonna pay for all this free love one day."

A speck of meat escaped his mouth and landed on the table. Apparently finding it too small to consume, he picked it up and smeared it on the side of his plate. "Marriage, family values, and a sense of community are what made this town upstanding and strong." He turned in his chair to face Faye. "In fact, back when I was coming up, a man like Harry woulda been run out of here for good and kicked out again if he came back. All this woulda happened as soon as he started acting up, too . . . before the situation got worse and he got himself kilt."

Faye thought Granddaddy was going to keel over. His little speech about Harry took all his breath. His outburst surprised her like a sucker punch to the stomach, making her wonder if he was the one who'd had a hand in her husband's death.

"Hush now, Willie," said Nana. "You'll get yourself all worked up, and the next thing you know you'll be lying in the county morgue . . . right next to Harry." The image of Granddaddy lying next to Harry was so ridiculous that it made them all snicker.

"That's not funny." Granddaddy took offense. "Besides, what I'm saying is true. And don't tell me to hush."

"Pass me the collard greens, please" was Faye's contribution to the conversation. Even though she wasn't hungry, it was all she could think of to say to get Nana and Granddaddy to stop fussing. Faye had never seen her Granddaddy so upset. She looked to Nana for help, hoping she could quiet Granddaddy and end the conver-

sation. Nana changed the subject to the quilting group
she was thinking about forming with Sadie, Theola, and
Vernelle, a few of the ladies from Mt. Zion Baptist
Church, and since it was a topic unfamiliar to Grand-
daddy, he didn't have much to say.

Sunday, the day after the Annual County Fair, Nana and Granddaddy were in church. As Pastor Lucas T. Walker was delivering the sermon, Nana was trying hard to mind her own business. Her grandson-in-law wasn't at the Fair yesterday, and as far as she was concerned, that was a downright disgrace; the man was deplorable. She turned her thoughts to Faye, hoping that would be a better place for her mind to go, but as it turned out, it wasn't. Her granddaughter had always been a dreamer and different from the other children her age.

Nana knew how her daughter's death had affected each of her grandchildren. But it was Faye who kept asking the question over and over again: "Why did God take my parents away?" Nana found it difficult to talk about the accident and always answered that question by saying, "God wanted your mother and father to be with Him in heaven to teach all the regular people The Rules so they'd know how to get along." She felt that was the best way to respond because she thought that was all an eight-year-old was able to understand. But after a while, she could tell her answer no longer satisfied her granddaughter.

One day, Faye set out to hear what God had to say for Himself. She wanted to ask him that question about her parents and hoped He felt like talking. She jumped on her bike and pedaled as fast as she could to the old hiking trail leading to Mt. Overpeck, the place where Pastor Benjamin T. Washington had received The Rules. If God gave the

pastor something on top of the mountain, maybe He'd give her something there, too. Since He'd already visited that area once, maybe He'd consider coming back again.

Faye rode her bike for as long as she could, until the road got too rocky and rough and the slopes became too steep and she had to get off her bike and walk. She walked past the waterfalls, through the spruce and fir forests, across the rickety bridge over the trout stream, and into the open field of blackberries. She recognized the totem cave and the shell of a cabin left by early settlers, and knew she was close to where she wanted to be. It wasn't long before she reached the familiar big boulder, and when she did, she pulled the kickstand down and parked her bike. Using her hands, she climbed on all fours to the boulder's precipice.

She squatted on the cliff that overlooked the valley of the sprawling green squares that made up the patchwork quilt that was Lemon City. Something about the welcoming wind moving through the pine needles of the evergreens and the leaves of the black tupelos down below, and the smell of the mountain laurels and the rhododendrons that splashed color throughout the valley, made her sink into a meditative state. The higher she was above the city, the closer she was to God. So she looked up at the sky.

She gazed through the clumps of clouds to see if she could find Him peeking down at her below. If there was any place where God was willing to speak, Mt. Overpeck was where she hoped to hear Him. She listened closely to the wind, stood still enough to hear her own breathing. His voice might only have been as quiet as a whisper.

Finally, when her mind was silent and her body was so relaxed it felt like it was part of the ground, she asked the question into the air: "God, why did you take my parents away from me?"

The answer didn't come right away. She was still in a

trance, about to fall asleep, when she heard, "I needed you to be strong." The message empowered her. She did not want to let God down. As Faye slowly left the trance, she felt a strength come over her that she had never felt before.

From that moment on, Faye was sure she could handle growing up as an orphan. After all, she had God's power and Nana and Granddaddy. She walked her bike back down the hill, thinking about God's words, and feeling loved more now than ever. It occurred to her how different she was from her brother and sister. While they all had the same instruction, Billy and Louise vowed to obey The Rules, but she always wondered what would happen if she didn't. She knew that Louise and Billy sensed her resistance, because she'd squirm when Nana went on about The Rules during home study, and as her siblings watched her get easily distracted, one or the other would make a mean comment so that Nana was sure to notice her quiet rebellion.

Then one afternoon, Faye remembered Louise reading her the fairy tale about a young girl and a prince. When Louise finished the story and Faye said that when she got older a black prince was going to ride into town, sweep her off her feet, and carry her away, Louise got so mad at the reference to Outsiders that she started to stutter. Louise, pointing a finger directly at Faye's face, told her she was never going to marry an Outsider and the only sweeping that was gonna be done was the kind that Nana told her to do, and while she was thinking about it, she should sweep the kitchen floor . . . now. Faye was stunned by her sister's outrage, thinking to herself that tomboys who were about to become teenagers were the worst.

Billy had his own way of keeping Faye's dangerous imagination at bay. The day her teacher discussed Frederick Douglass, Faye came home and tried to explain her enthusiasm for the lesson to Billy. She said that Frederick Douglass wouldn't have been able to accomplish

what he had if he had stayed in one city, that he was effective in helping Negroes because he had left his hometown. She wondered out loud what Douglass would have done if he had been born in Lemon City. Billy pointed a finger to the door and told her to get out of his room. She didn't understand why he was so upset. What had she said that was so wrong? To make matters worse, when she was halfway down the hall, he chased her with the Dr. Lyons tooth powder can until she screamed, and Nana came upstairs and bopped him on the head with a rolled-up newspaper to make him stop.

Dr. Lyons was the name on the container of the white tooth powder concealed in the medicine cabinet over the bathroom sink. Faye fantasized often about who this Dr. Lyons was. By day, Dr. Lyons was just an ordinary aluminum can containing tooth powder. But by night, Dr. Lyons was transformed into a real lion that only she could see, and Billy was responsible. With Billy shouting "Dr. Lyons is coming! Dr. Lyons is coming!" she was convinced the beast was approaching, which always made her holler and jump into bed, pulling the covers tightly over her head until Nana came to her rescue or until Louise fussed with their brother until he left their room.

Soon after Faye learned about Frederick Douglass, she saw a picture of him on the cover of a book Billy had borrowed from the library. It was in a pile of old junk in his room. He was a bushy-haired man who looked to her like a Negro version of Dr. Zorba from the *Ben Casey* show. She showed the cover to Louise, who identified the great man for her. Louise told her that as far as she knew, he was the greatest abolitionist and orator that ever lived and the most amazing author of his time.

Faye waited for Louise to leave the room before flipping through the pages of Billy's book. The print size was much smaller than she was used to reading and she had trouble understanding. But she ripped out a page that

didn't have too many words on it, folded it in half, and hid it inside her Uncle Remus storybook. She wanted to save the page for when she grew up and could understand its message. She had never violated a book before, but there was something intriguing about the man with the bushy hair that made her think his words were important enough to keep. Louise had made sure Faye understood what Mr. Douglass had done on behalf of the Negro people and this would always stick with her. She knew one day she'd make a contribution to her race, too.

After making that connection with Frederick Douglass, for the first time, she began to feel bigger than Lemon City. The thought was overwhelming, and when she swallowed, she felt she had passed a peach pit down to her stomach. Overcome by that peach-pit feeling, little did she know it was the beginning of a seed that had been planted and would take root and shape the rest of her life.

By the time Faye hit the flatlands, she felt better than she had felt in a long time. Feeling free for the time being, because she didn't have to worry about being an orphan anymore, she rode her bike as fast as she could to get home. The closer she got to the house, the more she was lured by the smell of Nana's biscuits. Just thinking about the butter and honey she would put on them made her mouth water. She had been out practically all afternoon, and she was starving.

That evening, she was feeling special because God had given her His blessing, and as a result, she wanted to make Nana feel good, too. When she volunteered to wash dishes and clean up the kitchen all by herself, even though it was Billy's turn to help, everyone looked at her as if she'd gone crazy, but she didn't pay them any mind. She scraped food from the pots, soaked them in sudsy water, and used Brillo to get them extra clean. She took

a dishcloth from the drawer and began to dry the dishes, then put the leftovers away.

Leaving Faye to clean up the kitchen, Nana headed outside to get some fresh air and watch the sunset. But when she opened the back door, she let out a scream that scared the night crawlers out of their holes. She yelled to Granddaddy to call the doctor, quick. When Faye ran to the door to see what the commotion was about, she saw Ole Miss Johnson sprawled out cold on the ground. Her legs were opened in a distasteful manner, and Nana told Faye to quit staring and get back into the house.

The next day, when Ole Miss Johnson came home from the hospital, Nana told Faye that she'd fainted because she had diabetes. Then she explained what diabetes was and how she'd have to inject herself with a hypodermic needle for the rest of her life.

The thought of doing something for life scared Faye half to death because that seemed like an awful long time, and she went next door to check on her neighbor. Ole Miss Johnson had left the door cracked and Faye walked in. The old lady was lying on her couch in the living room with a crocheted blanket covering her chilled, weak body. She had the TV on and was dozing in and out of consciousness to give her old bones a chance to regain their strength. When Faye asked her friend how she was feeling, Ole Miss Johnson, slightly delirious from the medication, thought she was still in the hospital, and responded as if she was talking to a nurse. She complained about having to lose weight and that she couldn't stop peeing, and she was always thirsty for water, asking, how was she gonna move on with her life when she was always in the bathroom? In her grogginess, she asked the dream nurse how she would feel if she had to always watch out and be extra careful about having a stroke, a heart attack, or her high blood pressure soaring even higher. Then she added in a whiny

voice that now she had to let her toenails grow, because cutting them too close might make her lose her foot. Then as if she remembered something, she said she couldn't afford to fall down steps anymore either—not that that was something she made a habit of doing to begin with. Frustrated, she threw her arm up in the air and went on about how the worst part was that she couldn't eat sweets and what was she gonna do without dessert breaking up the monotony of healthy food. Then the old lady opened her eyes and was startled to see Faye standing there. Faye looked terrified, not knowing how to react. The old lady was embarrassed, and politely ordered her young friend to go into the kitchen to brew some common foxglove tea to make her blood pressure go down, and then remembered to add, "just make it plain, don't give me no honey or sugar."

Faye was confused by everything her friend had just said, but she did as she was instructed. By the time the tea was ready, the old lady had closed her eyes and drifted back into sleep.

It was Faye's challenge to remember what she had experienced on Mt. Overpeck earlier that day. She had to remind herself to be strong, and already God was putting her to the test. Her old friend had scared her, and she couldn't bear to think about losing anyone else she loved in her life. When she went back home, she became unusually clingy. She followed Nana to the yard, she followed Nana to the Five & Dime, followed her to the TV room, the front porch, the back porch, to the pantry, to the kitchen. The only time Faye didn't follow Nana was to the bathroom, and her grandmother closed the door to prevent her from invading her privacy. For the most part, Faye didn't think Nana minded having a shadow. Both she and Nana knew it was only temporary.

CHAPTER SIXTEEN

It was the Monday after the Annual County Fair and Faye went back to work. She was so preoccupied with the way Harry had claimed to have gotten his black eye that she had accidentally cut off more of one of her customers' hair than she should have. The large, chubby-faced woman complained about the short haircut, and Faye tried to smooth things over by showing her the picture of a model with a similar hairstyle in *Essence* magazine. When the big lady likened herself to the skinny beauty with the layered flip hairdo, Faye knew all was forgiven and she was redeemed for her absentmindedness.

Now that she had agreed to live in Lemon City for one more year, she needed to give the new plan time to settle, and concentrate on her work. If she botched up hairdos, it would defeat the purpose of getting more practice before moving up to the big leagues in the big city. Already she'd started the countdown. Just two days after the Annual County Fair, she had 363 days left to go.

Business was always slow on Mondays, which was why the beauty parlor usually closed at around three o'clock in the afternoon. When she put the CLOSED sign on the door and locked up for the day, she didn't feel like being alone with her thoughts. Knowing Harry was probably still at work, she decided to drive over to Ole Miss Johnson's house first, then walk next door to Nana's.

DON'T LET THE MOJO LADY KNOW YOU GOT TROUBLES. IF YOU DO, SHE'LL GIVE YOU MORE. This was Rule Number Four, based on the notion that folks shouldn't complain about their problems, because their whining would have negative effects, leading to more worries that would keep coming back like the regeneration of a salamander's tail. Faye knew all about the Mojo Lady, but she didn't care. After leaving Hair Today, Gone Be Beautiful Tomorrow, she sought the solace of Ole Miss Johnson.

Just coming off of her sweet tomato victory, Ole Miss Johnson was dusting off her mantel, cleaning the spot that proudly displayed her red-and-gold crown. Humming Fats Domino's "I'm in Love Again," she picked up her headdress and kissed it, and then wiped the marks off the gold-plated metal and removed the smudge with a corner of her dress. Her mood was interrupted when the doorbell rang and she saw the sadness on Faye's face. If she were a betting woman, she'd swear on Easely's grave that whatever was bothering the chile had something to do with her Outsider husband. As she studied Faye, the old woman couldn't decide if she needed rosemary to bring her up, or chamomile to calm her down. She opted to give her the latter.

While she went into the kitchen to put the kettle on the stove, Faye looked around the living room, realizing how little had changed in the house since she was a young girl. Even the red-and-gold crown sat in its usual position on the mantel over the fireplace. As she surveyed the room from her usual seat, the same high-backed Queen Anne chair she'd sat in years ago, she realized the chair was in the exact same spot on the floor. The only difference was that the chair was worn, the cushions had sunk down lower into the frame, and the paisley fabric had faded. The house had the same scent of lemon, pine, and lavender, the oils Ole Miss

Johnson still used to clean her house and wash her clothes with every day.

Faye took comfort from the familiar surroundings. It helped soothe her as she surrendered to the fact that she'd have to spend another year in Lemon City. This transition time, the time she considered to be the waiting period, helped her identify with Ole Miss Johnson. The older woman's transition had been when she'd gone crazy and disappeared from the living after her husband died and resurfaced twenty-four years later, when pain and solitude were eventually replaced with acceptance and the will to carry on. It only *seemed* that she'd stopped caring about life. Faye had observed that when her neighbor had finally let go of everything that mattered in her past and acquiesced to her new situation, she'd appeared to be different. Her true self was gradually uncovered; she was finally able to allow a new day into her life. Although Ole Miss Johnson was basically still disagreeable, when she made an effort to be nice, she actually began to shine.

Perhaps Nana and Granddaddy had felt this way before they could accept her parents' deaths, and maybe Granddaddy felt this way the day he cut Easely Johnson down from the poplar tree. Others before her had lived through this difficult mental state, and so would she. However, at the beginning of the phase, getting used to this transition wasn't going to be easy. Right now, she felt there was a part of her that had literally passed away, as if when he'd insisted they stay in Lemon City, Harry had applied the pressure that cut off her circulation.

Faye leaned her head back and closed her eyes. She didn't want to undermine the magnitude of her feelings, but in that split second, she allowed herself to be at peace. Surely at the end of her transition time, things would turn out okay for her, too.

Sometimes when she wanted to get away from it all, she'd come to Ole Miss Johnson's. It was a place that she knew she could depend on staying the same, where she could find quiet from the outside world. As she relaxed her head against the chair, she closed her eyes. She longed for the motion she felt as a child when her mother stood behind her and pushed her on the tree swing in the backyard, higher and higher until her head fell back and she looked up and could almost touch the leaves. Faye let herself feel those feelings now. The leaves tickled her nose as they danced on her face. She could see the sky peeking out between them and feel the air brushing against her lashes as she pressed higher and higher into the wind. She closed her eyes and felt dizzy with pleasure, until she descended and landed back into her mother's arms and was pushed all over again. A faint whisper rolled off the wind into her ear as she sailed back up into the trees. "The Mojo Lady don't scare me. Tell me your worries, little Faye. I'll make them go away and bury them like june bugs in the field."

The whisper trailed off with the next passing breeze. She felt cheated out of hugs from her mother. Eight years of loving just wasn't enough. She was tired and wanted to be rocked to sleep, the way her mother had rocked her back and forth when she couldn't drift into darkness on her own. She slept. She didn't know for how long, but she fell into a deep sleep. When she opened her eyes, Ole Miss Johnson was cradling her in her arms.

"Don't worry, little Faye," she said. "I'm gonna fix you a nice tepid bath and rub you down with soothing cypress oil. I'll take good care of you."

Faye didn't argue. Even though she knew the old lady wanted to talk, she only felt like opening her mouth to swallow more tea. Conversation would have to wait. She wasn't ready to share her feelings. Her childhood caretaker was already running water in the tub, and she

could smell the fragrance of lavender growing stronger as it wafted down the stairs. She knew exactly where she would sleep. Because some things never change, when she heard the crisp white linen sheets being snapped and spread across the bed, she knew she would inhale the lavender until she dreamed of days gone by when she was loved unconditionally, when she was innocent and carefree.

When she awoke at around six o'clock that evening, she felt so refreshed that she gave her old friend a big hug. Faye knew that Ole Miss Johnson was aware of what she was going through, because the old lady could see the truth in her eyes, and sense her sorrow as soon as she stepped through the door.

"Thank you" was all Faye had to say to Ole Miss Johnson, and the old lady kissed her on her forehead and smiled.

"You gonna be okay, girl. Just be true to yourself and you gonna be okay." Ole Miss Johnson watched as Faye walked down the stairs before she closed her door.

Faye left her friend's house feeling as if she'd just received a blessing and went next door to see Nana. As she opened the gate in the white picket fence, Faye could smell Nana's home-cooking aromas escaping from the seams of the house, and she knew that if supper wasn't already on the table, it was about to be. When she walked through the front door, Nana was in the kitchen and Granddaddy was stretched out on the sofa reading the *Lemon City Chronicle* and peeking over the top of the newspaper to watch the news on TV. The first thing Faye noticed was that Ole Miss Johnson's picture was on the front page of the newspaper for winning the Tomato Competition twenty straight years in a row.

"Hey there, baby girl." He only called her that pet name when they were alone together because he knew it embarrassed her in public. "Good to see you." He put

down the newspaper and hugged her, and then patted the space next to him, gesturing for her to sit down.

As usual, Faye was happy to see her grandfather, but now she had reservations about being in his presence without Nana around, especially when she was in the process of devising a plan to gracefully decline his generous gifts. He seemed to have a way of reading her mind when they were alone, and she didn't want him to see her guilt.

"So how was your day, baby girl?"

"Can't complain . . . How you doing?"

"I'd feel better knowing you were happy about staying put."

Faye tried to be upbeat as she delivered the news. "You'll be happy to hear that we'll be here for a while . . . at least another year."

"Good. Finally come to your senses." He let out a chuckle. "I knew it."

"Granddaddy, you know this way of life is not for me." She was careful to keep her tone even, so she wouldn't get emotional.

"You've always been my baby girl . . . you know that." He looked at Faye and saw her cringe slightly, knowing she wasn't one to appreciate sweet talk, but he kept right on going. "Even smile like your mama. Have your mama's wide brown eyes, heavy eyebrows, soft cheekbones, and rounded face."

She liked being her grandfather's favorite, but it made her feel like she was ten years old when he talked like this.

"You even got the same expression she used to have when she pretended to be happy, but it was always obvious to *me* when something was nagging at her mind." He paused to let her take in his words. "You know you can always tell me if something ain't right." He put his hand on top of hers. "I know I might be scary some-

times. I ain't as cute and cuddly as your Nana, but this old ogre has got a soft spot right here." He placed his hand against his chest. "I love you more than you'll ever know."

Faye gave him a smile of gratitude.

"If I can help it, won't nothing bad happen to you," Granddaddy reassured her. "I won't let it. Period."

"I love you, too, Granddaddy," said Faye. "But don't worry about me so much. I'll be fine." She patted her grandfather's knee, leaving him to watch the news. He just shook his head after she got up and left the room, thinking about how little his granddaughter knew about life and how much she had to learn.

As Faye headed to the kitchen looking for her grandmother, Nana came out with a platter of smothered chicken atop a bed of hot, steaming rice. When she saw Faye, her face lit up. Immediately after that, she ordered her granddaughter to wash her hands, finish setting the table, and sit down to eat.

After the relaxing bath at Ole Miss Johnson's and the home-cooked meal at Nana's, Faye felt fulfilled. With love in her heart and stomach, she felt as if she could roll down the street into the cottage and into bed. She was ready to go home and unwind even more. She still hadn't caught up on her sleep after all the preparations leading up to the Annual County Fair and the long day she'd spent there.

Leaving Nana's at around seven thirty that night, she arrived home just in time to catch *The Flip Wilson Show*—because the other thing she needed besides love was a good laugh. Her favorite Flip character was Geraldine. "The devil made me do it," he would say in his falsetto voice. It was the excuse he used whenever he did something naughty. The more she thought about it, the more she felt the devil was behind Harry, too. There were too many occasions when he was late for dinner

despite confirming that he'd be home on time. There were even those times when he was supposed to be at work, and she called him, but no one answered the phone. When she'd confront him later, he'd say something about having an engine running, being out at the gas pumps, or taking a car out for a test-drive and not being able to hear. Faye wanted to give him the benefit of the doubt, but lately she was tired of being generous.

Although the sun had set, the heat it left behind was persistent. Humidity drove her to the refrigerator to get a tall glass of ice water. She dipped a dish towel into her glass and applied it to the back of her neck. Just as she was finding relief, the telephone rang. Now that she was beginning to cool off and relax, she didn't feel like answering it. All she wanted to do was collapse in the chair, put her feet up on the hassock, and let Flip show her a fun time. The phone stopped ringing, and then three seconds later it started ringing again. She kicked off her shoes, twisted the cork from a bottle of Mateuse wine, poured herself a glass, and sat down. The phone stopped ringing, and started again. "Damn you, Louise." She picked up the phone and snapped, "Who died?"

"Don't be silly," her sister said, ignoring her tone. "This is important."

Faye listened. One minute into the conversation, she couldn't understand why Louise was so bent out of shape about calling Medford. "Normally," she was saying, "we see each other once a year, but all of a sudden that's not enough."

"So call him. What's the big deal?"

"You think I should?" Louise asked the question as if she were sixteen years old and had never been on a first date.

"Dig it. Why not?"

"But what if the feeling isn't mutual?" When Faye didn't respond, Louise pondered the possibility and con-

sidered another option. "Maybe I'll send mous note."

"Don't be ridiculous. Call him. What h lose?"

"That's what I'm afraid of. It's so perfect now."

Faye thought the heat must be making Louise crazy. "What's so perfect about seeing a guy once a year just to screw his brains out? That's not perfect. That's obscene. Now call the brother and get off the phone with me. I've already missed the first part of my show."

Sometime in the middle of the night, the phone rang again. With her eyes still closed, Faye fumbled for the receiver and managed to bring it to her ear. The high-pitched falsetto voice on the other end said, "I'm just telling it like it is, honey. My name ain't Slugger, but your husband is still fond of the hugger . . . the orange Camaro, that is. If I were you, I'd kick him to the curb and say the devil made me do it." She heard a click and the line went dead. In her grogginess the voice on the other end had sounded like Geraldine, and she thought, *Now why would Flip Wilson be calling me at this hour?* She decided she must be dreaming. She reached over to find the other side of the bed still empty.

By the time Billy hung up the phone, the hugger orange Camaro that had been sitting in the parking lot at The Tap was gone. What kind of leech had attached itself to his sister? Although he had never played baseball—because of his bad knee—he considered the sport as a metaphor for life: This was Harry's second strike. The next time he wouldn't escape so easily. The next time he'd be out.

It was past midnight, and Louise couldn't sleep because she was obsessing about Medford. They made love over the weekend and he took her to heaven, and ever since then she had felt like she was floating on a cloud. Cooking breakfast for him on Sunday morning

⏌ having light chitchat was as refreshing as an ice-cold glass of fresh orange juice on a hot day in July. He was easy and made her laugh, even with his corny sophomoric jokes. So what if their conversation was simple? There were plenty of folk around town to engage in debate, to proselytize and philosophize with if she needed to because of her knowledge and interest in many subjects. Medford was comfortable, not like a pair of old shoes, but like something brand-new that was loose, like linen or cotton, that allowed you freedom of movement, room to breathe, and flowed with your body. He didn't expect anything from her—only what she was willing to give. He didn't pressure her to be anything, and that was beginning to make her want him more.

On Sunday, when Medford was naked from the waist up, chopping wood with an ax, Louise watched him from her window. His arm muscles, like clusters of rocks, were determined when they landed on their mark, yet she knew how gentle they could be. His chest was broad and she loved the way his shoulders provided a soft mantel for her head. His back was hard and she could see the definition of strength and recall how his sensitive skin had responded to her curious fingers. Although his hands were rough and callused, all she cared about was that he held her tightly and securely.

The age difference between them didn't really bother her. If anything, his level of maturity would be to their advantage. She had watched him as he labored hard for her all day. She knew he could feel her eyes on him, but he was resistant to her stares and stayed focused on the chore at hand. Not once did he acknowledge her presence while he was working, except when he needed a glass of water, or to sit down for a few minutes to take a break. Business was business with Medford until he was done for the day, and that's when he came to life.

After completing what he came to do, he swept her

into his arms and kissed her. "Louise Dunlap, you're one special lady. I'd do anything for you."

Louise was close enough to him to smell his salty sweat. "Don't say that," she teased, and slowly pushed him away. "Unless you mean it." She held him at arm's length. "With as many things that need to be done around here, I'd keep you busy every weekend."

"You mean to say, you wouldn't want to wait until next year to get all your work done?" Medford was hoping she'd fall for the bait and he'd catch her in his trap.

Louise hesitated, not quite sure how to answer, and decided to be objective. "Next year, I'll be on the block, so if you want me to clean and do chores for you, I'll be available. All you gotta do is come up with the dough." By the time Louise finished her last sentence, she realized how much she had offended Medford. The disappointment spread across his face and he tried to conceal it with a smile.

He shook Louise's hand and thanked her for the opportunity to serve her, then drew the back of her hand to his lips and kissed it. "Until next year," he said, and was on his way. When he reached the dirt road, he turned back and waved.

Louise had stood in the doorway wanting to kick herself for being such a jerk, and that's why she was sitting up in bed losing sleep over Medford at this moment— because she couldn't get him out of her mind. Maybe there was more to sex than just having it, she thought— Medford was the only man who made her curious about that. There was always tomorrow, and the next day, and the next. She had time to think about how she would deal with Medford. If he stayed on her mind, maybe she'd decide to call him first.

"Faye, who you got handling the funeral arrangements?" asked Nana, helping herself to some white meat since there was no dark meat left on the platter.

"When the coroner finishes the examination, they're taking Harry to King Funeral Home."

"I wouldn't pay for a funeral for that low-down, no-good, dirty, rotten snake in the grass," said Billy.

Granddaddy interrupted. "Billy, that's your sister's dead husband you're talking about . . . show some respect."

"I'd cremate him . . . in the backyard," said Billy. "If you want to economize, light up a big bonfire. Nana could use the organic material to fertilize her tomatoes."

"Can y'all please stop talking about this while we're eating?" Elvira pleaded. She was nibbling on the strands of string beans hanging over the tines of her fork. Everyone was showing signs of slowing down at the table. They were at the part of the meal where they continued eating just because the food was there.

"I understand how you feel, but we all know the best time to plan a funeral is when the family is all together," Granddaddy responded reassuringly. "So now's the perfect time to talk."

"I know you haven't had a chance to look at caskets yet, dear, now have you?" asked Nana.

Faye shook her head.

"I know where you could get a casket real cheap,"

Louise said. "There's that cardboard box Nana kept when the new refrigerator was delivered."

Faye rolled her eyes at her sister. Louise continued, "I know you want to do the right thing, but it doesn't make sense to spend a ton of money on something that's going into the ground. Let's face it. Expensive or not, maggots are invincible."

Elvira ran from the table with both hands covering her mouth. Despite her abrupt departure, the conversation continued.

"Well, I certainly hope y'all don't treat us that way," said Nana. "When me and your Granddaddy pass on, don't be putting us into no cardboard box. That's all I can say."

"And don't think you can economize by putting us together either, just in case y'all was planning on being that cheap. We want our own space," said Granddaddy. "Separate, ya hear?"

"If the County Sheriff releases us tomorrow, I'll go down to King Funeral Home with you," Louise said to Faye.

"Thanks. I could use the company."

"What about the boy's father?" asked Granddaddy. "Anybody contact his father?" He looked at Faye.

"I called the number Information gave me, based on the return address from the letters he sent me." She let out a deep sigh. "It was the number to his dad's cleaners on the corner of Seventh Avenue and 158th Street. I've called there several times, but no one ever answers the phone." She shrugged her shoulders. "They all must be busy in Harlem. I've left several messages, but no one's called me back." She paused, looking down at her plate and deciding what to eat next, and her fork landed into the mound of mashed potatoes. "Billy sent a telegram to his dad, so hopefully we'll hear from him soon."

"That's the answer," Billy shouted, as if he'd heard the

solution to the problem. "Send his dead ass home. Ship his body up North and have his daddy pay for his funeral."

"No way. That would definitely be more expensive," said Louise, "'cause now you're talking about buying a casket to ship him in."

"No need for a casket—pack him on a block of ice and put him in a cooler. Shoot, he's already frozen, ain't he? Half the job is already done."

Elvira came down from the bathroom and resumed her position at the dinner table. Billy gave her a comforting hug, and she acknowledged that she was okay.

"What time does the game start?" On behalf of his wife, Billy changed the subject and directed his question to Granddaddy.

"I believe it starts at five thirty," Louise blurted out, letting the menfolk know that they didn't have the exclusive on sports.

"I can't wait to see ole Bear Bryant kick the stuffing out of Louisiana State." Billy ignored his sister and continued talking to Granddaddy, who grunted and nodded his head in agreement.

"I betcha he'll take them Bamas straight to their five hundredth victory, too," said Louise, finally getting Billy's attention.

"I believe that'll set a new national record for a college team," said Granddaddy, adding, "and y'all know I'm not a betting man" as he put a five-dollar bill on the table. "But what quarter y'all think he'll take the game in?"

"Bear's all right. But you know, he can't hold a candle to Coach Eddie Robinson," said Billy.

"Nope. Nobody can," confirmed Louise.

"But Grambling ain't playing today, so y'all decide on your quarter and don't be cheap. Cough up some money."

Relieved to give the subject of Harry a rest, the women soon turned the conversation to shopping at all the

Thanksgiving Day sales going on tomorrow—until they remembered they were under house arrest and weren't going anywhere. This made them upset all over again with Harry for intruding on their annual shopping spree, even when he was dead.

CHAPTER EIGHTEEN

The fall of 1972 represented the second-biggest adjustment that Faye had to make in her life. She had gone from anticipating freedom to actual entrapment during the course of the summer, and now she had to put in the time to complete the one-year sentence. As if that wasn't bad enough, the leaves were severing their lifelines from the trees, falling to the ground to shrivel up and die. It was the time in nature to be a witness to the process of death, and that did nothing to help cheer her mood. Even though autumn was only temporary, things falling down around her, the sun barely making its way through the clouds, the darkness cutting into the light of day, all reminded her of the state of her own life, added to her depression. It was the season of desolation, and it accurately described her mood.

The only thing that kept her going through this period was looking forward to the next Annual County Fair and creating a formula for Nubian Silk.

The back room at the hair salon was the perfect place for her makeshift laboratory. In October, she'd converted the area from a storage space, pushing the old broken equipment and antiquated salon chairs aside. She had considered calling Billy to come pick up the junk, knowing he'd find something to do with it, but decided against it because Elvira would kill her if she did. After cleaning the cabinets and the countertops to give herself a proper work space and gain access to the sink,

she had claimed the back room as her own. All she had left to do was to unpack the herbs and oils she'd bought from Ole Miss Johnson. Rosemary, jasmine, lavender, almond, and geranium oils, soy proteins, and other natural ingredients lined the shelves. Once she organized her stock, she had everything she needed to experiment and refine Nubian Silk.

If she had to stay in town, the best part was having access to unsuspecting customers. She tried out different mixtures on various heads to see what worked best on which types of hair. She experimented with conditioners, moisturizing creams, and scalp treatments. In between appointments, after hours, and on weekends, she fussed with formulas in the back room. When she'd used her concoctions on customers, they never suspected a thing, because she put what was being tested into jars and containers marked Professional Use Only. And her products worked. Results showed the women's hair was generally easier to manage, shinier, and soft. She wanted them to be happy with what they had to work with, whether they inherited coarse, straight, or wavy hair. Proud of her accomplishments, Faye felt confident she was getting closer to finding the perfect recipes for Nubian Silk.

Once again, Faye was a fixture in town. She was getting regular customers, and she was good at identifying them, even with her eyes closed. It had gotten to the point where she'd play a game with herself to break up the day. She'd purposely turn her back while a customer was getting into her chair, then she'd turn around with her eyes closed, touch the kink in their scalp, feel their natural roots and new growth, run her fingers through their hair, and automatically know who the customer was. Eight out of ten times, she'd guess right. By the Annual County Fair next year, she'd probably be batting a

hundred, but it wouldn't matter because she'd be gone by then.

She was standing behind the chair, giving a teenage girl a perm, when she realized that being the owner of Hair Today, Gone Be Beautiful Tomorrow was a dream come true, and that she should be grateful for the gift. But she wasn't. For her, coming to work in the town she grew up in, day after day, was like eating the same meal over and over, but at this time, it was more like being force-fed, and her gag reflexes were activated and she felt like she was going to puke. She wondered if she'd ever be completely satisfied with her life or if "having more" was something that only happened to Outsiders.

If that wasn't enough to contend with, she sensed the Lemonites had mixed feelings about her being in town, believing that her presence upset its PH balance, or People's Harmony quotient, which they considered to be off cadence and way below normal. Most people were happy to claim her for another year because it gave Lemon City a chance to wrap itself around her like ivy growing up a flagpole. There were others who were confused with her indecisiveness about coming and going and wished she'd make up her mind, because the back and forth nonsense was giving them tension headaches. There were those whose emotions ran high, ranging from pitying her to claiming that by leaving she would be committing treason. It was obvious that some of the church folks felt sorry for her. Whenever she'd run into them in town, their patronizing expressions looked down upon her as if she were a stray dog they were tempted to pat on the head and take home for discipline and training. There were folks who she ran into at the Piggly Wiggly who stared at her out of curiosity, as if she were an oddity worthy of residing in a museum. The Town Council held a vote and the outcome was unanimous in their support for Faye to stay. The Ladies of Mt.

Zion Baptist Church were determined to win their daughter back, and held prayer vigils once a week. There was a tiny faction in the town who wished she would leave and get it over with, for fear that other young people, or children with impressionable minds, would be influenced by her unethical attitude and immoral ways. The women who frequented the salon were happy she would remain. They wanted Faye's undivided attention on their hair, and behind her back, secretly whispered that they wished her husband would go.

Despite everyone passing their judgment on Faye, and regardless of anyone's individual opinion, the town collectively was of one mind and one soul, and the heart of the town—its citizens—would never abandon Faye. It was its nature to forgive and be possessive of its own.

If the truth be told, the men didn't appreciate Harry's scent in their territory, and the women for the most part, felt violated by his presence. The only thing Harry could do for them was fix their cars. As his business grew to be a success—even though it was more of an "in and out" establishment, someplace where you'd prefer to stop by or pass through, as opposed to a place to linger, feel at home in, or chat—Faye saw him less and less. While she locked herself away in the back room of the salon, he kept himself busy at The Shop six, sometimes seven days a week. Sometimes he didn't make it home at all, and Faye was certain that Harry had someone else on the side to occupy his time.

As the weeks went by, Faye had a breakthrough. She was so excited about a new combination of chemicals, herbs, and oils that she drove to The Shop to share her good news with Harry. But all he could say was, "Check out this 1969, eight-cylinder hugger orange Camaro Z-28 hardtop coupe." He rubbed his hand along its curves. "Isn't she a beaut?"

Faye felt a chill when he complimented the car as

though it were a woman, and the pieces began to fall into place. She wondered if there was a connection between her husband and his cars that had more to do with just his attention to mechanics.

"Harry, are you cheating on me?"

At first, Harry's eyes widened at the inquiry, then he put down his ratchet and embraced her. Though she felt foolish for blurting out the question without reason—at least not one that was substantiated with physical evidence or associated with having proof of infidelity—she had to say it just the same to get it out of her system. Harry swore he was faithful and that he gave her all his love, but Faye wasn't so sure. The truth was, Harry was so in love with his cars that she didn't think he even noticed her leaving the garage.

Instead of freezing cold for the New Year, the temperature was unseasonably warm. By the end of January, seventy-five degrees was the all-time high, and the temperature was still rising. It was as if the seasons had shifted, playing musical chairs, each one making a move four months to the right. Some people believed this strange phenomenon, this sudden solar invasion, was punishment for sheltering and accommodating the Outsider. Others thought it was a warning that meant the Outsider had to get out now, before the earth began to shake, lightning struck, hail began to fall out of the sky, and things got even worse.

As a result, in the dead of winter, people preferred to stay inside, cooling off with the comforts of air-conditioning in their homes, instead of adding oil to their boilers for heat. Some folks ventured to climb Mt. Overpeck, so that at a certain part of the day, if they stood under a big boulder or shaded ridge and timed it just right, they could catch a quick, natural breeze and find relief.

As the months passed, the weather didn't get any better. By April, it was so hot that drugstores had to stock up on anti-itch cream because of the heat rash the children kept getting in the folds of their elbows. Doctors' offices were busy treating the elderly to prevent them from getting heatstroke, giving them advice on ways to keep their body temperatures down. The Piggly Wiggly

and the Five & Dime couldn't keep up with the demand for ice chests and Styrofoam coolers every day, and ice trays, and the ice itself, became the fastest-selling commodities in town, more so even than toilet paper and milk.

The heat waves warped the vision of the streets, giving drivers the illusion they were looking into distorted mirrors at a fun house. Meadows, pastures, forests, and farmlands were brown from being scorched by the sun. Wildflowers, bushes, and trees retreated into a state of dormancy from the shock of dehydration. What the landscape needed was less sunburn and more generosity from the clouds to provide the town with some rain. Tree frogs stopped jumping; birds didn't have any energy to sing. The animals, instead of carrying on at their normal pace, just moseyed along, and the fish swam downstream while they still had the energy, looking to be refreshed in the Roanoke River. It was as if the sun had gone haywire. The whole town had turned into a living furnace and everyone was worried about how they were going to survive the real summer.

Although it was late and Nana and Granddaddy were ready for sleep, the humidity was keeping them awake. A big fan was blowing in the corner of the room. Granddaddy had propped himself on his pillow, reading a hunting and fishing magazine, while Nana licked some S&H green stamps into her book. She was saving the stamps for a toaster oven. When she finished putting the stamps into place, she picked up her needlework. She was in the process of knitting another sweater to add to the collection she had stored in the hope chest at the foot of her bed for her great-grandchild. Whenever it would come, whoever it would be, she would guarantee the baby would be warm. She had already made two blue sweaters, and now she was working on the pinks. "Oh,

I forgot to tell you." Nana looked up from her needle-work, but her fingers kept going.

"Forgot to tell me what?" Granddaddy took off his reading glasses to give her his attention.

"The bank called yesterday, saying you were late and short on last month's loan payment."

"I ain't never been late or short on my loan payments. I always pay 'em on time. Someone must have made a mistake."

"Well, they claim you're the one who made the mistake."

Granddaddy put down his outdoor magazine and got out of bed to double-check. He knew he was starting to be forgetful, but he would swear on a stack of Bibles that he wasn't that bad, not yet. He dug through his dresser drawer where he kept his underwear neatly folded, rummaging for his checkbook. The ledger indicated he had paid his half of the loan—two hundred and fifty dollars and forty-three cents—on the fifth of the month. "How much did they say I was short?"

"I believe they said two hundred and fifty dollars and forty-three cents."

"I'll pay it tomorrow." Granddaddy slid his check-book back underneath his boxer shorts. So Harry had reneged on his commitment.

Nana knew Harry must have cheated her husband, and she didn't like him covering up for that Northern sewer rat, not one bit. No longer could she hold back from speaking her mind. "Willie, I don't quite know how to say this, but I'm gonna let it out the best way I can." She put aside her needlework to make room for her emotions. "You know I don't like getting into folks' business, never mind tellin' 'em how to act, where to go, or what to do, 'specially grown folks. You know how we was raised to abide by The Rules of this town, right?"

"Umm-hmm," said Granddaddy, looking at her over his reading glasses.

"I mean we got Rules for a reason. Good reasons, I might add. And Lord, forgive me for what I'm about to say, but I don't like that man. I don't like that man, not one bit. I hate the way he's treating our granddaughter, and I don't have no proof. I ain't seen nothing, mind you. I just sense it and I get a wormy feeling whenever I think about him. I feel downright creepy, crawly, and slimy and I wish she never married the snake in the grass in the first place. There now, I said it. I feel better, like I just swept all the dirt off the porch." After taking a deep breath, she picked up her needlework again. "Now, Willie, dear. What we gonna do?"

"Don't you worry about a thing. I'll take care of it." He patted Nana's thigh, which he knew had a way of calming her nerves. He returned to his outdoor magazine and came across an ad for a new Winchester bolt action repeating rifle and realized his hunting gun was getting old and needed to be replaced. As he thought about this turn of events, he couldn't help but reflect on Rule Number Two: IF YOU CAN'T BE HONEST, YOU MIGHT AS WELL BE DEAD.

Nothing in Nana's life had prepared her for dealing with an Outsider. She had never wished death on anyone. Not even Ole Miss Johnson. But Harry was on his way to becoming a first. Her fretting so much over the situation had made her work up such a sweat that she got up and stood in front of the fan. She lowered the top of her cotton nightgown and leaned into the forceful air so it could blow-dry her bosom and she could finally get some sleep.

Along with the heat wave of 1973 came the Republicans back into office. Faye always thought that hair and politics were like oil and water—they just didn't mix—but she was finding out that the opposite just might be

true. Who would have thought the newly elected party would have such a major influence on hair? Perhaps it was a coincidence, but as the country was becoming more conservative, the trend was for sisters to return to straightening their naturals. The problem was that with all the heat in Lemon City, there wasn't a perm strong enough to prevent the various levels of kink from curling up or snapping back. Faye knew she had to keep up with the times in order to be successful.

It was Sunday afternoon. She was accustomed to Harry being at The Shop; she was used to him not being at home, not even on the official day of rest. Since he wasn't around to give his opinion on the change that was about to occur with her hair, she decided to trade her easy natural products for the pain of the chemical burn on her own.

She went to Hair Today, Gone Be Beautiful Tomorrow and left the CLOSED sign on the door so she wouldn't be disturbed. As she permed her hair, she watched it stretch at least three inches longer than usual, until it draped below her shoulders. When she applied a dab of Nubian Silk to her scalp and brushed it through her hair, she discovered it was way too thick for her new look. What she needed was a second version of her product to be used primarily for fine, straight, chemically treated hair. Nubian Silk II would be her next challenge. She divided her hair into small sections and wrapped each piece around a hot curling iron to give it some body and bounce, but she discovered the time and effort had been all in vain the moment that she walked out the door. Humidity grabbed her and didn't turn her loose until it destroyed all the work she had just completed. It released her only when it was satisfied that her hair was limp, like the strings hanging on a wet mop.

She went to Nana's for dinner that night, and when Louise saw her new do, she went berserk.

"I don't care if the country is becoming more conservative," said Louise. "I'm keeping my 'fro. I don't give a rat's ass about those damned elephants."

The more Faye ignored her sister, the more upset she became.

"You sellout," said Louise, who was wearing a colorful dashiki and wooden beads woven into her cornrows, which went clickety-clack every time she moved her head. "Afros aren't a fashion statement. They're a cultural statement. They're part of our identity of black being beautiful . . . you sellout." For Faye, Nubian Silk was indeed about selling, and if the product did sell out she'd consider herself a profitable success.

It was so hot these days that Nana resorted to preparing light meals, except for Sunday dinners, when the family got together. Sunset brought some relief. After dessert, around eight o'clock, they plopped themselves down in the living room to watch *The Mod Squad* on TV. It was Billy's favorite show, and his sisters teased him because they all knew he wished his life as a crime fighter could be as interesting as Lincoln Hayes's.

But on this night, just as the show started, Granddaddy motioned for Billy to come upstairs. His grandfather's timing couldn't have been worse. Why couldn't Granddaddy let the matter wait until the show was over, or at least until the first commercial break? But judging by the look on his grandfather's face, he could tell that whatever he wanted to discuss was urgent. Billy obediently followed him upstairs. Elvira and Louise exchanged meaningful glances. Whatever was going on must be serious. Faye watched Granddaddy and Billy disappear. She glanced over at her sisters. The way their eyes turned downward, she had a sneaky feeling they knew more about what was going on than she did. Saint distracted her by climbing into her lap to use it as a pil-

low, and she stroked the animal's furry head while wondering what on earth was going on.

"I got this from the bank yesterday," said Granddaddy. He handed a letter to Billy. "It seems your sister's husband missed part of his loan payment this month. This is the second time he's tried to pull something like this."

"Second time? How come you didn't tell me about the first?"

"Now, you know this can't go on," Granddaddy continued, as though Billy hadn't spoken. "He tried to cheat me before. What's wrong with this man? What's he take me for, a horse's ass?"

Billy tried to answer at least one of his grandfather's questions, but he couldn't get a word in.

"I got my new shotgun sitting right here in my closet." He walked to the closet and took out a long box that was stamped COD.

"No need for that," Billy said, waving his hand. "I'll take care of everything." He handed Granddaddy back his letter.

"I'm sure you will," said Granddaddy, somewhat relieved. "And I really want to say, don't hurt him too bad. But the words are stuck in my throat and won't come out."

Lemon City continued to smoke like a Virginia ham roasting on the middle rack of an oven. By April, the one-hundred-and-ten-degree weather was more heat than they usually got in summer and more than their tempers could bear. The drought had made the ground so cracked and barren that it was impossible for a pickax to penetrate. If anyone had tried to plant a seed in the earth, the dirt would have crumbled in their fingers, and the already existing plants—the perennials and the annuals—couldn't push their way from underneath the ground to get some air. It was so hot that even though the birds had already flown south, they had to fly farther south, away from Lemon City, to get a reprieve.

The only two subjects talked about were the heat and the Tomato Competition. Rumor had it that for the first time in Lemon City history, the Town Council might actually move the Fair. *The Old Farmer's Almanac* predicted that by the fall, weather patterns would change and be perfect for harvest. Right around August was the supposed turnaround, and right around Thanksgiving was when the crops would be ready for picking.

Billy was in the bathroom, splashing cold water on his face and dreading going out into the day, when he heard the news on the radio about the possibility of moving the Annual County Fair.

His talk with Granddaddy the night before had been

resolved by following the dictates of <u>Rule Number Six:</u>
<u>WHAT GOES AROUND WILL ALWAYS COME BACK AROUND</u>
<u>AND HIT YOU IN THE HEAD</u>. Billy didn't know what made
him hotter, the mercury rising in the thermometer or the
blood boiling in his veins because Harry had tried to get
over on his grandfather. It was an act he took as a per-
sonal offense against his entire family.

Just like he promised Granddaddy, Billy drove to The
Shop first thing in the morning. He took the long way
around town just to cool his head for fear of what he
might do when he saw Harry. He loosened the top three
buttons of his starched short-sleeve uniform shirt and
rolled down the windows, but the humidity was so in-
tense that it smacked him in the face and he had to turn
the air-conditioning on. He had never experienced
bizarre weather like this before. The roads were so hot
that heat waves were rising up from the tar, making the
highway look like it was about to warp like a vinyl
forty-five left out in the sun.

On the side of the road, he spotted a discarded piece
of furniture. As he got closer to the polelike object, he
could tell it was an old hat rack with only a few broken
hooks. He pulled over and brushed the dirt off the stand
with a rag that he always stored underneath his front
seat for these occasions. He could use the old rack for
something, even if it was just to throw his clothes over
when he was too tired to hang them up. Or maybe he
could use it to beat Harry with when he saw him. But he
left the rack where he found it. He'd pick it up later.
Business first.

He pulled up to The Shop. Harry's white Pontiac
GTO was parked on the side of the building. "Harry Lee
Thompson, I'm calling you out."

Harry was in the garage beneath the hood of a 1971
Plymouth Gold Duster 340. He stood up, wiping his

hands on a dirty rag. "Yo, what's happening, my man? What brings you all the way out here?"

Billy ignored Harry's outstretched hand. Before Billy realized what he was doing, his elbow lurched forward and crashed into Harry's neck, flinging him back against the wall, and putting him in a choke hold that left his feet dangling a few inches off the ground. "Now you listen to me, Harry Thompson. I done talked to you about my sister. Now I'm gonna talk to you about my grandfather. I want a check in the amount of two hundred fifty dollars and forty-three cents written out and delivered to him by the end of the day. And if you ever try to pull a fast one like this again"—he took the gun out of his holster, cocked the trigger, and held it to Harry's head— "don't bother showing up for work."

Harry couldn't move. All he could do was shift his eyes from left to right to see if his customers had witnessed what had just happened, knowing a situation like this could be bad for business.

Billy slowly released his grip. As he walked back to his car he warned, "Your time is up! They may tolerate that crap up North, but it don't work down here." Billy decided on the spot not to wait for Harry to strike out. He had a plan for when he got back to the office and if his hunch was right, Harry was a dead man.

Harry straightened up his work clothes and rubbed the soreness around his neck. He made sure Billy was in the car before he opened his mouth. "If you didn't have that gun, you wouldn't be so big now, would you? Just 'cause you own a piece legally, you think you the man, huh? Well, maybe you are the law, but this is the state of Virginia, and I got weapons, too."

"You want me to put you in the Lemon City Jail? I'll bring you in for petty theft." Billy was lying through his teeth. Paying a bank loan late wasn't a crime, but he knew a guilty person shrank at even the hint of arrest,

and he had a hunch somewhere, sometime, Harry had broken some law. He wasn't surprised when Harry backed down.

"Okay, so I made a mistake. It ain't no big thang. We still cool, brother. Don't you worry, I'll get a check to Granddaddy today." He waited until Billy was out of sight before telling the three people he had waiting inside that he'd be right back. But two of the three men who had just seen what had happened got into their cars—no matter how broken and disabled they were—and drove them home as best they could. The one man whose car was still on the lift was sorry that he had no choice but to stay and wait for the Outsider, who was in major trouble.

When Billy returned to his office, he got the number for a police station close to New York's 125th Street. An Officer Hopkins answered the phone. After identifying himself and where he was calling from, he asked the officer if he had a file or any information on a Harry Lee Thompson, black male, approximately five feet ten inches tall, late twenties, no distinguishing features that he was aware of. He gave as much of a description as possible, knowing that every little detail helped. Officer Hopkins took down the information and told him he would be busy over the next couple of weeks working on a homicide case, that he couldn't make any promises to get back to him before then, but that he'd look into it as soon as he got a chance and give him a call. Billy was hoping to get the information sooner, but he was content that he was at least on the road to bringing Harry down.

Just like everyone in Lemon City knew exactly where they were when Dr. Martin Luther King Jr. was assassinated, so did everyone in Lemon City know exactly what they were doing when they first heard the news that the Annual County Fair had been moved to November. Shock waves penetrated the town as fast as a nail being drilled through wood paneling on drywall. Even though everyone had ample warning to prepare for the adjustment, the realization hit them that for the first time in one hundred years, something in their lives would change. For many Lemonites, the thought of finding something else to do on that September weekend was unbearable. The population would have to modify their routines and adjust their schedules to accommodate this new chapter in history. A few of them wondered aloud what the world was coming to and doubted that they'd ever be the same.

Nana was caught between watching *As the World Turns* on TV in the living room and stirring a hambone and white beans in a Crock-Pot in the kitchen. When the commercials came on, she'd retreat to the kitchen, stirring, and when her soap opera came back on, she'd return to the living room. The third time she did this, she heard the earth-shattering news. She always kept the kitchen radio on and tuned to the town's gospel station. Just as she was taking the first taste of the beans, the news broke into Pastor Lucas T. Walker's daily program: The Annual County Fair was going to move to the third week of November.

Walking back into the living room in a daze, as if having a delayed reaction, the news hit her so hard that when she flung herself against the back of the La-Z-Boy, she nearly ejected herself from the seat. Moving the Fair until the weather changed would give her a new chance, a fresh start to compete. Based on the timetable the local emergency bulletin gave her, she should be planting around August and harvesting close to Thanksgiving. It would be strange to have two important holidays back to back, but she couldn't worry about that. All she cared about was getting the right seeds so she could plant some prizewinning tomatoes and give her neighbor a brand-new cause for concern.

Outside, Granddaddy was sitting on the porch, listening to the transistor radio and playing checkers with Bootsie, while Clement was squatting on a stool, waiting on the winner. When they made the announcement, Bootsie jumped up and started carrying on like red fire ants had marched up his pants, which made him lose his concentration. Granddaddy was able to jump him three times and land a king.

Ole Miss Johnson had taken to growing herbs indoors since the heat wave began. She was gently running her fingers through the basil, parsley, and dill she was raising on her kitchen windowsill when she heard Bootsie next door hollering about a report on the radio. All she could make out was that it was something about moving the Annual County Fair. She turned on her radio to listen for herself. She couldn't believe her ears. After she pulled herself together, she unfolded a blueprint of her garden she kept hidden in a drawer in her kitchen and sat down at the table to carefully strategize how she would change her tending of the tomatoes so she could maintain her status as Tomato Queen.

On the way back from The Shop, Billy heard the special announcement on his CB radio. He had to pull over

onto the shoulder of Route 23 to catch his breath. Once the news sank in, he cranked the car back up and headed to the office, hoping there wouldn't be any emergency phone calls waiting for him when he got there, because when people were looking for answers, if they didn't call their pastor, they tended to call the police. If he could help it, he didn't feel like dealing with any more stressful situations today.

By noon, the town had declared that businesses and schools could be closed to give people and families who might be distraught over the situation an opportunity to come together to grieve, console each other, or to discuss the recent changes and organize support groups as needed. Elvira and Louise were happy to get the rest of the day off.

Only one thing bothered Elvira: She was worried about juggling the Annual County Fair and Thanksgiving dinner at the same time. She wasn't used to cooking for large groups, but it went without saying that Nana's priority would be reviving her tomatoes. Faye wasn't the best at wheeling and dealing in the kitchen, and while Louise could throw down, out of the three of them, Elvira felt she was definitely the best cook in the family, second to Nana. Based on this, she decided she should get ready to do the food shopping when the time came and prepare herself for having to make the meal, just in case.

Louise was freaked out because delaying the Fair meant postponing the next time she'd see Medford. She had not yet gotten up the momentum—or maybe even the nerve—to call him. This monumental turning of events forced her hand.

Faye closed down the beauty parlor. Most of the women cancelled their appointments, and those who were in the shop went home crying, dazed, or confused because they didn't know what to do with themselves while they waited for the Annual County Fair.

Faye didn't overreact, but she was extremely disap-

pointed. Delaying the Fair for two months meant she had
to spend more time in Lemon City, and she didn't want
to do that—she was ready to leave. Harry was avoiding
her at all costs these days, as if not bumping into her or
speaking on the subject would make the issue obsolete
and the problem disappear. What she needed was a sign
to tell her what to do, something conspicuous that would
hit her over the head on what decision to make—
something as obvious as the lightbulb going off on the ju-
rors who'd acquitted the Soledad Brothers two years
ago. She knew she wouldn't receive an answer to her di-
lemma from her family; she'd have to get it from God.

Nana was taking her garden tools and hose out of the
shed, dusting them off, preparing the weapons she'd
need to engage in the tomato battle. If the dry spell
broke, as predicted, she was going to be the first to turn
the soil. Faye appeared just then in the parched, barren
garden. The expression on her face told Nana every-
thing her granddaughter was feeling. While she did not
know of Faye's plan to leave Lemon City, she assumed
Harry's despicable behavior was causing her grand-
daughter pain. She hated the effect Harry was having on
her family; it was time to do something about it. She de-
cided to do what she should have done long ago. It was
never too late to combat evil.

"How's your husband?" Nana asked, sharpening her
flat rake. When Faye hunched her shoulders and didn't re-
spond, Nana knew exactly what she had to do. At that
moment, doing the Lord's work came to mind and Rule
Number Seven came into the picture: HELP THOSE IN NEED
AND NEVER JUDGE THEM BY THE HOLES IN THEIR SOCKS.

During the next week, Nana took it upon herself to or-
ganize how she was going to help Harry. Late Satur-
day morning, in a last-ditch effort to save his soul, she
rounded up the Ladies of Mt. Zion Baptist Church to form
the traditional Council Circle. Despite the one-hundred-

and-five-degree heat, they all pulled up in a caravan, in front of The Shop. Then they all got out of their cars, Bibles in hand, formed a circle around the building, and started to pray. Nana led the group. The Ladies turned and said in unison, "Husbands, love your wives just as Christ loved the church and gave Himself up for her. He who loves his wife loves himself."

Harry was mortified. He pleaded with Nana to call off her minions. He walked over to where she stood in front of the group and whispered, "Nana, what are you doing?"

"Praying for you, son." She looked at him over her wing-tipped glasses. "Everyone needs spiritual healing, everyone needs food for the soul. Blessed are those who hunger and thirst for righteousness, for they will be filled."

"Nana, I don't hunger for anything. I don't need to be filled." He was nervous about the scene she was creating. The Shop had already taken a hit when Billy had assaulted him. "Only my gas pumps need to be filled. Only my garage needs to be filled. Only the wallet inside my pocket needs to be filled. Please go away. You're scaring off my customers."

"The Bible is nothing to be afraid of, son. The good book and the good word never scared nobody but the devil." Harry stood there, helpless. There were no cops to call. He was on his own. And he knew that when his customers saw the Ladies in a circle, they understood he was a marked man.

Nana continued on her mission. "Proverbs chapter four, verses fourteen and fifteen," and the Ladies turned their pages and read in unison. "Enter not into the path of the wicked, or walk in the way of evil men. Avoid it, do not travel on it, turn from it and go on your own way."

By noon, the Ladies had worked up such a sweat that their wigs, hats, and scarves had to come off. Those who

had chosen to straighten their hair as part of the new trend now had hair that was reverting to its natural state. There were a lot of regrets about not keeping Afros.

A pretty young woman in a gold-colored car caught Nana's attention. She and Harry were staring at each other at the gas pumps. This inspired her next reading: "First Corinthians chapter seven, verse four." The Ladies turned their pages and again read in unison: "The wife hath not power of her own body, but the husband: and likewise also the husband hath not power of his own body, but the wife."

Upon hearing this, the pretty young woman in the 1971 Plymouth Gold Duster 340 with an 8-cylinder engine sped away.

Harry had had enough. He couldn't take it anymore. He called his wife at the beauty parlor to get her to call off her grandmother, but the line was busy, and when he tried her at home, no one answered the phone.

That same afternoon, Louise finally got up the nerve to call Medford. She paced the kitchen floor until she mustered up courage, and then launched her fingers into the holes of the rotary phone. He caught her off guard when he picked up on the first ring, and she hung up. She couldn't call him back right away because then he'd know it was her.

She waited five minutes before dialing again. When she got him on the phone, she did everything she could not to stutter. Before she could manage a sentence, he said he was glad to hear her voice, which made her relax. After that, her words began to flow and she was able to tell him the reason she called. She said that *Buck and the Preacher* starring Sidney Poitier and Harry Belafonte was playing downtown and asked if he would be interested in taking her on a date. He agreed, but only on one condition. Conditions always made her cringe,

but this one was easy: He wanted to do the asking next time. Louise was relieved. When they hung up, she hollered and did a happy dance and let out a shout like she had just been touched by the Spirit. Anyone who happened to be home at the time could hear her carrying on all along Tuckahoe Road.

Faye had just gotten home from the beauty parlor, and was exhausted from all the jawboning about the Annual Fair. Louise screamed out the window that Faye should call her right away. Faye was dying to know what all the fuss was about.

"Faye, you won't believe it," Louise said, all out of breath.

"What in heaven's name is going on up there?"

"I made a date with Medford." Her hands were so sweaty, she nearly dropped the phone.

Faye hadn't heard this kind of excitement from Louise since last year when they acquitted Angela Davis of murder, kidnapping, and conspiracy charges. "See? Every now and then you've got to take a chance, especially when it comes to following your heart." As she heard herself advising Louise, she almost choked on her words because if she were looking into a mirror, she could be expressing those same sentiments to herself. Deep down inside, she knew she had to take a chance and follow her heart, too, but there was one big difference between her and her sister: Whereas her sister wanted to get close to the man she wanted, Faye was questioning whether or not she wanted her man when she knew he was pulling away.

"Thanks, baby sister. You're all right. I'll let you know how the date turns out. Love ya."

She hung up, leaving Faye wishing that her problem could be solved as easily as picking up the phone, making a request, and having it granted. "Hello, Harry, how would you like to move up North with me? You would? That's great. Let's go." Click.

When the news of the Annual County Fair finally sank in, she was beginning to see it as something positive. With this new extended deadline, she was grateful for the two extra months it gave her to work through her situation. It wasn't easy to resolve. Despite the fact that there wasn't a Band-Aid big enough to put over the hurt that she had experienced for nearly a year, she was conflicted about what to do. She wanted to move to the city and be settled in time to attend the National Black Business League Convention in New York in December. She'd read an article titled, "Black Economic Progress: How to Do It Yourself," which read in part: "Without economic freedom, there is no freedom," "Business ownership would help black people out of poverty," and "it has to be accomplished without economic aid from the city, state, or federal government." If she went up North by herself, it would be the end of her marriage. If she stayed in Lemon City with Harry, it would be the end of her life. Loving Harry was draining her like water being squeezed out of dirty clothes on a washing machine's spin cycle, and she was tired of feeling wrung out and spun.

In the bedroom, she pulled off her top and freed herself from her bra. The only evidence of Harry having been home was the greasy work clothes he'd dropped in the middle of the bedroom floor. When she used her foot to toss them to his side of the room, something fell out of the shirt pocket. Upon close examination, she saw it was a matchbook from The Tap. Inside the cover in his handwriting were the words "Dodge Challenger R/T" and a phone number. Normally she wouldn't do such a thing, but curiosity and suspicion got to her and she dialed the number anyway.

A woman answered the phone. She hung up. This was no great surprise. Either he was cheating on her, or that was just the number of a customer that he had written

down hastily on the spur of the moment because he wasn't near his service directory phone book. But deep down inside, Faye was struggling with the facts because her first thought was likely to be more accurate. She was tired of covering up for Harry, and pretending that everything was fine took more energy than facing the truth. Denial was starting to take its toll. Exhausted from the heat and feeling bummed out by reality, she put on a nightgown, turned on the air conditioner, and crawled into bed. It was late afternoon and the sun was still blazing, but she'd try her best to take a nap.

She still hadn't received the sign she was looking for, and before she drifted off to sleep she remembered there was something she should do. Climbing out of bed, she fell to her knees and prayed to God for guidance and direction. At that exact moment, the phone rang. She was certain God wasn't calling and He was the only One she wanted to talk to so she didn't answer, just continued along with her prayer. Before she was done, Harry rammed through the bedroom door like a bull moose charging after a deer. She scrambled to stand up.

"Your grandmother has lost her mind," he yelled at the top of his voice. "She and all her church friends were praying around me all afternoon, scaring away my customers. I tried to get her off me, and when I couldn't, I called you at the salon and at home. Where the hell were you all afternoon, anyway?"

Faye saw the temper flare in Harry's eyes, and he looked so mean, she thought she saw the devil. "I was working just like you, and then I came home. I heard the phone ringing, but I was too tired to answer it." Harry fought to contain himself, treating her like she had done something wrong. She caught herself responding out of fear. She didn't like being the object of Harry's wrath, but while he was home and she had his full attention, she fired off a question of her own.

"All I want to know is, are we moving?"

Harry was so mad that he couldn't prevent the venom from spewing out of his mouth. "No. No, we ain't moving. And you can quit asking me that question because I'm buying The Shop from Granddaddy, and we're staying put whether you like it or not."

Faye was so stunned she couldn't move. She couldn't even speak. Only her eyes shifted to follow Harry when he slammed the door behind him. His words hit her so hard that she could've sworn he'd raised his hand and actually slapped her square across her face.

On top of Mt. Overpeck, just past the big boulder, there was a ridge jutting out from a low hill. As a child, Faye would ride her bike as far as she could, then walk it the rest of the way. She'd made the place her placid retreat, and Nana knew that if she wasn't playing in the backyard or down by the creek at the end of Tuckahoe Road, she'd be in her private sanctuary. It was her summit, her safe haven, and now she was drawn to it, to the solace she once knew when she was a child and the feeling she once had of being on top of the world.

She hadn't thought about Mt. Overpeck for years, but now memories of her time spent there flowed over her. Perhaps this was the start of God's plan. It was where she had asked God why her parents had to die. And God had replied. Her spirit was always opened when she came to this place, even before she was able to know the meaning of the word "spirituality." She came to believe that the higher you are in the world, the closer you are to God. And she'd lain on the grass and looked for Him through the clouds.

After Harry stormed out of the door and she was sure he was gone, she packed a light lunch, changed her clothes, and drove up to the mountaintop. The afternoon sky was an overcast grayish blue and looked like for the first time this year it might treat the earth to some

rain. She spread out her lawn blanket and made herself a picnic. When she finished eating, she lay back on the blanket and stared up at the heavy sky. All she needed was a sign, something to let her know that leaving Lemon City—even if it meant leaving her husband—was the right thing to do. She identified a few shapes in the clouds as she searched to find God again. In her relaxed state, her body fell limp, and she drifted into sleep.

At first the busy images in her head were a blur, but they gradually came into focus. Civil Rights marchers young and old were carrying protest signs as they walked down a main street in what appeared to be a big city, a strange-looking city that seemed more suburban than urban, more quiet than noisy, more littered with houses than with trash. When she looked down at herself, she was on the sidewalk. She was envious of the marchers, with their determined faces and steadfast gaits, and she desperately wanted to be among them, picking up their pace. But whenever she stepped down into the street to join them, some invisible force pulled her back. She made several attempts to break free from the sidelines, to enter the steady stream of people, but all she could do was watch. Frustrated, she searched the crowd for a familiar face. As she scanned the protesters, she read their signs: POWER TO THE PEOPLE, THE BLACK MAN CAN, IT'S NATIONTIME, and DECENT HOUSING NOW.

She ran along the sidewalk, trying to get ahead of the march, but she felt herself moving in slow motion. Her feet had become stuck in a sticky substance like honey or molasses. The protesters got ahead of her and passed her by as she read their signs: LAW AND JUSTICE; WE SHOULD STAND BEHIND OUR MEN, NOT AGAINST THEM; BURN BABY BURN; WE SHALL OVERCOME. She tried to get the gooey stuff off of her shoes and begged for help, but everyone's ears were deaf to her cries. Suddenly she noticed a little girl being carried by a man who was proba-

bly her father. Her skin, the color of black willow-tree bark, stood prominent against her frilly white dress. She wore pink ribbons in her three thick brown braids that matched her pink patent-leather shoes. She couldn't have been more than eight years old with her arms draped around her father's neck and her head hung over the back of his shoulder. The little girl looked directly at Faye with large brown eyes that twinkled in the sunlight, and waved.

In her dream, Faye looked behind her to see if the child was waving to someone over her shoulder, but there was no one there. The little girl waved again and smiled at Faye with a warmth that was like a quilt wrapping her with comfort, and she forgot all about her anxiety and frustration. Then the little girl began to speak to her, only it wasn't normal speaking. She realized that she could actually read the child's lips. As she mouthed the words, Faye heard the child's voice inside her head, and the understanding between them was clear: "Don't worry if you miss this march," she said. "Not everyone needs to be caught up in the flow of a movement. There is more than one way to liberate our people." In a flash, a sign suddenly appeared in the little girl's hand: GO NORTH, TAKE WHAT YOU KNOW, MAKE IT GROW. Then she smiled and waved good-bye and the strange little girl and her father disappeared in the steady stream of the crowd. Faye awoke to find that she was wet from rain. She had just received the sign.

Faye let the heavy raindrops fall on her until she felt completely cleansed, until she was certain all the worry had washed away, and all became as clear as looking through a brand-new window. Feeling refreshed and totally renewed, she left Mt. Overpeck. She felt a spirit of light pass through her and lift her into the air, sweeping her off her feet and carrying her all the way home.

August brought on the first rains and the cooling of '73. Nana put on a wide-brimmed straw hat, tied a burlap pouch around her waist, and grabbed a pair of garden gloves. She paused at the back door and tilted her head to the sun, testing its strength as if she wasn't quite sure it could be trusted. But the day was beautiful and the temperature mild. The tomato seeds she'd planted a few weeks back had grown, and it was time to tie the stalks to the six-foot-tall stakes that marked her rows. Saint followed right behind her.

Nana dragged her garden stool from the shed, sat down, pulled out a pair of used nylons she'd stored in her pouch, and began to tie. Saint reared back on her hind legs and scampered up the stakes one by one, as if she had inhaled catnip or thought she was climbing trees. Nana was tickled as she watched her cat get her spunk back, trying to make up for the months of exercise she'd missed because of the unbearable heat. After a few mad dashes, Saint was clawing her way to the top of the poles. She soon tired herself out and curled up in the shady spot underneath Nana's stool.

From the kitchen window, Ole Miss Johnson flinched as she gave herself an insulin injection. Having just seen Saint carrying on next door made her worry about the safety of her garden. What if that crazy cat got to climbing up her trellises and stakes and eating her tomatoes like last year? She'd have no choice but to shoot it. She

was tired of chasing the animal around her yard, and she didn't like cats to begin with. Liquid on the stove began to bubble, breaking her concentration, and she spun around to turn down the flame underneath the pot. Then she dropped her needle into the boiling water to sterilize it for the next time she needed to take her insulin.

Nana tied one of the stalks too tight to the stake. Her mind had drifted into a daydream: Her fingers began to bend, her hands started to shake, then raised themselves to shoulder level, and she squeezed her fingers as tight as she could. Before she knew it, she was thinking about strangling Harry. She loosened the nylons from the plant's neck, and then sprinkled water over the stalk to make amends for her mistake. As much as she wanted to focus her efforts on winning the Annual County Fair Tomato Competition this year, she was still wondering how she could get rid of that man, her mean and trifling grandson-in-law, for good.

Saint noticed a nylon toe dangling outside Nana's pouch. Every time Nana moved, the nylon toe moved, too. For Saint, the flaccid pendulum was a signal that it was time to play. She swung at it with her paw until her claws caught on the seam, and then she yanked the whole leg from the pouch and ran with it across the yard.

"Quit it now, Saint," Nana said. "Bring it here."

Ole Miss Johnson came to the window just in time to see Saint headed straight for her garden.

"Come back here, now. Don'cha go over there." Nana stood up and looked over the fence to see how far the cat would go.

Rejuvenated by the moderate temperatures, Saint was feeling friskier than usual. She heard Nana calling, but there was no turning back. Already up for the challenge and for some mischief, little did she know that Ole Miss Johnson was, too.

"That animal is trespassing," Lurleen yelled. She grabbed the loaded pellet gun stored in her pantry and fired a shot through the kitchen window.

"Lurleen Johnson, you put that thing down before I call the police," said Nana.

"Keep Billy out of this. This is between you and me. Git that cat offa my property. Git it outta my garden!" she hollered, taking another shot.

Saint was too fast and Ole Miss Johnson too near-sighted for anything disastrous to occur. With all the excitement going on, Saint dropped the tattered nylon in Ole Miss Johnson's garden and darted back to Nana's side.

Satisfied that her point was well taken, Ole Miss Johnson retreated into the house and put the gun down on the kitchen counter. As long as Saint was outside, she felt it necessary to keep guard over her tomatoes. Pulling her rocking chair right up to the screen door, she sat and waited, as alert as a sentry.

The next few weeks managed to be equally as stressful for Nana. With all this excitement, her blood pressure was gradually beginning to rise. Stress from gardening the perfect tomato, anxiety over winning the Tomato Competition, Saint being out of control, and her grandson-in-law getting on her nerves inspired her to make some adjustments in her life. Nana went directly to her neighbor, whom she believed to be at least half the source of her health issues. She found the old lady sprinkling water on her plants in her backyard, as if she were performing a baptism with holy water.

"Lurleen. I need to speak to you." Nana, who was in her yard, had walked to the fence, which was as close as she wanted to get to her neighbor.

"What is it, Ernestine? Can't you see I'm busy?" Ole Miss Johnson glanced at Nana out of the corner of her eye and continued to refresh her garden. When she saw

Saint standing next to Nana, she pointed her hose at the animal, and snickered and snorted under her breath when it scampered away.

"Lurleen Johnson. You didn't have no right to do that, and no cause." Nana wanted to snatch the old lady right out of her yard, but instead she shook her finger at her. "You getting mean and spiteful in your old age, and you know who don't like ugly, Lurleen."

"Tell me what you want then, and git it over with." Ole Miss Johnson turned off the hose and faced Nana. "I ain't got all day."

"I don't want us to be at each other's throats this year. Let's try to compete in a civilized manner."

"So what's preventing you from doing that?" Ole Miss Johnson, bored with the suggestion, started watering again.

"Lurleen, it's both of us. Each of us is driving the other to the edge."

"I ain't driving nowhere. You the one driving yourself crazy." Ole Miss Johnson waited for Nana to say something, and when Nana didn't, she softened her tone and added, "All right, then. I'll try to be neighborly, but I can't make any promises if you can't keep control over your cat and make it stay out of my yard."

Nana picked up her beloved pet and retreated to her house, unsure whether or not she had achieved a truce with her neighbor.

September started off with Nana and Ole Miss Johnson putting aside their differences. They both tended their gardens daily—composted, mulched, added limestone, and tested the soil to make sure the pH balance was just right. They both examined the leaves for pesky beetles, worms, whiteflies, aphids, and other bugs, and watered their tomato plants so they could reach their fullest potential. Both backyards were filled with the rich scent of manure, and the women took to inhaling

the smell like it was the sweet breath of life. However, this year the only difference between the Dunlap and the Johnson gardens was their choice in style of row covers, and each woman regarded her row cover as her secret weapon.

Nana was absolutely certain her secret weapon—her tunnel row cover—would change her streak of bad luck and make her this year's Tomato Queen for a Day. It was a lightweight plastic that she draped over wire, shaped like a cylinder, giving her plants more protection against insects, sunscald, tomato puffiness, and cracks, especially against diseases such as Blossom-end rot, which she was determined never to get again. The instructions she'd read on the side of the box said the tunnel row cover would allow her plants to thrive in the fall and continue to help them grow even when the weather got cool. As she laid the individual covers over the rows of her sweet little tomatoes, she felt like she was spreading blankets over newborn babies in a nursery, tucking them in for a good night's sleep.

Her neighbor's row cover, on the other hand, was shaped like a tent, and was tacked to six-foot-tall stakes. From what Nana could see, the plastic that was hanging over the tomatoes had flaps and air vents to prevent unwanted elements and insects from coming in, at the same time minimizing soil moisture and temperature fluctuations, just like the instructions indicated on her row-cover box. According to the salesman at the store, the tunnel row cover was this year's model and the tent row cover debuted a few years ago. Nana didn't know why her neighbor preferred the tent-style cover, and hoped the old lady wasn't privy to information she didn't have. She hoped Ole Miss Johnson had based her decision solely on the fact that she was cheap, and because it was an old model, it was on sale.

By the end of the month, Saint was bored with being

on her best behavior and the truce between the neighbors came to a halt. Every now and then, she'd leave Nana's side to sneak off and sniff Ole Miss Johnson's tomatoes like she was taking a whiff of a newly opened can of Chicken of the Sea. While her adventures never lasted very long, Nana understood that Saint was doing what came natural to cats, which was to be curious, but Ole Miss Johnson didn't buy into that behavior. Saint was nipping on her tomatoes and gnawing on her last nerve. It was getting to the point where Nana was fearing for her cat, not trusting what the old lady would do behind her back if Saint moseyed into her yard by herself and she wasn't outside to protect her.

Nothing could have guarded the Dunlap family against the mail hand-delivered by the United States Postal Service one Friday afternoon in October. The envelope marked CONFIDENTIAL and addressed to Billy was from an NYPD precinct in Harlem.

Billy emptied the papers from the envelope and laid them on his desk one by one, as if he were dealing a deck of cards. He called each offense out loud: petty larceny, assault charges, embezzlement, breaking and entering, mail fraud, car theft. Practically the only things that weren't listed on Harry's rap sheet were manslaughter, murder, or sex crimes.

Now Billy knew why Harry didn't want to move up North. There was no extradition treaty between Lemon City and the rest of the world; no one would ever find his sorry ass in Lemon City. Billy lingered on that thought. He contemplated making sure that no one ever did. Since there had been no Outsiders to consider, the founding fathers had determined that Lemon City law enforcement people would take care of their own business. This decision was in accordance with Rules Two, Five, and Six: IF YOU CAN'T BE HONEST, YOU MIGHT AS

WELL BE DEAD; CHEATING MAKES YOU LOWER THAN A DOG SCRATCHING UP A WORM IN THE DIRT; and WHAT GOES AROUND WILL ALWAYS COME BACK AROUND AND HIT YOU IN THE HEAD. If Harry returned home, he'd be arrested. Billy had always known that he served as the family's patriarch-in-waiting. With this responsibility in mind, he decided to call an emergency meeting at his grandparents' house to alert everyone to the situation and get their feedback.

The first person he contacted was Louise.

"Good afternoon, Lemon City Library," she said with a cheery smile in her voice, as she was looking up a book title in the Dewey decimal card system for a patron.

"Louise." Billy sounded slightly panicked. Since he never called her during the day, he knew she'd be concerned.

"Billy?" She cupped her hand over the receiver and whispered, "What's the matter? You never call me here. Who died?"

"No one died, but what I'm calling about may be worse than death."

"Whatcha mean? What's going on?" She looked around the library to make sure her conversation remained private.

"I can't tell you over the phone. Just get to Nana's right away."

"I'm working. Quit playin' around. I can't just up and leave before the end of the day."

"Believe me," Billy said as he tried his best to calm his sister down, "this is an emergency. It's about family. All I can say is, I'm calling everyone except Faye."

"Uhmm . . . Ohhh . . ." Louise squinted her eyes as she began to catch on. "So this is about Harry, huh?"

"Everyone is meeting at Nana's. Be there," Billy said abruptly. Then there was a click, and the last thing Louise heard was the dial-tone hum.

Elvira was on the playground, rounding up the kids after recess, when the principal called her in to answer the phone. The first thing Billy told her was that no one had died, but there was an important matter. She must go to Nana's right away.

Twenty minutes later, he left the office. When he arrived at Nana's, they were gathered around—Granddaddy, Nana, Louise, Elvira—anxiously awaiting the news. Not much explanation was needed. Billy dumped the contents of the confidential brown envelope on the table and waited for their reactions.

The family passed around the documents like they couldn't believe what they were seeing, but the facts were before them in black and white—Harry was as crooked as railroad tracks crisscrossing at a train station.

Billy waited for their horror to pass, and for fury to replace it. Given the circumstances, Granddaddy was remarkably calm. What he said was, "No sense in notifying the authorities over this. I think we have all the authority we need to rectify the situation right here at this table. It's obvious the Outsider needs to be taught a lesson. We will waste no time feeling any remorse. He played us all for fools; worse, he broke Rules Number Two, Three, and Five, made a mockery of Rule Number Ten, and will suffer the consequences of Rule Number Six." Granddaddy patted his wife's hand, rested his hand on top of hers, and continued. "Let's not allow this situation to spoil our celebration of the County Fair. I suggest we wait until the Fair is over to decide how to handle this recent development."

"What if he finds out we got the word on him and splits?" Billy asked.

"Don't you worry, he won't get away. He's not going anywhere without us getting to him first," Granddaddy assured him.

"Me and Elvira will keep an eye on him," offered Louise.

"Remember, we were supposed to figure out a payback for him last year," Elvira whispered as she nudged Louise with her elbow.

"You just stay away from this guy. He's a criminal," warned Billy, looking directly at his wife.

"What about Faye?" Louise was concerned not only for her sister's safety but also for her heart.

"She's not in any danger. He's not a murderer."

"Not yet, anyway," said Elvira.

"He won't be if we get to him first," said Louise.

"That's enough from you young'uns," Granddaddy continued. "Now y'all go on with y'all's day, ya hear?" He shooed his grandchildren away with his hands. "Focus on your business and think about what we should do to remedy this thing as a family. Family has always come first with us."

As they all got up to leave, Granddaddy added, "Don't nobody jump the gun before then. It don't make no sense to do anything you'll regret."

CHAPTER TWENTY-THREE

It was strange to see everything in full bloom in November when it was normally the time of year when everything should be dying or already dead. That's exactly how Faye felt when she called the Ladies of Mt. Zion Baptist Church. A part of her had died when she hung up the phone after asking them to put out a search for someone to manage the beauty parlor. She told them she was expanding the business and needed some extra assistance—and what she told them wasn't completely a lie. It was just that the business wasn't expanding in Lemon City. With a manager in place, taking over the day-to-day responsibilities for Hair Today, Gone Be Beautiful Tomorrow, it would be easier for Granddaddy to find a suitable, dedicated owner.

She set her Samsonite suitcase on the bed. Opening her drawers, she started packing up the memories, stacking the special moments, neatly folding the good times away, making room for her valuables and most important possessions. Locking them safely inside her suitcase, she held on tight to the key. These would be the only things she'd bring with her on her long-awaited journey. Everything else, the items that didn't fit into her luggage or into her new life, like clothes that were old or too plain to wear in the city, or dusty shoes with rundown heels that were inappropriate for walking down stylish city streets, she deliberately chose to leave behind. She shoved the suitcase underneath her bed and

went into the kitchen to pour a glass of dandelion wine. After that, she decided to give herself a refill.

With only one week left before the County Fair, Nana was spending more hours per day toiling in her backyard, and so was Ole Miss Johnson. While Nana was tending her tomatoes, Saint was minding her own business, resting under her stool until she heard the scurrying. The cat looked up in time to see the last part of a slender gray tail pass through the picket fence, and she let out a war cry that startled Nana and scared the bejesus out of Ole Miss Johnson. Saint instinctively did what any other cat would do under the circumstances. She chased the mouse.

Ole Miss Johnson didn't see the varmint and didn't care about Saint's reason for trespassing. She picked up her pellet gun and started to shoot. When she ran out of BBs, she ran outside with a broom to hunt down the moving target, trampling over whatever got in her way. Nana stood up as straight and as tall as her arthritis would permit, bringing her pruning shears with her because she didn't want to go into her neighbor's yard unarmed. It was too close to the competition to allow herself to be distracted from her preparations. *Don't start no s—h, and there won't be no i—t,* she thought to herself, because she would never cuss out loud. Nana had no idea what she was going to do when she reached the old lady's yard, so she was relieved when Saint came charging back through the fence, dropping the dead mouse at her feet. She scooped the shaken animal into her arms and carried her into the kitchen.

Ole Miss Johnson assessed the damage she'd caused to her own garden and cursed the cat. She picked up the handful of green beefsteaks that had fallen from their branches and scattered across the ground. She brought them into the house and rinsed off the dirt. These would be perfect for what she had in mind. She reached into

the dark drawer where she stored the plants she rarely used and located the smelly herb that resembled parsley. Nothing was going to stop her from winning the competition this close to Saturday. She had to take action. As she broke the leaves from the stalk, she waved the stench away from her face. She ground the leaves into little pieces and boiled water to make the tea that would turn into a potent liquid. She filled her syringe with the substance, injecting it into three green tomatoes, then she placed them neatly on the windowsill where they would gradually turn red and ripen. *That cat's days are numbered*, she thought.

The weathervane on top of the Dunlap house was spinning frantically until the breeze caught the arrow and pointed it in the direction where the winds were heading—southeast. A bad storm was coming. If it weren't for the dampness that made Granddaddy's arthritis hurt so bad that he could feel the pain down to his bones, he would have given Harry's punishment more thought. But the ache in his body was diverting his attention away from his efforts to decide the best method of discipline for his grandson-in-law. He decided to use his energy where it was currently needed and put Harry on hold. All he knew was he had another week to come up with an appropriate action for Harry's behavior, hopefully one that would hit him where it hurt.

Ole Miss Johnson smelled the rain getting closer. In an attempt to protect her cherished tomatoes, she put on her parka, throwing the hood over her head to guard herself against the increasing winds and streaming rain. She hauled the heavy-duty plastic made especially for these occasions from her toolshed and proceeded to cover her garden. As the winds started picking up speed, she struggled to nail the corners of the plastic into the ground. When she finished, she stood in the kitchen,

peering through the window to make sure her garden was safe from nature and that there was no sign of the cat.

By late afternoon, Nana's tomato stalks were no match for the strong winds that were passing through and the sharp rains hitting the ground like pellets. When it looked like the row covers over her tomatoes were going to need more protection, she and Granddaddy fought the nasty elements to shield their garden with heavy-duty plastic as well, holding down the edges with stakes and reinforcing them with bricks to keep the tarpaulin in place. They were soaking wet as they carried in as many tomatoes that had been sideswiped by the wind as they could find. When they were finished, they took off their ponchos, sat in front of the lighted fireplace, and anticipated the worst. Nana would consider herself lucky if half her tomatoes survived the storm and made it to the competition, which was six days away.

Thunder pounded its fist against the sky and lightning spread its arms across the city. Faye looked out the window in time to see the intermittent aura of the storm's fury spread over the mountains like a giant shield. It had been twenty minutes since the power had gone out. All the houses in Lemon City stood in darkness, except for the flickering of candles and kerosene lamps that cast shadows, which danced against windowpanes.

Harry was washing the dinner dishes by candlelight while Faye sat in her slip on the edge of the bed, quietly staring out the window at the storm. Since their last big fight, he hadn't mentioned the move, and Faye was determined not to raise the subject. She assumed she was on her own. As she sat at the window, drifting further away from him like the storm that was passing over the city, she wondered if anyone could ever truly love her, or if she'd ever find love again. Now she felt empty, aware that loneliness wasn't too far behind. She didn't know

how she'd let herself fall into such a worthless state, or how she'd abandoned herself in the process of what she thought was love at the expense of someone else. Just thinking about it made her body go limp. Right now, she just didn't care. Nothing seemed to matter anymore as she became more numb and her feelings began to shut down. Once she hit rock bottom with her emotions, she had nothing left to lose. The only thing that would help her get ahold of herself was reclaiming her self-esteem, rediscovering her power, and pursuing whatever pleasure she could so she could feel alive again. As the storm headed over the mountains, she closed her eyes and imagined herself being carried away with it. Jumping into the storm's saddle, controlling the reins, and taming the wildly dark and disgruntled clouds would give her satisfaction.

She heard the Jiffy Pop kernels rattling like marbles in their tin pan, bursting full against the aluminum foil on the propane grill. Harry appeared with the popcorn in a bowl and handed it to her as if it were a peace offering. However, peace wasn't what she needed, and love was the last thing on her mind. Sex was what she was interested in. She didn't know when she'd be with a man again. She wanted to take him now. That much he owed her.

She reached into the bowl and picked out a single kernel, placing it against his lips, letting him taste the salt and lick the butter from her fingers. When he attempted to pull it into his mouth with his tongue, she snatched it back and ate it. She took another piece of popcorn from the bowl and placed it on his lips and teased him until he couldn't stand it anymore and kissed her. When she unzipped his pants, he sank into the mattress as she swallowed him whole. When she was ready to ride, she charged with the fury of the storm. Jolted by a surge of energy, she moved as if she were in control of the light-

ning, owned the rain. The clouds wouldn't move unless she called. When Harry looked up, a quick flash hit the room, and he swore for a split second he saw a halo of light around his wife's head.

Up the road, the power was still dead where Louise and Medford sat playing Scrabble by candlelight to the tune of a transistor radio. With every crash of thunder, Louise fought the urge to roll off the beanbag chair and move closer to him so he could hold her in his arms and she could nestle between the curve of his neck and the ridge of his shoulders. But she promised tonight would be different. She wouldn't look at him as a sex object anymore. Instead, she'd see him as her object of affection and as a means to learn to trust.

Billy and Elvira were in bed reading *Black Bourgeoisie* and debating the pros and cons of integration versus segregation. When they couldn't agree on the impact of Marcus Garvey's "Back to Africa" movement and whether or not it was successful, they blew out the candles and did the only thing they could agree on—made another attempt at making a baby. Since Nana had knit quite a few blankets and sweaters by now, they felt they were behind schedule and made a conscious effort to keep up with supply and demand.

In the middle of the night, Ole Miss Johnson heard an unidentifiable noise coming from her garden. She threw open her bedroom window to assess the impact the storm was having on her tomatoes. No sooner had she held out the lantern into the darkness than the rain spit on her flame, and the wind blew it out. A corner of the plastic covering had torn through the nail and was waving in the wind. She cursed the strength and the speed of the wind that made a storm treacherous and unpredictable, because without the power of the gales, a storm would only be a breeze with light drizzle.

Dressed in her long white cotton gown, she could have

been a ghost against the black of the night as she ventured outside on an emergency mission to rescue her tomatoes. Holding her arms across her face, she tried unsuccessfully to shield her eyes against the downpour. But her vision wasn't good to begin with, and all she could hear was the flapping in the wind and the creaking of branches. She followed the annoying sound, and just when she was underneath it, she reached her arms high in the air to capture the runaway corner and tie it back down to the ground where it belonged. When she jumped up again to claim the covering, she heard a snap. She knew she was in trouble. There was no way of knowing where to turn in the darkness; she waved her hands in front of her to clear her way back toward the house. She heard a louder snap, and then the sound of something breaking just overhead. Before she was hit, she let out a scream. Then she was knocked to the ground. The last thought she had while lying in the cold mud, getting soaked to the bone, was how tragic it would be to have to relinquish her Tomato Queen crown.

Next door, Nana and Granddaddy woke up to a sound they knew wasn't thunder. Granddaddy jumped out of bed. He was barely able to see out the window, so he went downstairs with a flashlight and scanned its beam across the backyard. He heard a groan that sounded like a wounded animal coming from the yard next door and turned the light in that direction. A tree had fallen on Ole Miss Johnson. He yelled upstairs for Nana to bring the first-aid kit and a blanket.

The next day, the sun successfully fought its way through the clouds. The sky was clear as far as the eye could see, and the cardinals were visible as they swam across the broad blue canvas.

Faye had had the best sleep she'd had in years. If it weren't for the truck engines groaning, hauling away debris, and the men working on the telephone lines, giving

each other instructions and sounding as if they were standing right outside her window, she'd still be dreaming. How Harry could sleep through all that racket she'd never know. She guessed she had knocked him out cold with exhaustion from last night's activities.

Without electricity, the closest thing she'd get to coffee this morning was to boil some water and make herself some instant. She was stirring two teaspoons of sugar into the piping-hot brown liquid when the phone rang.

"Hello."

"Morning." Nana sounded worried. "You all right? Is everything okay?"

"We're fine. Just a few branches came down, that's all. How about you?"

"We did okay, but Ole Miss Johnson wasn't so lucky."

"What happened?"

"Well, in a way, she was lucky. She didn't die."

"Nana, what happened?"

"A tree came down on her, broke her shoulder bone, and cracked a couple of her ribs."

"Oh my goodness. How'd that happen?"

"I told you. It was a tree."

"I mean, why was she outside in the first place?" Faye took a sip of coffee, but it was too hot and burned her lips.

"Plastic came off her tomatoes, and she tried to save them by tacking it back down, but she was no match for the storm, poor thing. You should see her garden. Looks like all hell broke loose in there. No chance of her winning anything this weekend."

"Nana, how could you think about the Annual County Fair at a time like this?" She could see her grandmother grinning through the phone. If she pulled back the husk, Nana's rows of teeth would be lined up like kernels of corn.

"I'm just describing the damage that was done, that's

all," Nana continued, trying to wipe the smile off her face and to sound more serious over the phone. "The doctor's been over there all morning, and the Ladies from Mt. Zion been over there, too, but I'm sure she'd like to see you as soon as you get a chance. I'm making some chicken soup with dumplings for her now. Come by here first, and carry it over to her."

"I'll be right over." Faye had never heard Nana so cheerful in a conversation about Ole Miss Johnson. She was so happy about the state of her neighbor's garden that she was actually making her chicken soup. With her competition out of commission, she was beside herself.

Faye put down the receiver and went straight to the bathroom to take a shower. Standing naked, she examined herself in the mirror. Since last night's storm, she realized how different she'd become and wondered how she had turned into this new stranger. She rotated sideways to the left, then to the right, looking at her lean body. She pulled back her shoulders so that her chest could expand into perfect posture, then sucked in her stomach. She stared at herself until she saw goodness and beauty staring back at her, and she smiled. Putting on her shower cap, she turned the nozzle in the shower and tested the water with her hand. When the temperature was just right, she stepped in. She was tired from everything she'd been feeling over the past year, and then some. She relaxed her arms across her breasts and closed her eyes. She took deep breaths, pulling oxygen into her lungs, filling them up with air and expelling it slowly until her head was light and her body absorbed the benefits. When her breathing turned to a steady rhythm, she leaned into the water to let the stream caress her nipples. Her head rolled back as she immersed herself under the showerhead, surrendering to the cascade, allowing herself to be seduced. Slowly, she began to move her hands over her nakedness with deliberation.

When she was ready to be cleansed, she reached for the bar of Dove soap, and let the warm steady stream wash off the previous night. Soaping her body all over, she paid special attention to her private places to take away any remnants of her husband. Removing her shower cap, she shoved her head into the water, no longer caring if her hair got wet, only concerned that she was completely cleansed. All that mattered was that she be purged of him and rid of any leftovers that might decide to creep into a crevice and stay. When she was satisfied with the purification, she did one last rinse with her hands and made her fingers visit all the places that made her happy. She had never explored herself that fully before, but there would be a lot of things she'd have to do in her new life that she'd have to get used to, especially those that would make her content.

When she got dressed, she left a note for Harry on the refrigerator door, letting him know what had happened to Ole Miss Johnson and that she'd be home later in the day.

Ole Miss Johnson's backyard was worse than Faye had imagined. If she didn't know any better, she would think a tornado had ransacked the old lady's garden. Two Ladies from Mt. Zion were already in the backyard, on cleanup duty, when she arrived. They told her that two other church members were holding a vigil over the fragile woman.

Faye walked into the kitchen to find eucalyptus oil simmering in a pot on the stove. The scent purified the air. She assumed one of the church ladies knew about the medicinal remedy, because Ole Miss Johnson was in no shape to even tell anyone how to treat her. All the doctor could do was to make sure she was comfortable and give her a narcotic to make sure the pain didn't get too bad, because the best way to recover in a situation like this was over time. She was drowsy and weak, but

she opened her eyes when Faye entered, obviously sensing a familiar presence walking into the room. Faye held Ole Miss Johnson's bony, withered hand, startled by how cold it was. She rubbed it to create friction, as if she were starting a campfire with two sticks. Faye pulled the handmade quilt at the foot of the bed over Ole Miss Johnson's slight body to provide her with extra warmth. She whispered into her mentor's ear that everything was going to be okay, and that she had all the time in the world to heal.

Ole Miss Johnson couldn't move, and for now it took too much effort to speak, but her mind was still active, and she was frustrated that the words she wanted to come out of her mouth wouldn't. But what she was thinking was that she wasn't worried about her own healing. She was as strong as a bear and as stubborn as a mule, and in a few months' time she'd be back to being as good as she could possibly be at her age. What worried her most was Faye's healing, because what the young woman was going through was much more traumatic than being ambushed and side-whacked by a tree.

Faye told her dear friend to rest while she went to the basement to find the arnica and comfrey to soak a bandage for bruises and brew a pot of elderberry tea to bring down the fever and get rid of the cough that also had assaulted Ole Miss Johnson.

As Faye prepared the healing herbs, she couldn't help but think about how much the old lady had taught her and how grateful she was to her for influencing her life. She felt guilty about leaving her friend at a time like this. The thought occurred to her to use the tragedy as an excuse to prolong her stay, but she dismissed the idea as quickly as it came.

When she went back upstairs, the old lady forced out a whisper: "When you leaving town?" Faye had to lean

in close to hear her as she applied the warm arnica and comfrey compresses to her battered and swollen body.

"Who said I was leaving?" Faye asked, glancing at the two church members to see if they were eavesdropping. They quickly turned their heads away.

"I just know," Ole Miss Johnson said softly. "It takes two people to be married, not one." Ole Miss Johnson paused as if to gain more energy to move her mouth again. "If a person can only be married to himself, and sees the other person as invisible"—she paused, to allow her chest to rise as she took a deep breath—"sometimes it's best for the other person to be alone, or at least be with people who see her." Her chest went up high as she took another breath, then it settled down again. "Besides, the other person can get more accomplished that way."

"I'm leaving next Monday . . . a week from today." Faye leaned down so she could whisper. She took her old friend's hand and with the other, she gently stroked her forehead.

"Have you told anyone about it?" Faye felt Ole Miss Johnson relax as her body responded to the touch.

"Not yet."

"Don't be afraid. You doing the right thing, chile." She began to cough herself into a fit, and Faye put her finger to her mouth to shush her so she'd save her strength, but Ole Miss Johnson wouldn't be quieted until she finished what she had to say. "By yourself ain't such a bad thing to be, and leaving Lemon City ain't the worst that could happen." The old lady made a loud, throaty noise to gather what she had in the back of her mouth and let out the contents in the spittoon next to her bed.

Faye laid the arnica compresses across her shoulder and badly bruised legs. Now she cooled the hot tea by blowing over the cup. When the liquid was cool enough,

she raised Ole Miss Johnson's head so she could sip the elderberry tea. When she started to choke uncontrollably again, Faye told the old woman, whom she regarded as a mother, to lie quietly now and go to sleep. After a while, when the snoring became steady and consistent, and the church members left for the day, Faye dropped to the floor and kneeled against the bed as if she were going to pray. But instead she buried her head in her arms and let the hot tears that she had been holding back run freely down her face.

When she regained her composure, she went out to relieve the Ladies of Mt. Zion from their yard duty. By that time, she had already decided to spend the night. When the long day finally ended, she thought to call her husband, but walked down the corridor to the guest bedroom in Ole Miss Johnson's house and decided to call it a night instead.

Ironically, during the past couple weeks, Harry had been nice to her, granting little favors, running small errands, bending over backward, obviously trying to make up for his bad behavior. But Faye knew where he was coming from. Her mind was winning the power struggle over her heart, and she had no problem taking advantage of his new disposition. Harry agreed to rebuild Ole Miss Johnson's gazebo and restore her garden without giving her any resistance. He rented a 1972 red Chevy Cheyenne pickup on Tuesday to transport the loads of lumber and equipment.

When Harry drove down Tuckahoe Road and pulled up in front of the old lady's house, he surveyed the devastation. Her backyard looked like it had been blown up by a land mine. The cat was eating a crushed tomato amid the rubble and he kicked some dirt over in its direction to make it scat. There were hundreds of little round red bodies thrashed about, randomly scattered across the yard. He snapped open a large trash bag, put

on a pair of gloves, and began to throw the dead toma-
toes inside.

Nana was sitting on the stool in her garden, whistling
and humming to herself, when she looked over her
neighbor's fence and saw the top of Harry's head. She
was in the process of both admiring and scrutinizing the
individual tomatoes, the cream of her crop that she'd se-
lect to enter into the Annual County Fair. She was care-
fully removing the specks of dirt from their skins, spit
shining them against her smock, and placing them into a
red velvet-lined wicker basket. She knew it was selfish,
but she couldn't help feeling exhilarated. Her moment of
glory would come in four days. But now that she had
spotted her grandson-in-law within close range, she quit
whistling and humming and watched him like a beady-
eyed squirrel stopped dead in its tracks by a car coming
down the road. She'd have to work quietly now and not
speak. She didn't want evil to know she was nearby and
disturb the happy mood she was in.

Harry finished discarding the wasted tomatoes and
useless stalks. He sawed the fallen trees and branches
into fireplace-sized logs and kindling and stacked them
into neat piles near the hole in the fence to prevent the
cat from sneaking back into the yard. When the ground
was finally free of debris he smoothed over the earth
with a rake. After putting in several hours of work, he
started collecting his tools from the yard. Shielding his
eyes with his elbow, he glanced up at the sun to deter-
mine the time of day. He looked up at Ole Miss John-
son's house just in time to see one of the Ladies of Mt.
Zion staring down at him from a top-floor window. He
rubbed the back of his hand across his forehead to wipe
the perspiration from his face and waved to be polite.
The lady looked at him with disdain and walked away,
first pulling down the shade and then lowering the sheer
white curtain into place.

He was dying of thirst, and since the back door was open, he invited himself into the kitchen for a cold glass of water and made himself at home. With his glass tilted toward the ceiling, his eyes explored the unfamiliar surroundings. He spotted three tomatoes on the windowsill that were just ripe for eating. He took a bite out of one of them and finished eating it, and put the other two tomatoes in a brown paper bag that he found in the pantry. When he was done packing up his snack, he collected the trash bags that were filled with mutilated tomato remains, loaded them into his truck, and headed home.

Faye drove home from Hair Today, Gone Be Beautiful Tomorrow for the last time. Glancing out the window, she was thinking about how much she was going to miss Lemon City, and how much more she was looking forward to the adventure that lay ahead. She absorbed the scenery like a tourist would, taking a mental picture of the landscape to keep for the lonely days she knew lay ahead. It was weird how everything had turned upside down and topsy-turvy. The orange-yellow leaves that usually fell from the sycamores in autumn were holding on tight to their branches, still intensely green. At this time of year, it was peculiar for the azaleas and the dogwoods to be in full bloom and the smell of fresh gardens and clean mountain air to penetrate the senses. It was as if summer was now where fall used to be.

She turned down Tuckahoe Road, and spotted Harry's white GTO through the thickness of the leaves and his rented red Chevy pickup parked next to it. It was odd for him to be home on a Tuesday afternoon. Besides, this was the day he was supposed to help out Ole Miss Johnson. Then a thought occurred to her that brought a smile to her face. Maybe he was home early because he'd changed his mind, opened his heart, and couldn't wait to greet her at the door to tell her himself. She

imagined him running out of the cottage, getting down on his knees, begging for her forgiveness, pleading to go with her up North, promising never to stay away from her for too long ever again.

But she immediately snapped back to reality. This fantasy wasn't his style. It was not going to happen—she was beyond wishful thinking and happy endings by now. But she appreciated anything that would make her smile these days, and she laughed out loud when her fantasy ended, knowing how ridiculous and absurd it was.

There was nothing funny about what she saw when she parked her car and walked through the cottage door. Harry was lying on the living room floor. He looked like he was dead. No sound was coming out of him. His chest was not moving. Not a twitch. There was a big, red blood clot stuck on his mouth, and his face had turned ashen. That was all she could tell from a distance, so she decided to take a few steps to get a better look.

Tiptoeing to her husband as if she were afraid to disturb the dead, she stopped short when she was beside him and hovered. Upon examination, she identified the speck of leafy green on his lips as part of a stem. Then she leaned in closer and realized the blood clot was actually a tomato. She called out his name, thinking this was his idea of a joke, but he didn't respond. Kneeling over his body, she shook him. "Harry! Harry!" she yelled, as if he were hard of hearing. He didn't budge from his catatonic state. She tried to raise his arm, but it was stiff and weighed a ton. She stood up and held her hand over her mouth as if to scream, but nothing came out. She nudged his leg with her foot, but there was no reaction. Nothing she did had any effect on him. Just to be sure, she stepped back, swung her leg forward with full force and kicked him as hard as she could for all his meanness and for his game of ho-of-the-month and the specialty muscle cars that turned him on.

But Harry didn't feel a thing. He couldn't hurt any-
one anymore. He had joined the ranks of the dearly de-
parted.

Then reality hit her like an unexpected blow to the
head, catching her off guard and unprotected. The
scream finally found her voice, and she sank to her knees.
Tears began rolling down her face as she wrapped her
arms around herself, rocking back and forth until the
drool came, and she wiped her mouth with the back of
her hand. Then her sobbing stopped and her ears perked
up as she looked around the room. Listening to the still-
ness, it occurred to her that she might not be alone. Pull-
ing herself together, she got up and threw open the living
room closet. No one. She ran into the bedroom, opened
the closet door. Nothing. She opened the bathroom door
and flung back the shower curtain. Just water dripping
from the nozzle. She looked underneath the bed. Only
her suitcase. Supporting herself against the doorway be-
tween that main room and the bedroom, she looked at
Harry, lying limp on the floor, and felt sorry for him. If he
had kept his word over a year ago, they would have been
long gone and he wouldn't be left in this condition.

She ran to his side and shook him. She wanted him to
wake up immediately so they could start their lives all
over again. She was too young to be a widow. "Harry!
Harry!" She looked at her husband. "How could you do
this?" She waited a beat, then raised her head to the ceil-
ing. "Why did this happen to me?" She looked back at
Harry. "What went wrong?" She turned back to the ceil-
ing. "Why did this have to happen now?" Sobbing to
the point of convulsion, she flung herself over her hus-
band and jumped on him like he was the last bus leaving
Lemon City.

While she was on top of Harry's body on the floor, her
head began to spin and the room began to swirl. Her
stomach began to hurt and swell with sadness. Failure

and fear began to weaken her knees and regret was de-
termined to drop her to the floor. She started to gag as
all the emotions began creeping their way up her throat,
making her feel like she would vomit. She rushed to the
bathroom, fell over the porcelain fixture, and heaved.

When she released the rancidness in her stomach, her
eyes caught sight of the box of Kleenex on the coffee
table. She plucked a few tissues, blew her nose, and
then, with all her might, she threw the box against the
wall. Instead of landing on the floor, it hit the reproduc-
tion Tiffany lamp. It wasn't just the sound of the impact
that startled her. Broken glass scattered across the floor,
shattered in bits and pieces. She ran over to the lamp,
picking up the remains, desperately trying to match the
pieces together in order to make it whole again. But the
shards were too small, making the lamp irreparable. She
looked at what was left of the fallen lamp, then turned
her attention to her husband to see what was left of her
life.

Leaning over Harry, she looked down into his face,
which was slightly contorted with the tomato in his
mouth. His expression of agony wasn't becoming. Or
was it sheer ugliness, reflecting her husband's true self
that she was seeing? She couldn't tell which. Although
the longer her eyes stayed on him without interruption,
the more she began to see clearly.

It took a while, but it finally sank in. And when the
thought occurred to her, the corners of her mouth turned
up and broadened into a grin. What was she thinking?
Harry's dying actually solved her problem. Instead of
grieving, she should be celebrating, grateful for this last
gift he had given her. Grabbing another tissue from the
box, she dried her eyes and wiped her face clean. With
her husband dead, now she could go up North and begin
her journey guilt free. Now that the ball had been
removed, all that was left was the chain—Nana and

Granddaddy. After dragging them through her marriage to an Outsider, and all the incumbent disasters that he had brought the family, she felt sure her grandparents would have a new perspective on her move up North. She would bet they'd much prefer her to focus on her business and what they considered this strange business of Black Power than to be miserable in Lemon City and get involved with an Outsider ever again. She was sorry that Harry was dead, but if there was ever a sign from God that she should proceed with her plans, this was it.

Her moods swung back and forth like a pendulum on a grandfather clock. Sadness came over her like a window shade being pulled down to seal out the night. When she realized she was left alone in the darkness, she put both hands to her face and cried whatever tears she had left. She was sad about everything that had ever happened to her in this world, thinking how pitiful her life had become, losing her parents, and now losing her husband. No matter how bad Harry was—Harry living or Harry dead—either way, the result was that she was back to ground zero, all by herself.

Once all the feelings had a chance to run through her, and she felt able to speak, she picked up the phone to notify the police. Billy's voice immediately comforted her.

For reasons that couldn't be explained, no one had ever died the day before the big celebration. Instead of granting another postponement out of respect for the dead, for the first time in Lemon City history, the Town Council voted to cancel the Annual County Fair. Nana passed out when she heard the news. Granddaddy used smelling salts to revive her.

No matter how full they were with turkey and all the fixings that went along with it, they all saved room for dessert. Nana brought out peach cobbler with vanilla ice cream, blackberry pie, coconut pineapple cake, walnut brownies, and raisin bread pudding with warm vanilla sauce. Eyes widened and stomachs expanded to accommodate. They had much to be thankful for. While they each had their own reasons for gratitude, the origins were similar because they revolved around air—all of them could breathe easier. Faye in particular felt a new-found sense of freedom.

Just as Nana saved the best part of the meal for last, Faye also saved something for the end of the meal. While Nana placed sliced samples of homemade sweets onto plates and passed them around the table, Faye said, "I've decided to proceed as planned and use my train ticket to head up North." She bit into her brownie, anticipating the worst.

"Oh, no," said Elvira, sounding as if Faye had announced she had a terminal illness and a short time to live.

"That's right." She cleared her throat. "I'll be leaving this Monday." She glanced sideways at Granddaddy because she couldn't dare look at him head-on.

"Your husband's dead. You ain't got to go nowhere now, ain't got to run away no more." Granddaddy passed the vanilla ice cream to Billy, keeping his atten-

tion on Faye. "All you got to do is stay right here, keep me and your grandmother company. In fact, that's the only thing all y'all got to do." Granddaddy swirled his index finger, pointing around the table to reinforce his position just in case it had slipped anyone else's mind. "Life is simple when you don't go out your way to complicate things."

Faye turned to Nana for help, but by the look on her grandmother's face it was clear that at this particular juncture, she was on her own. "I wasn't leaving Lemon City to move *away* from Harry. I was supposed to leave Lemon City *with* him. That was our plan when we first came home, remember?" When Granddaddy didn't answer, she felt like she was under silent attack. In this war without words, she refused to be rendered helpless. "And you know that . . . so don't pretend you don't."

"You better quit putting sass into your mouth, young lady," interrupted Nana, not giving Granddaddy a chance to respond. "Just you remember, a spider can't trap the bug by biting its head off if it's on the other side of the room. It must first weave an intricate web and carefully approach the bug in order to make the connection." Then Nana proceeded to throw her head in Granddaddy's direction, which she kept doing until Faye finally caught on.

"What's wrong with your neck?" Granddaddy thought his wife had suddenly developed a tic. "This twitching thing, this must be something new," he announced to the group as if it were just another old-age ailment to add to his ever-increasing list of pains.

Faye took the spider story and the head signal from Nana to mean that if she wanted Granddaddy to listen to her, the first thing she should do is calm down. In getting him to understand her feelings, she thought the next step and the best way to connect with him would be to tell the truth. It wasn't going to be easy for her to admit

the real reason she married Harry. To herself she acknowledged that in the end it seemed Harry had a hidden agenda, too. Now that she had found the courage to depart on her own, she was depending on her grandparents feeling sorry—sorry for her marrying an Outsider, sorry for her having gone through all that trouble, and sorry because her husband just died. After their feeling sorry, she hoped they'd give her their blessing and let her go. Maybe Harry still had a chance to play an important role in helping her escape Lemon City.

"The truth is, I married Harry because I wanted to leave Lemon City and live up North. I never thought you'd let me leave on my own, so I married someone who was from the North who I thought wanted to return to the North, and of course, since he was my husband, I'd have to go with him, but things didn't work out that way."

"Oh, no," said Elvira, still going with the terminal illness reaction.

"Lawd have mercy," said Nana.

"That explains a whole helluva lot," said Granddaddy.

"Even so, he still needed a good ass whuppin'," said Billy.

"Dag, that's pretty messed up," said Louise.

"I did love him," Faye said as she looked at her sister, "but, I did have an ulterior motive when I met Harry Lee Thompson." She faced both grandparents. "And now I feel it's partly my fault that he's dead." She looked directly across the table at Billy.

Faye saw the disappointment wipe across her grandparents' faces, which made her feel as rotten as mold spreading over stale bread.

"What's that you say about a motive?" Billy didn't want to believe it, but since Faye was in the mood for a confession, he had to ask the question. "Did you do it?"

"What do you think?"

"You coulda made up that story about finding him coldcocked on the floor and put him there yourself."

"Well, I didn't."

"You know, it just doesn't seem fair." Granddaddy poured so much warm vanilla sauce over his bread pudding that it looked like a chicken dumpling sitting in a bowl of soup.

"What doesn't seem fair, Granddaddy?" asked Louise, examining her blackberry pie as though addressing her question to the filling.

"'Cause as far as I'm concerned, justice has already been served. Just like this here dinner." As he took a bite of his bread pudding, he closed his eyes, savoring the taste and momentarily forgetting about Faye—and everything else—altogether.

He swallowed a few bites before saying, "Don't matter how it happened. I'm glad he's dead."

"Willie, show some sensitivity," Nana said as she waved her hand at her husband to make him shush. "Regardless of how you feel, remember our Faye is still in mourning."

"Speaking of mourning . . ." Billy leaned over his dessert plate and began to eat. "In the morning, Sheriff Taylor is coming to ask us questions about this murder and all I know is, y'all better have your stories straight."

"Beauregard Taylor. Ain't that Sheriff Jethro Taylor's son?" Since the name had finally registered, Nana looked at Granddaddy to see if it rang a bell for him, too, and it did.

"Yes, ma'am."

"If he's anything like his father, I don't reckon he'll give us much trouble."

"Nana, a man's gotta do his job no matter who his family knows and how long he's known 'em."

"Never mind that, let's just enjoy the last course of

this last supper with all of us together for what might be the last time and just hope for the best." Granddaddy was anxious to turn his attention to the TV. The football game was coming on and he didn't want any more talk about Harry to spoil his pregame enthusiasm. Tomorrow would be here soon enough.

After the women cleared the table and washed and dried the dishes, they sipped dandelion wine and played Pokeno until Elvira won everyone's quarters and energy. All the while they were playing, Nana couldn't get over the fact that Faye had actually married a man to get out of Lemon City, that she'd felt so trapped, she would apply such imagination and attempt to leave at any cost. If moving away from her home and her history meant so much to her granddaughter that she was willing to compromise love, then maybe she and Granddaddy should consider making an exception to The Rules. It wouldn't be the first time—after all, Faye had gone away to college. Common sense touched her heart and hinted that breaking The Rules might somehow be preferable to breaking her granddaughter's spirit.

Nana made up her mind she would talk to Granddaddy as soon as the football game ended. It was late, and for the most part they were tired because of the effects of the dandelion wine, the hollering over the football game, and the general anxiety. With a big day ahead of them, she announced it was time to go to bed and everyone agreed to call it a night.

As her grown children marched up the stairs like they had long ago, and she and Granddaddy stayed behind to turn off all the lights, check the stove to make sure the gas was shut off, and look around to see that all the food was put away, she couldn't help but get a little weepy-eyed over all that was now just precious memories. When she thought about Faye breaking with tradition, which triggered the thought that one of her children

might also go to jail, that was enough to elevate the weepy water in her eyes to flood levels. After releasing a few drops, she turned her eyelids into dams that kept her emotions under control. She couldn't let Granddaddy see her in this state; it was critical that she be composed. She had to convince Granddaddy to let Faye live her life outside of their protection. Most of all, they had to trust in God, the Supreme Maker of all Rules, to keep her safe.

CHAPTER TWENTY-FIVE

Faye and Louise hadn't slept in the same room together since Louise had graduated from high school and moved into the two-family house across the street. Not much had changed, except the room seemed half as big, and the twin beds looked really small. On Louise's side of the bedroom were faded posters of Jimi Hendrix and Angela Davis taped to the walls. Underneath the poster of Angela, Mick Jagger's full-size lips were spread across an album cover. On the adjacent walls were posters of the Jackson 5 and Gladys Knight and the Pips, a magazine photo of Madam C. J. Walker, and a small photograph of Malcolm X marked Faye's half of the room. Against the far wall was a long wooden bookcase they shared between them, which fell into neutral territory.

"Did you really love him?" Louise asked as she pulled her sweater over her head to undress for bed.

"As much as Harry would let me, I loved him."

"Answer me truthfully. Why do you still want to leave us?" Louise found a pair of cotton pajamas in the dresser drawer. Unzipping her skirt, she let it fall to the floor. When she sat down on the bed to put the bottoms on, she slid off the mattress and caught herself before hitting the floor. The wine was taking over.

"I don't want to leave *you*, silly. I have to leave *here*. It's just something I gotta do."

"Aw, you ain't gotta do squat." Louise put her pajama top on and fell sideways on the bed into the pillow.

"Every time I get scared and tell myself, 'Okay, I'll stay,' I get this feeling in my stomach like someone's reaching inside and grabbing my guts with a fist, squeezing and turning them like a doorknob they're trying to yank open."

"Dag. That sounds awful," Louise mumbled into the pillow.

"And when I tell myself, 'Okay, I'll go,' all the cramping stops and I'm at peace. I don't know. It's weird." Faye began putting on her pajamas.

"*You're* weird." Louise rolled over, pulled the covers over her head, and before Faye knew it, Louise was asleep. As she started to snore, Faye wondered how she was going to settle down with all that racket. It was a good thing she wasn't too tired. Looking for something to do, she sat at the foot of her bed, dusted off the bookshelf, and started browsing through the books. On the top shelf she found *Up From Slavery*, Booker T. Washington's autobiography, which she remembered Louise reading to her when Louise was in high school and she was in sixth grade. Scrolling her fingers across the bindings, she found one of her very favorite books, *Their Eyes Were Watching God*, by Zora Neale Hurston, and right now, she was feeling like Janie Crawford, the main character, because she might also have to have three marriages before she finally finds happiness too. There was *The Souls of Black Folk* by W.E.B. DuBois, about race in America, which was required reading for her honors English class in high school. Her finger found *The Living Is Easy*, a book by Dorothy West, which was one of Nana's favorite stories because it was about folks "passing" and the lives of the black upper class. There was *Native Son* by Richard Wright, which was about Bigger Thomas, whose story she could have sworn would have turned out differently had he been around during the time of Black Power. On the second shelf,

there was *The Lost Zoo*, her favorite children's book of poems by Countee Cullen, about the animals Noah didn't take with him on his ark. When she pulled out *The Lost Zoo*, there was an old newspaper stuck against the back of the shelf. As she carefully dislodged it from behind the book, its pages practically disintegrated in her fingers. The front page of the newspaper read *The Journal of Negro History* by Carter G. Woodson. *Oh, my goodness*, she thought. *He was the famous historian from Buckingham County.* She could barely read its frayed pages, but she could make out that it was published in February of 1917. She was dumbfounded that the discovery had survived this long, and even more amazed that Nana's meticulous cleaning hadn't uncovered the lost treasure after all these years. She could hardly wait until morning to tell Louise.

Next door in Billy's room, Elvira was tiptoeing over stuff on the floor, careful not to disturb the mess that Billy had left when he'd moved out years before. Nana always kept the door closed so Billy's junk never had a chance to get in her way. But right now it was preventing Elvira from reaching the bunk beds on the other side of the room. As Billy walked in front of her navigating a clear path, she was holding on to his shirttail, careful not to break anything more than it was already broken. When she reached the beds without incident, she plopped herself down on the bottom bunk and kicked off her shoes. From where she sat, she scanned the posters of the female R & B groups plastered on the walls: Martha Reeves & the Vandellas, The Marvelettes, The Shirelles, The Supremes, and The Ronettes. She thought that compared to the other things he held on to, these posters might be the only normal part of his collection.

"I don't know about you," Elvira said, "but I think Faye should stay in Lemon City. I get worried for her when I think about her moving to the big city. Too many

people up there, all of 'em strangers, you don't know their families. And I hear they don't even have enough home training to say hello, good morning, how you doing, or nothing. I hear you can be laying down dead in the street and they walk over you. I hear you can be screaming for help 'til your face turns purple and they just turn their backs. Being around folks like that is just no way to live."

"Don't worry about Faye, she's never been far away from home for too long. She'll be back." Billy started taking off his shirt and to Elvira's surprise, he actually put it on a hanger and hung it up in the closet.

At the far end of the hallway, Granddaddy was in bed reading a *Jet* magazine while Nana was knitting a navy blue sweater.

"What you think about Faye moving up North?"

"I don't think about it."

"You can't bury your head in the sand on this one, Willie."

"What do you want me to do?"

"Let's give her our blessing."

"Just like that?" He nearly tore the page out of his magazine trying to turn it over to continue reading the article on the other side. "We got Rules."

"I know we got Rules, but we also got a granddaughter who's different, who's being called by something, who for some reason is being drawn to the Outside world."

"And it's up to us to keep her in."

"If we make her stay, I don't think she'll ever recover. I'd put my hand on a stack of Bibles and swear she'd never be the same again."

"It'll pass. She'll get over it."

"If she leaves without our blessing, I just know something bad will happen, something awful terrible, that we'll always regret."

"There's no reason to think the worst."

"But if we let her go with our blessing, I just know she'll come back to us. Don't ask me how I know it; I just do."

Granddaddy couldn't help but reflect on his old friend Easely, and how he'd gone outside the city limits and Granddaddy had never seen him alive again. It brought back the fear in him so bad that he had to put down his magazine and stare into the air, thinking about what his wife had just said. Granddaddy hated it when she made sense, but The Rules had value, too, and he told her he'd have to sleep on it and give her his answer in the morning. Nana went back to knitting with a smile on her face, knowing that her husband sleeping on things usually worked in her favor.

At the other end of the hallway, the tranquilizing effect of the dandelion wine was creeping up on Faye. Since tomorrow would be another long day, she avoided thinking about the outcome too much by diverting her attention to the bookshelf. Even if someone in her family was to blame for Harry's timely demise, because he was an Outsider, she rationalized the penalty wouldn't be too severe. And if the Ladies of Mt. Zion had anything to say about it, the county authorities might even overlook the cause of death altogether. Thumbing through the bindings, looking at titles, she was searching for something to read to pass the time between drowsiness and slumber. The lonely sound of a whippoorwill calling from the woods pierced through the silence, making her wonder what kind of sounds pigeons made when they talked to each other in the busy city.

She leaned over to see what was underneath the heavy atlas on the bottom of the shelf and came across her favorite old Uncle Remus storybook. Blowing the dust off the cover made her sneeze. When she opened the book, a folded piece of yellowish paper fell from its pages. She

unfolded it carefully so she wouldn't tear the frail paper. Once she focused on what she held before her, she remembered: it was the Frederick Douglass page she'd torn from Billy's library book years ago. She read the paragraph again and now that she was older she hoped that she would understand it:

The history of civilization shows that no people can well rise to a high degree of mental or even moral excellence without wealth. A people uniformly poor and compelled to struggle for barely a physical existence will be dependent and despised by their neighbors and will finally despise themselves.

She had no idea why she'd stored this piece of paper in safekeeping, other than the fact that she felt a connection to the man with the bushy hair. She studied the words, trying to apply them to her own life, and then something clicked.

Way before the Black Power movement, there was Frederick Douglass, and what he spoke and wrote about was economic freedom—that's exactly what she was striving for with Nubian Silk. Economic freedom not just for herself, but if she could become successful, she would spread the wealth and ultimately help more of her people. Looking back, maybe Frederick's message was the original source of her inspiration. Even though she didn't fully understand the meaning of his words, maybe he'd just crawled into her psyche and stayed until she had. The combination of this new revelation and the dandelion wine was enough to make her head spin. Feeling overwhelmed, she lay down on the bed and turned out the light. Then she succumbed to the night.

When Nana woke up the next morning, the first thing she did was nudge Granddaddy.

"Willie, this chile is gonna leave. How are we gonna send her out into the world?"

"We gonna give her our blessing. I'm gonna sell The Shop and give her twenty-five thousand dollars to get her business started. She might know someone to take over the salon. We're gonna give her as much food as she can carry and pray she won't have any more hard lessons to learn."

Nana reached over and hugged her husband so hard he could barely breathe.

When Faye woke up to the smell of Nana's cooking and her ordering everyone to come down to eat, Frederick Douglass was still resting facedown on her chest.

Beauregard Taylor woke up with a hangover on the morning after Thanksgiving, dreading what he had to do that day—not because he had drunk more bourbon than he should have the night before, but because the last time he'd made the trip to Lemon City, it was due to unpleasant circumstances and unresolved business.

When he was a boy, his father had made a point of dragging him around in his patrol car, preparing him for what he'd call "the real world" and the bad people in it. He hated his training to become a sheriff back in those days, and now that he had become one, he hated it even more.

It was the judging part that bothered him: He couldn't care less about good and evil. He'd never had the passion for it that his father had. The more evil he saw, the more angry he became, convinced that bad people didn't need jail, they just needed to die. Simple as that. Why waste time locking evil up when in most cases it would be let back out in the streets again anyway? Might as well get rid of it for good.

Even though there wasn't much evil in Jefferson County, what little there was was still an inconvenience and he didn't feel like driving to Lemon City on a beautiful day like today to deal with it. He heard there was suspicion that someone in the family had killed Faye's husband, although he found that hard to believe. He knew the Dunlaps were honorable folks, but he also knew how much Lemonites hated Outsiders, so anything, he guessed, was possible. But

he dreaded being the one to have to cart one of the Dunlaps away. Besides, it would be a terrible way to end his career.

He walked into the bathroom and looked at the shadow on his face that had grown prickly overnight. Staring into the mirror, he picked up his razor and moved it back and forth like a manual lawn mower trimming new grass. How was he going to look Willie Dunlap Sr. in the face today? Dunlap Sr. had been the Lemon City sheriff way back when his father was enforcing the law for the whole of Jefferson County. It had been a gray day long ago when he and his father were making the rounds and they came upon Willie Dunlap crying uncontrollably, banging his bloodied fists into the ground next to a poplar tree. The sight of the Negro hanging gave him the chills. It downright made the hair stand up on the back of his neck and him sick to his stomach, and he swore he never wanted to see anything like that again. He never wanted to become an officer of the law after that, but he'd never had the nerve to tell his father.

Now that his old man had passed away, there was no need to pretend he liked doing this job. By now, he was just putting on his uniform every day out of habit. Maybe instead of delivering bad news, he'd do something honorable like becoming a postal worker and delivering the mail. He'd just turned forty-three last month. Maybe it was time for him to begin to think about retiring and opening up that little hardware store like he'd always dreamed of doing.

They never did find out who hung Willie Dunlap Sr.'s friend, and ever since then he'd felt he owed the old man something, but had never found a proper way to repay him. That was another reason why he hated what he had to do today, and swore when it was over, the first thing Monday morning, he'd turn in his resignation. Sick and tired of being in this business, he was ready to do something else.

* * *

Nana had finished cooking a banquet for breakfast. She warmed up leftovers from the day before, and it felt like Thanksgiving all over again. They finished stuffing themselves—not because they were hungry, but because of bad nerves due to the fact that one of them might not get a home-cooked meal until he or she was up for parole.

At eleven o'clock, the doorbell rang, and Billy opened the door to Sheriff Taylor. Everyone was sitting around the dining room table doing their best to be calm and composed.

The sheriff removed his hat. Nana offered him some breakfast and he smiled and politely declined. Granddaddy offered him a seat, but he told them he preferred to stand.

"How y'all doing?" Sheriff Taylor asked. Everyone just nodded their heads, wishing he'd skip over the formalities and get down to business. "I got some good news and I got some bad news." He ran his hands through his sandy brown hair then searched their faces for signs of guilt, but no one flinched; they all looked like expert poker players from what he could tell. "Which do y'all want to hear first?"

Billy wasn't in the mood for playing games, but they had to humor the sheriff since this was how he wanted to conduct his investigation.

"Let's hear the bad news first," said Billy, wanting to get it over with.

"The bad news is, based on the coroner's report, Harry Lee Thompson was poisoned." He lowered his eyes to the floor, then quickly lifted his head to see if he could catch anyone off guard. Detecting criminal behavior was something he was naturally good at, but the family looked genuinely surprised to hear the news, so he continued. "Autopsy report shows it was a powerful herb—a lethal dosage of hemlock—that did him in. Any of y'all in possession of any hemlock?"

"We don't have any hemlock here," Nana volunteered. When the sheriff kept staring at her, she took that to mean he was second-guessing her response and added, "I'm sure of it."

She folded her arms across her bosom in a way that both embarrassed and intimidated him, and made him reluctant to confront her.

"What's the good news?" Billy asked.

"The good news is our office got in touch with Mr. Thompson's family, and they're gonna pay to transport his body up North."

"How do you like that?" Faye turned to Louise. "He refused to go up North when he was alive, now he's got to go because he's dead."

"Excuse me?" Sheriff Taylor was confused by the remark.

"Never mind," Louise shot back at him. She shook her head to let Faye know now was not the time to have that discussion.

"The tomato had the hemlock in it," Sheriff Taylor continued. "It appears as if the hemlock had been injected directly into the tomato. Y'all know anything about that?" This time he addressed his question to Granddaddy.

"I'm not the expert on tomatoes. Talk to my wife, here. She'll tell you everything you want to know."

Beauregard Taylor wasn't ready to address Nana directly again so he spoke to the general audience. "Unfortunately, the tomato was in such a bad state of decomposition by the time we were able to examine it that we couldn't find any fingerprints."

Knowing that hemlock was an herb and knowing that there was an herb garden in the vicinity, Nana looked around that table to see if anyone else was thinking what she was thinking. In unison everyone tilted their heads in the direction of next door.

"Beau Taylor . . . ," Nana said, as if she'd known him all his life.

"Yes, ma'am," he said respectfully.

"You said the tomato had decomposed, and you weren't able to get fingerprints."

"Yes, ma'am." It made him uncomfortable the way Nana was starting to question him and he shifted from one leg to the other.

"But were you able to tell what kind of tomato it was?"

"I believe the county coroner mentioned that it was a beefsteak." He pulled a notepad from his back pocket and checked his notes. "No, I'm sorry. It was a Bragger. Beefsteak . . . Bragger . . . they're all the same to me."

"Not to me they ain't. And I don't grow either. In my garden, I only grow Big Boys, Mountain Prides, and Jubilees. But Lurleen Johnson next door, now she grows beefsteaks *and* Braggers, so you may want to take your questions over there to her." Nana pointed her thumb in Ole Miss Johnson's direction.

"Nana, you know she's not well." Faye didn't think the timing was right to use Ole Miss Johnson as a scapegoat.

"I know she's bedridden, but she can answer the question, 'Did you put hemlock in your tomatoes,' can't she?"

Sheriff Taylor agreed to go next door and Faye went with him to make sure his presence didn't scare the old lady to death.

They returned shortly. While they were gone, the group in the living room stayed still. Nana prayed silently. Twenty minutes later, Taylor and Faye returned. Before the sheriff even opened his mouth, it was clear to Nana from his body language and Faye's great big smile that her family was safe from the law.

"Here's my understanding of the murder . . . the crime . . . the accident." The sheriff stumbled over his words trying to come to terms with what to call the unfor-

tunate occurrence. "Lurleen Johnson had injected a hand-
ful of them Bragger tomatoes with hemlock, then she left
them on the windowsill to ripen. Her intention was to scat-
ter them throughout the garden to kill the cat . . ."

"Now wait a minute . . ." Nana got up from her chair
so quickly that she startled the sheriff, who almost
reached for his gun.

She was furious that Saint had been the target of Ole
Miss Johnson's fatal attack. "I'm going next door right
now. And Sheriff, you may as well stick around, 'cause
there's about to be a real murder that you can witness
for yourself."

"Wait, Nana." Faye restrained her from walking out
the door. "Ole Miss Johnson was wrong, but Saint isn't
dead. Harry's the one who's dead."

Calmed enough to see the wisdom in Faye's reasoning,
she sat back down in her seat. Maybe she should thank
Lurleen for giving her the family back intact.

Sheriff Taylor took the handkerchief from his back
pocket and wiped away the sweat that was beginning to
surface on his brow. "Anyway," he continued, "accord-
ing to my notes, Harry Lee Thompson did some work
next door the day he died. That's when he must have
picked up the Braggers and eaten them. Shortly after
that, he expired. I'll write that down in my report. Far as
I'm concerned, this case is closed. Death due to acciden-
tal poisoning, that's what I'll say. I've got a sworn con-
fession from Miss Lurleen Johnson right here regarding
them bad tomatoes, but since they were in her house and
no one put a gun to his head to eat them, y'all are free to
go and do as y'all please."

And with those words, Sheriff Beauregard Taylor tipped
his hat to the room, shook Granddaddy's hand, and was
gone. In some small way, he felt vindicated from the un-
solved crime years ago. Regardless, first thing Monday
morning he would send in his resignation and retire.

To show her appreciation, Nana picked Saint up off the floor and rubbed her back just the way she liked it. As it turned out, Saint was not only loyal, but in keeping with her name, had provided the family with divine protection.

Now that they were officially free from house arrest, Nana and Granddaddy announced that Faye would be free to leave Lemon City.

Faye ran to Nana and kissed her. Tears mingled. Both women cried from sadness and joy.

Her siblings, each one of them, felt the same mixed emotions. It was left to Louise to put it into words. "You better make us proud, Faye Dunlap Thompson. Because you're representing us—not only the family but all of Lemon City."

"Power to the people," Faye vamped, and all her siblings laughed out loud.

Then it was time for Faye to thank Granddaddy, only there weren't any words. What could she say to the man who had given her all of his loving care—and then, finally, her freedom? "Granddaddy . . ."

Before Faye could finish her sentence her grandfather interrupted. "I just knew that you, being the youngest in the family, would be the one to stay here with me, watch me get old . . . older." He smiled. "Where you got all this nerve . . . all these crazy things trapped in your head, I don't know. But if you think your life will be better with strange people in it, unknown dangers, unwelcome surprises and chaos, with no family around to help and protect you, then you must be hell bent on going and who am I to stand in your way?"

"You're my hero, Granddaddy." She kissed him. "You're the best grandfather, father, and friend rolled into one that a girl could ever have, and I love you." She hugged him and he held on tight to her for a while. And as everyone went on about their business, Granddaddy thought about his baby granddaughter, who looked just

like his daughter, Aurelia, and as he lost his daughter long ago, he was afraid that he might lose his granddaughter, too. With this thought, a droplet of water rolled over his cheek and he wiped it away before anyone could see.

When Faye released her grandfather, she went next door to leave a note for Ole Miss Johnson.

Dear Ole Miss Johnson,
You helped give me the courage to fulfill my dream. I only hope I can be as strong as you. I love you and thank you for everything.

She signed it "daughter."

Faye stayed at Nana's for the rest of the weekend. She didn't want to go back to the cottage; it gave her the creeps. She asked Billy to bring her Samsonite suitcase.

On Monday, they all piled into the 1962 Ford Galaxy station wagon and drove down to the train station to see her off. Nana packed her a big picnic basket of leftovers: turkey soup, turkey casserole, sliced turkey breast for sandwiches, smoked turkey wings, and turkey cutlets for the trip. Granddaddy was sad to see his baby girl go, but with the money he gave her and the food from her grandmother, at least she wouldn't have to worry about where she would sleep and what she would eat. And if his wife was right, which she usually was, he was already mentally preparing and looking forward to her triumphant return even if only for a visit. This had been a god-awful year, and it would have been even worse if one of his family members had been convicted of first-degree murder or manslaughter, which is why all things considered, the saga of the Outsider had somewhat of a happy ending. Granddaddy honestly didn't understand what his granddaughter was looking for in life, or what she felt was missing that he and Nana couldn't give her.

He only hoped she'd find it soon so she could stop over-achieving and feeling responsible for this crazy world and finally find her own peace. What he wanted most for his granddaughter, more than anything else, was for her to know there was value in The Rules, that they weren't just restrictions that put people into confinement, that they had a purpose—ten dern good ones, to be exact. And he hoped that Faye was smart enough to see that, yes indeed, the boll weevil did bite her back.

With the help of a Pullman Porter, Faye lifted her trunk, filled with the chemical and herbal ingredients to make Nubian Silk, onto the overhead rack, and placed her Samsonite suitcase in the luggage compartment behind her seat. A picnic basket filled with food sat by her side. She waved as she watched her family, standing on the platform, gradually disappear. As the train pulled off, tears clouded up in her eyes until everything became a silvery blur, and her heart sank just a little because she was leaving behind the support that helped hold it in place. When her neck started to crick from its twisted position as she looked back at her family, she turned around to face forward to the challenge of her new destination. Thinking about the unknown that lay ahead made her grip the arm of her seat and close her eyes, preparing for the ride of her life.

The movement of the train as it traveled alongside the mountains had a back-and-forth motion that made her feel like being rocked in a cradle. As the rhythm made her relax and leave certain memories behind, Harry became smaller and smaller until she was able to shrink her deceased husband to a size of a pea, and flick the thought of him away.

Epilogue

It took five years for Faye to establish herself in her own hair-care business. By 1978, Nubian Silk was distributed in beauty salons and beauty supply stores in all five boroughs of New York City, as well as a few suburban towns in Westchester and northern New Jersey. She paid off her small business loan, and repaid Granddaddy his generous investment, even though he refused to accept her money until she begged him to take it back.

Although she was riding high in the hair-care business, something major in her life was missing. Based on her personal observation, it seemed the Black Power movement was dead, and she had missed the biggest opportunity of her life.

Then one day, one of her customers, an active member in the National Urban League, gave her a copy of Vernon C. Jordan's "State of Black America" report, which had just been released to the public. According to the report, the nation's economy was bad; unemployment continued to rise, and the income gap was widening for African Americans. Vernon C. Jordan had stepped in and asked President Carter to do something about it. As she turned the pages of the report, the underlying message became clear—it was in bold black print, nearly jumping off the page. What hit home the hardest was one line in particular, and she read it over and over again: ". . . much more was needed by way of federal actions to assist poor people in cities." And that's when

it clicked, and everything came together, and the messages of Vernon C. Jordan and Frederick Douglass merged into one idea and a brand-new plan came to her mind. She was so excited about this new revelation that she couldn't wait to call Granddaddy first thing in the morning. All she would need to execute her plan would be a little help from her family and friends.

The next day she called Granddaddy to ask him to arrange for her to purchase The Tap and all the surrounding property. Then she asked him if he would be interested in being a primary investor and stockholder in her new business. By the end of the week, the fifty acres of real estate were owned by the Dunlap family.

The next step was to initiate phase two of her plan. She called the renowned African American architectural design and construction firm Smallwood and Associates to draw up the plans and to act as main contractor and consultant for the project. Samuel Lamont Smallwood Jr. with his subcontractors, and Medford, whom Faye hired as manager for the site, worked together to make the infamous watering hole history. In its place she instilled the first African American–owned and –operated Nubian Silk manufacturing plant and distribution center, and a housing complex that would contain all of its employees' families. Faye had figured out a way to help poor people in cities, which was Vernon's idea, and to provide them with a way to develop wealth, which was Frederick's idea. By combining these two ways of thinking, she made a lot of people happy.

In September 1980, just in time for the Annual County Fair, Faye led these Outsiders, representing the largest relocation of people to the Lemon City area since the Great Migration of 1875, to the east side of Route 23. Since the new folks planted themselves just outside of the city limits in Jefferson County proper, the Lemonites didn't mind accepting them as their neighbors. As long as the new

folks stayed outside where they belonged, the townspeople were content. Sponsor or no sponsor, they weren't getting in.

Just as construction was about to be completed, Faye went to the top of Mt. Overpeck and looked down at the brand-new commercial and residential development adjacent to the patchwork quilt of farmlands, forests, and meadows. In that moment she realized she'd created her own Black Power movement, because she'd moved many of her people toward financial independence and freedom. There was no limit to what she could do, living within the confines of Lemon City. It was a box that she now felt comfortable in, because she was free to open and close the lid as she pleased, by her own will.